MW01254980

THE
DUKE
OF
LIES

⚜ *The Untouchables* ⚜

DARCY
BURKE

The Duke of Lies
Copyright © 2018 Darcy Burke
All rights reserved.

ISBN: 1944576290
ISBN-13: 9781944576295

Book design: © Darcy Burke.
Book Cover Design © Carrie Divine/Seductive Designs
Photo copyright: © Period Images
Editing: Linda Ingmanson.

For Lynda

*I may have inspired you to write a book,
but you've returned the gift many times over.
Thank you.*

Chapter One

Blackburn, England, April 1818

As VERITY BEAUMONT, Duchess of Blackburn, watched her six-year-old son cuddle the baby goat, she wondered if they would soon be adding to their menagerie. She'd come here to hopefully gain a steward, not another animal. Yet, if Beau asked her, she'd be hard-pressed to say no. He was her entire world, and she was unashamed to admit it.

"He seems to have made a friend."

Verity turned to the former steward of Beaumont Tower, Percival Entwhistle, who went by the far less formal name of Whist, and gave him a plaintive stare. "Please do not offer a new pet. I can't support one more animal with the dogs, cats, rabbits, and most recently a squirrel we already have."

Whist laughed and held up his hand. "I give my word, Your Grace." He tilted his head toward the stable yard, where his grandson was dismounting from his horse. "Ah, here's Thomas now."

Straightening, Verity patted the back of her head. She knew Thomas well as Whist's grandson, but saw him less often since he'd gone to work as steward at a neighboring estate. Since then, she'd seen him on a few occasions, including at last week's assembly, and was impressed with the knowledge he'd gleaned from his grandfather and the experience of being steward the last four years. If she were honest, she was also charmed by his pleasant demeanor and his dancing ability. But since she'd been alone these past six and a half years, perhaps she was easy to charm.

After tending his horse, Thomas strode toward them, his mouth tipping into a warm smile. He swept his hat from his dark head and bowed to Verity, his lean frame bending easily. "Your Grace, it's a pleasure to see you."

"And you, Mr. Entwhistle."

"Should we go inside to conduct our business?" Whist asked, gesturing toward his small cottage, which sat on the Beaumont Tower estate. Verity had provided him the home upon his retirement nearly seven years ago.

She glanced toward Beau's nurse, who stood nearby. The nurse nodded and returned her complete focus to her charge. Verity turned to Whist and Thomas. "Yes, let's."

Whist motioned for her to precede him and followed her into the cottage. She took a seat in a chair that allowed her to see her son through the window. Whist and Thomas also sat, and watched her expectantly.

"I do appreciate you meeting with me today," Verity said, feeling suddenly nervous. Though she'd been the duchess for nearly seven years, she hadn't fully inhabited the role. The steward, Cuddy, managed the estate almost entirely without her input, and while she oversaw the household, the staff was so efficient as to make her practically unnecessary. She rarely entertained visitors, and for the most part they only supported Verity and her son. It was, overall, a simple existence and one for which Verity was grateful because it allowed her to be relatively independent. Only relatively because her father still tried to exert his influence from time to time.

He'd done a fair job of controlling things after Verity's husband Rufus had disappeared, and Verity had endured his meddling for quite some time before asking him—firmly—to stop. She suspected, however, he still kept a hand in things because of Cuddy. Her father had referred him to Rufus when Whist had retired, and it seemed that Cuddy was still her father's man. She could be wrong about that, but she wasn't wrong about one thing—Cuddy wasn't *her* man.

Verity straightened her spine as she glanced out at Beau chasing a rabbit in front of the cottage. Suppressing a smile, she focused on the business at hand. "I asked to meet with you both because I'd like to make a change at Beaumont Tower."

Whist inclined his head. "And what would that be?"

"I believe it's past time I hired my own steward—someone I've selected and whom I can trust to manage things as I see fit."

"As you see…" Whist's voice trailed off, and he coughed. "Am I to understand you wish to participate in the management of the estate?"

"I am the duchess," she said. "And in the absence of the duke, it is my responsibility to do so. In just a handful of months, my husband will likely be legally declared dead and my son will inherit the title. I owe it to him to ensure the estate is running smoothly."

Thomas's brow creased with concern. "Do you have reason to believe it's not?"

"I'm not sure. When I ask Cuddy to review the accounts with me or to inform me how the tenants are faring, he promises to do so at some indeterminate time in the future. Only, that time never comes to pass. And when I visit the tenants on my own, it's clear Cuddy isn't spending much time with them."

The furrows in Thomas's forehead deepened as he exchanged a look with his grandfather. "Have you insisted he show you the account books?"

Now she felt mildly embarrassed. "I haven't *insisted*, no."

Thomas blinked, his dark lashes sweeping briefly over his bright blue eyes. "I didn't mean to imply you should have. I beg your pardon. I was only trying to ascertain the tone of your communications with him. He should've showed them to you the first time you asked." He pressed his lips into a firm line.

Whist scoffed. "He should've shown them to you without your asking." He looked at Verity with kindness and understanding. "What do you wish to do?"

"I'd like to replace him." She gave her sole attention to the younger man across from her. "With you, Thomas."

Whist's mouth split into a wide grin. "That's my boy. You've made an excellent decision, Your Grace."

A bit of color bloomed in Thomas's cheeks. "I'm... I don't know quite what to say. Thank you for your confidence, Your Grace."

"I know your grandfather trained you well, and while I hate to take you away from Bleven House, I need you more than they do." She had no idea if that were true, but she *did* need him. Most desperately. It was past time she took control of things.

Whist angled himself toward his grandson. "You've done an excellent job there, but this is an incredible opportunity. Entwhistles have been stewards at Beaumont Tower for over a hundred years."

The only reason an Entwhistle was no longer the steward was because Rufus had encouraged Whist to retire. Whist had demurred, but in the end, Rufus hadn't given him a choice. Then, at her father's behest, he'd installed Cuddy.

Thomas turned his humbled gaze to Verity. "I'd be honored to accept the position. Of course, I'll need to inform my current employer, and I wouldn't want to leave immediately."

Whist nodded. "Certainly not. In the meantime, I can help take up the slack." He looked to Verity. "That is, if you'd want me to."

Verity smiled warmly as some of the tension left her shoulders. "I should like nothing more. But only if you think you're up to it."

He let out a soft chuckle. "I can do what needs be done while Thomas gets his affairs in order. When do you plan to let Cuddy go?"

The anxiety that had just left returned to Verity's frame with disturbing force. She oughtn't be afraid to exert her authority as duchess, but she was nervous about telling the man he would no longer be employed at the estate. It wasn't just his size—and Cuddy was a towering fellow with more than a bit of brawn—but his demeanor. He was always courteous and deferential, yet Verity had never felt comfortable around him. He possessed a nervous energy that put her on edge. She assumed it was just her but now found the courage to broach the subject.

"How do you think he'll take it?"

"In a professional manner," Whist said. "As he should. Why, do you have reason to think he'll behave otherwise?"

Then it *was* just her. But then she interacted with him far more than Whist did. "Not really," she said, deciding not to pursue what were probably just silly concerns. She'd been isolated the last several years at Beaumont Tower, content to focus on her son. But now she was eager to break free of her constraints and exert her duty—and her power—as duchess. She owed it to her son if not herself.

Thomas gave her an earnest stare. "If Cuddy gives you any trouble, I hope you'll let us know immediately."

"I will, thank you." She rose, and they stood along with her. "I'll plan to speak with him tomorrow morning, so Thomas, if you'd like to inform your employer tomorrow, I'll leave that up to you."

Thomas bowed. "I am deeply honored and grateful for the opportunity to serve you and the fine estate of Beaumont Tower, Your Grace."

"It is I who am honored and grateful," Verity said with a smile. "Now, do stop that as I've never been one to appreciate obsequiousness."

Her new steward grinned as he straightened. "I'll endeavor to remember that."

She liked his smile. It made her feel a bit more at ease at the coming change. "I should tell you that I plan to be very involved in the management of the estate—as involved as my husband would have been, if he were here."

"I find that an admirable enterprise," Thomas said with a gleam in his eye. "I will ensure you fulfill the role you desire."

"Has it really been nearly seven years since His Grace went missing?" Whist asked.

"It will be in August, yes." It seemed a lifetime, and she supposed it was—their son's lifetime. Rufus had not only never met his son, he'd never even known she was expecting. He'd left for London to bow before the king and hadn't returned.

Whist gave her a caring look that bordered on pity, something she was used to receiving and eager to cast aside. "It can't have been easy, but soon you'll be able to move on and let him go."

Oh, she'd let him go quite some time ago. Not long after he'd left, if she were honest. She was certain the marriage had been orchestrated by her father. A man she loathed had wed her to a man she'd come to detest. Thankfully, she'd had to endure Rufus for only a little more than three months before he'd vanished. She'd thanked God every single day and felt absolutely horrid for it.

The mild smile she'd perfected over the past six and a half years rose effortlessly to her lips. "Thank you. I am quite eager to move on, and this sets me on that path." She looked to Thomas. "I'll send a note confirming the date of Cuddy's departure."

Thomas nodded. "May I walk you out?"

"Of course."

The trio left Whist's cottage, and Beau ran directly into Verity's skirts. "Mama, can we take the baby goat home?"

She widened her eyes at Whist in silent appeal.

The former steward coughed. "I'm afraid not."

Thomas squatted down to Beau's level. "If you took her with you, she and her mother would be very sad. It would be like you leaving your mother. You wouldn't wish to do that, would you?"

Beau looked up at Verity, his green eyes wide. "No, I wouldn't wish that at all." His hand found hers, and she gave his fingers a squeeze.

The boy snapped his head back to Thomas. "Then her mama will come with us too."

Thomas was quiet a moment, his expression thoughtful as he contemplated Beau's earnest face. "That would certainly solve one problem, but I believe it would create another." He glanced toward Whist. "You see, these are my Grandpapa's goats, and he loves them dearly. He would be sad if they left. Perhaps you could come visit them?"

Beau expelled a breath and looked longingly toward the goat pen. "I could." He turned his gaze to Verity. "Can I, Mama?"

"Of course." And because her son could melt her heart like no other, she said, "Perhaps we should consider keeping a goat herd closer to the castle. Then you could help tend the babies."

Beau's eyes lit, and his mouth spread into a wide, gleeful smile. "Oh yes! Let's make Cuddy do that right away."

Verity laughed at his excitement while at the same time delighting in the fact that she soon wouldn't have to "make Cuddy" do anything except leave. And she hoped that would occur without upset. "*I* will make sure it happens, my dear." She looked down at Thomas, who gave her a firm nod.

Her new steward grinned at Beau. "It seems we've come to an excellent conclusion for everyone."

Beau nodded. "Thank you for helping me solve this problem. Mama says solving problems is one of the most important things we must learn."

Thomas tipped his face up to Verity. "Your mama is right, and what a lucky boy you are to have her." His gaze was warm with respect and perhaps something else that made Verity think of him in a different light— as a gentleman and not just her new employee. Well, that wouldn't do.

Before she could say it was time to go, Beau asked, "Where is your mama, Thomas?"

"Oh, she died some time ago." His voice held just a tinge of sadness.

"My papa might be dead," Beau said rather matter-of-factly. "But I think he'll come home someday." He leaned close to Thomas and lowered his voice to what he probably thought was a whisper but that was barely below a regular speaking tone. "I think he was kidnapped. Someday when I am big, I will rescue him and bring him home."

It was moments like these that pulled at Verity's emotions. She'd never even hinted that Beau's father had been awful, and the staff hadn't either. They had to have been cognizant of the cruelty he'd heaped on Verity, but they'd never openly discussed it. She could only imagine the type of father he would have been to Beau. That was the primary reason she was grateful he was gone—she would have hated to see him mistreat her son. In fact, she wasn't sure she could've borne it.

So while she appreciated Beau's need to romanticize his father, she remained somewhat neutral. Only in the last year or so had she begun to prepare Beau for the probability that his father wouldn't return. Soon she would have to explain that Rufus was dead and that he—Beau—would be the duke. That wasn't a conversation she looked forward to.

"I have no doubt you will rescue him," Thomas said solemnly. "And how fortunate your father is to have you as his champion."

Beau let go of Verity's hand to put his hands on his hips. "Yes, I am his champion. Like a knight! I like to play knights."

Thomas chuckled. "I do too. Do you have a wooden

sword?"

Beau gave Verity a rather mutinous look. "No. Mama won't let me have one because I kept running through the drawing room with it."

"Well, we must listen to our mothers." Thomas gave her an apologetic nod.

It was past time to save the gracious Thomas from her son. Verity couldn't help but be impressed with how he'd interacted with Beau, and she looked forward to having him on the estate. Perhaps he would be able to provide Beau with some of the fatherly direction he was lacking. "Come, Beau, we should be on our way. It's nearly time for your luncheon and then afternoon lessons with Mr. Deacon."

His nurse moved toward the coach and nodded toward the door. "Come along then, your lordship."

Beau waved to the Entwhistles. "Good-bye!" He lingered briefly at the goat pen before clambering into the coach with the nurse's help.

Verity turned to Thomas, who'd risen to his normal height, which was a bit taller than her five feet seven inches. "Thank you for your kindness to my son. I daresay he will enjoy having you on the estate."

"It will be a pleasure. He's a charming boy."

"In need of a fatherly figure," Whist put in as he looked between them with a half smile.

Thomas threw his grandfather a scandalized look. "I wouldn't dare to presume."

"Your grandfather vocalized what I'd been thinking," Verity said. "Beau is in need of someone to show him some things, such as how to care for a baby goat. Several members of my staff assist however they can." She thought of her butler, Kirwin, who doted on Beau. "I'd be remiss if I didn't tell you that part of your job will likely include instructing Beau in the ways of the estate." She'd mentioned this to Cuddy when Beau had turned six in January and she'd hired his tutor, Mr. Deacon, but the steward had done what he always did—put her off.

"I would be honored to teach him," Thomas said. "And as you know, I learned from the very best." He shot a smile toward his grandfather, who laughed before moving forward to clap his grandson on the back.

"You were an easy student, my boy. Truly, Your Grace, the estate won't be in better hands."

"I think so too." She nodded toward them. "I'll see you both soon."

She went to the coach, where the coachman helped her inside, and a moment later, they were on their way.

Beau scooted close to her side, his warm body tucked against hers. "Mama, can I come back to visit the goats tomorrow?"

"I don't know about tomorrow, but soon. And I will see about having a goat herd closer to the house."

"That will be ever so nice," Beau said with a sigh. "I'm going to be a good duke someday, Mama, because I will know how to care for all the animals and all the people at Beaumont Tower."

She dropped a kiss on his head, inhaling the sweet scent of boy. "Yes, you will. You'll be the best duke Beaumont Tower has ever known."

The castle—Beaumont Tower itself—was situated on a hill with lower and upper courtyards, both of which were ringed by the castle proper. The main part of the castle that contained their living quarters encircled the upper courtyard. It had been a medieval stronghold and had since undergone several refurbishments in an effort to modernize. It was large and drafty and beautiful. To her, it was home.

A few minutes later, the coach drove through the entrance tower and into the lower courtyard, where it stopped at the base of the steps that led to the upper half of the castle. They stepped down, and Verity leaned down to hug and kiss Beau. "I'll see you after lessons."

"But first to luncheon," the nurse said. "I am famished! Shall we race upstairs? Carefully," she added, with a glance toward Verity.

Beau was already tearing off toward the upper gateway of the castle. "Try to catch me!"

Verity smiled after them as the spring sun warmed her head and shoulders. Closing her eyes, she tipped her head up to the sky and let the rays wash over her, basking her in the promise of a new beginning.

Ever since her dear cousin Diana had come to visit five months ago, Verity had been unsettled. Diana had come with her husband, though they hadn't yet been wed—Verity had the pleasure of attending their wedding at Gretna Green. It had been the most romantic event she'd ever beheld. Their love and passion for each other was palpable, and Verity couldn't have been happier for her favorite person.

And yet, it had only served to inform her that she was lonely, that she was without love or passion. Oh, she had Beau, and for him, she would be eternally grateful. For six years, she'd convinced herself that she didn't need anything more. Until she'd realized she did.

Perhaps she wouldn't find love or passion, but she would take charge, and she would make it possible for herself *to* find those things, if she were lucky. But she'd already been lucky, she reminded herself. She had Beau, and she didn't have Rufus. Fate had been quite kind, and she really had no reason to complain.

Not that she was *complaining*... She shook her head as she walked up the steps to the wide path and veered to the right side of the garden that flanked both sides of the stone walkway. How she loved the gardens—three of them—at Beaumont Tower. These were the places where she'd reigned, and they never failed to buoy her spirits. She searched now for the courage she needed to take the next step, to let Cuddy go and get Beau used to the idea that his father wouldn't be coming home.

She had leaned down to smell the budding bloom of her favorite rose when the sound of a horse coming into the courtyard drew her to turn her head. The lone rider was large, broad shouldered, with a hat that shielded his face.

Verity walked back to the path and retraced her footsteps to the stairs. The rider steered the horse to the base of the steps and swung himself from the animal's back. The hair on Verity's neck stood up, and the warm spring day turned suddenly cold.

The man put one foot on the first step as he swept his hat from his head. Faint recognition was quickly chased by dread as his gaze found hers.

"I'm home."

Chapter Two

❦

VERITY STARED AT the man—her husband, apparently—and felt an overwhelming urge to run into the house and bar the door against him. Could he really be here? After all this time?

A groom rushed toward them, alleviating the need for her to speak. In any case, she wasn't sure she could.

Rufus turned toward the approaching retainer, who came to a dead stop several feet away. Even from this distance, Verity could see the shock register in the groom's expression as his eyes widened and his jaw dropped.

The groom fumbled a bow. "Your Grace." He sounded as disbelieving as Verity felt.

"Would you, ah, mind tending my horse?" Rufus sounded uncertain. And not at all like the man she remembered. Did she remember? It had been so many years, and she'd long ago forgotten the cadence of his voice, let alone the planes of his face. "And please have the saddle bags sent to the house." *Please?*

The groom nodded, then took the horse toward the stables. Rufus watched the animal go before pivoting back toward where she stood near the top of the stairs. Then he slowly climbed toward her, each step a definitive click of his boot against the stone.

As he neared the top, Verity took a step back. Then another. When he reached the path, she had to lift her gaze to his face. Was he taller than she remembered? Again, she wasn't sure she could rely on her memory at all, and yet that was all she had.

What did she remember? His light brown hair, his piercing hazel eyes, his firm, sometimes cruel jaw, his slender, aristocratic nose, his wide shoulders, and his long fingers—yes, she remembered those biting into her skin when he grabbed her.

She shuddered as the air around her turned colder still. "Where have you been?" It was the only thing she could think to say. And the question came out low and strained.

He took another step toward her, and she edged backward once more. "I beg your pardon?" he asked in a polite tone she would never have imagined him using.

She cleared her throat and willed herself to have courage. "Where have you been?"

"That is, ah, a long story, as you can probably guess. May we go inside?" He stared past her at the castle, and the look in his eyes was one of longing and perhaps…disbelief.

Well, that was one thing they had in common then. Good Lord, her husband was standing in front of her.

He'd asked to go inside. She wanted to scream that no, he couldn't come inside, that he couldn't come anywhere near her or Beau, but she didn't. She couldn't. This was his house. The fact that he was asking her was…odd. The Rufus she'd married would've stamped past her and expected her to fall in step behind him. If she didn't, he'd simply go back, grab her by the arm, and drag her along.

She folded her arms across her chest and wrapped her hands around her biceps, as if she could ward off his touch, should he try to thrust it upon her. "Of course." She turned and walked along the path, leading him toward the upper gate. Her back tingled as she expected him to do something untoward—make a denigrating comment or seize her in some way. But she made it all the way to the upper gate, where she paused and looked back at him. He was several feet behind her, moving quite slowly, it seemed, as his head swung this way and that, taking in every bit of his surroundings. It had to be quite strange to be home after all this time.

Where *had* he been? For the first time since seeing him, an emotion other than shock and fear crept over her: curiosity.

She continued through the upper gatehouse and across the upper courtyard to the back of the castle. She climbed a small set of rounded stairs and opened the door to the King's Hall. With the family crest hanging over the wide hearth, the room was the most formal in the castle. Suits of armor stood in the corners, and an impressive array of medieval weapons hung from the walls amidst portraits of Beaumonts from eras gone by.

There was no formal portrait of Rufus, just the small painting that hung in Beau's room. It had been commissioned, along with one of her, after their wedding, and had been completed after Rufus's disappearance. Because of that, she'd never thought it was a true representation. The artist had made him look far more affable than he was.

She moved to the windows that looked out over the back lawn. He went directly to the portrait of the former duke—his uncle—and stared up at Augustus, for whom Beau was named, captured in his thirties. She hadn't noticed before, or perhaps she'd forgotten, but Rufus bore a striking resemblance to the man.

Except Rufus was bigger. In fact, he seemed bigger

to her than he had seven years ago, and back then, his size had frightened her. Now, however, his shoulders were broader, and he *was* taller than she remembered. But perhaps her memory was faulty.

When he finally turned from the portrait, his gaze traveled the room, looking a bit as if he'd never seen it before. But that was absurd. Perhaps his memory was just a bit hazy.

"Do you want refreshment?" she asked. "I've no idea how long you've been traveling."

"You deserve to know where I've been. Will you sit?" He gestured to the seating area in front of the hearth.

Again, he asked politely. In the past, she would've done as he instructed without thought, but that was a long time ago. Still, she couldn't suppress the tingle of apprehension that danced along her flesh.

Summoning a bead of courage, she went to the seating arrangement closest to her that overlooked the back lawn. She perched on the edge of the settee and waited to see what he would do.

He walked slowly toward her and sat in the chair angled to her right. He set his hat on the arm of the chair. "You look well."

"Thank you." She ought to tell him the same, but it was hard to make idle conversation with a man she regarded as a beast. She managed to say, "You do too." Which only made her imagination run wild. Why had he come back now? Why couldn't he have stayed gone? Her insides clenched with a distress so fervent that it bordered on pain. What she wouldn't give for him to disappear again. Everything had been so perfect—

He interrupted her thoughts. "You will likely want details, but I won't provide them. I prefer to put what happened behind me." That sounded more like the authoritarian she knew.

Verity braced herself, clasping her hands together and squeezing them in her lap.

"I was taken by an impressment gang and forced onto a privateering vessel."

The tension pulsing through her stopped as she tried to make sense of what he was saying. "You were kidnapped?"

"That's another way of putting it."

"But you're a duke." Who would kidnap a duke?

"I told them that at every opportunity, but they didn't give a damn," he said wryly. He rushed to add, "Pardon my language."

Who was this man? That bit of humor—both in his tone and in the tilt of his mouth—was perhaps more shocking than his revelation. And then he'd asked her to *pardon his language*? He'd said far worse in her presence. He'd *called* her far worse.

She struggled to take a deep breath as anxiety rolled back through her. "You've spent the last six and a half years on a ship?"

"For the most part. I fought in the war with America. It was horrific. I'd prefer not to get into the specifics, if you don't mind."

Again, he treated her with a deference she would never have expected. Her eyes narrowed as she stared at him intently. He looked like her husband. Mostly. Except for his size. He had the same strong, square jaw, the same sandy brown hair, though she now realized it was a bit lighter, probably from spending so much time out in the open air on a ship. And the same nose, or so she thought. Damn, but it was difficult to summon an exact picture of him. If he yelled at her or bared his teeth in anger, then she would know for sure…

She froze for a moment. Did she think he wasn't her husband? That was beyond absurd.

"No," she finally said, recalling that they were supposed to be having a conversation, however bizarre after all this time apart. "I'd rather not know the specifics either. But how is it that you are now here? Did you break free of your captors?"

"Yes. The ship caught fire, and I was able to get away and find my way here." He glanced around again, drinking in his surroundings as if they were water and he was dying of thirst. "Home."

"You look as though you can't quite believe it." She wanted to bite the words back as soon as they left her mouth. They didn't say such things to each other. He wasn't…amusing or, God forbid, *charming*, and she wasn't conversational.

"I can't, actually. I never imagined I'd return to Beaumont Tower." He said nothing of her. Or Beau.

Beau.

Verity's heart sped until she feared it would catapult from her chest. What was she going to say to him? What was Rufus going to say? Did he even know? She should tell him, but couldn't bring herself to form the words. She wasn't sure she could expose her boy to this monster.

"I realize this is…awkward or strange or both. And probably many other things," he said, again with that half smile that made him look as attractive as the day she'd met him at the house party she'd attended here with her father when she was just nineteen. As attractive as she'd believed him to be until their wedding night six months later.

She closed her eyes briefly and directed her attention to the window and the lawn stretching away from the house. "It is many things, yes," she said softly. "I don't know what to say or how to react. I am…shocked."

"I can well imagine. It's a bit of a shock for me to be here. And a relief."

She heard it in his voice. He sounded almost vulnerable. She turned her head back toward him. "What happened to you?"

"I told you—"

"Yes, and I understand you don't wish to speak of the specifics, but you are vastly different."

He cocked his head to the side and took his time answering. "In what way?"

"In every way." She stopped herself before she categorized his improvements.

Improvement? She couldn't think like that. He was still Rufus Beaumont, the Duke of Blackguard, as she liked to call him in her mind. "This is more than awkward or strange. I've spent the last six and a half years mourning you." The lie came easily. "And moving on with my life."

"You can't have taken a husband?" he asked.

"No, but neither am I ready to welcome you as such. I can't…" She was afraid to say what she wanted, but it had to be said. "Things can't go back to the way they were." She meant that in every sense and braced herself for his anger. Only it didn't come.

He nodded easily. "I understand. Completely. I don't wish to force you into anything. I'm looking forward to reacquainting myself with the estate. Is there a new steward? I should like to meet with him."

"No, it's still Cuddy." *God, he is here.* She still couldn't believe it and suspected it would be some time until she could. "Of course you can meet with him." Except she'd been about to dismiss him. Her plans were going up in flames! Why did he have to come back?

She abruptly stood, needing to move so the nervous energy flowing through her could have an outlet. As she paced toward the hearth, she ignored the prickle of apprehension that danced along her nape. Would she never be able to turn her back on him without feeling a sense of dread?

At the fireplace, she turned and realized she'd had good reason to be concerned. He'd gotten up from the chair and prowled toward her on silent feet. This was different too. She'd always heard him coming, his heavily booted feet clomping over the floorboards with an impending doom.

He stopped a few feet from her, his brow creased with concern. Concern! "I'm sorry for this—for what you must be feeling. I can't imagine how difficult this must be."

She absolutely didn't know what to do with his care. It was as if he was a completely different person. She kept coming back to that. Because what else would explain his utter change? She blinked at him. "Were you injured?"

"Many times." He said this without inflection, and she wondered how he'd been hurt and to what extent.

She shrugged her curiosity away. She didn't want to care about what happened to him. She didn't even want to *know* him.

And yet she must. He was her husband, by law, and he was here. He could claim his marital rights, and she'd have no quarrel. She could try to sue him for divorce…a near-hysterical laugh bubbled in her throat, and she worked to swallow it down.

He took another step toward her, and she shrank back. He held up his hands. "I don't mean to upset you. You need time to adjust. I understand. I do too."

The tension between them was palpable—her anxiety and his...surprise? Surely he would know how she would react to him? He'd delighted in frightening her, in keeping her in a state of wariness if not outright fear. He'd liked watching her cower.

But this Rufus—for he was *not* the same—seemed to be in a state of wariness too, as if he wasn't sure what to expect from *her*. Maybe he'd forgotten, and maybe whatever had happened to him had changed him enough to... To what? Make him tolerable? She couldn't believe that was possible.

They were thankfully interrupted by the arrival of the butler, Kirwin. His pale blue eyes widened as he saw Rufus. "Your Grace." The words came out in half surprise and half question. He was so startled that he apparently forgot to bow.

"Kirwin, it's good to see you."

Verity blinked at her husband—that was going to take some getting used to. Had he really just said it was *good* to see someone?

"And you, Your Grace. Your bags arrived from the stable, and they said they belonged to His Grace, but I didn't believe them."

"And why would you?" Rufus said with that almost charming smile. "I've reappeared out of nowhere. Well, not nowhere, but it may as well have been. Suffice it to say I was taken away against my will, and it has taken me this long to return home."

Kirwin glanced toward Verity, and she could see he was still in a state of shock. As they all would likely be for quite some time. "Welcome home, sir. I'll have your bags taken upstairs…" His voice trailed off as his gaze moved back to Verity.

"I can move my things out of the ducal chamber." She kept her eyes averted from Rufus. "I took the larger chamber a few years ago."

"That makes perfect sense, and I won't ask you to leave it. Kirwin, put my things wherever you see fit." Rufus looked to Verity. "Unless you have a preference?"

He was asking for her *preference*? Oh, this was going to take more than getting used to. This was going to require a complete shift in her behavior and her thinking. *If* he remained like this. Perhaps as he settled back into his routine, he'd revert to the beast she'd married.

Both Kirwin and Rufus watched her expectantly. "The Blue Room." That was the bedroom next to the drawing room and the farthest one from her chamber.

Kirwin nodded before shifting his attention to Rufus. "Do you require anything, Your Grace?"

"A bath would be welcome. If it's not too much trouble."

"Not at all. I'll have it prepared at once." Kirwin turned to go but then pivoted to look at Verity, his brow raised. "His lordship will be upstairs in the Guinea Room," he said softly.

Verity nodded at the butler. "Thank you, Kirwin."

The butler left, and she took a deep, sustaining breath.

Rufus looked at her in question. "His lordship?"

"The Earl of Preston." When he seemed nonplussed, she said, "Your son."

He nodded briskly. "Of course. I'd forgotten he would hold the courtesy title." He wiped a hand across his brow. "I was remiss. I should have asked after him directly. As I said before, this is all so strange."

"You know that you have a son?" He'd disappeared before she'd told him she was expecting.

"I'd…heard."

She supposed that made sense. "Where did you come from? I mean, have you been traveling all over England?"

"No, I arrived in Liverpool about a fortnight ago. I would have come sooner, but I wasn't…in the best of shape."

Again, she wanted to know what he'd endured. A horrid part of her was glad he'd suffered. She could think of no one who deserved it more. But the thoughts made her feel small and wretched.

She refocused on Beau—nothing mattered next to him. "So you heard of Beau on your way here."

"Beau?"

"That's what we call him. His name is Augustus Christopher Beaumont."

His eyes widened in surprise. "Christopher?"

"That was his great-grandfather's name. Have you forgotten?"

"Not at all. I'm just surprised. I would've expected Archibald to be one of his names."

She went completely still, expecting him to rail at her for not using his father's name. However, Augustus was the one who'd been kind to her. If only he hadn't died just a month after she'd wed Rufus. His presence had kept Rufus from devolving into a complete blackguard, and once he was gone, things had changed for the worse.

"I like it very much," he said softly, surprising her more than anything else that day. And that was saying quite a bit. Was this how it was going to be? She would stare at him in disbelief as he continued to behave completely out of character, all while her insides curled in turmoil, awaiting the snap in his temper.

"He's a very good boy," she said cautiously. "I need to speak with him, to prepare him before you can meet."

"I would expect nothing less. I will let you decide when and where."

"Your kindness and understanding is more than I could have hoped for. I'll talk to him after his lessons. If all goes well, you can meet him this evening."

"I should like that, thank you. And now, I believe I'll have that bath." He turned toward the stairs that rose against the far wall, and she watched a frown crease his profile.

"The Blue Room hasn't changed," she said. "Do you remember where it is?"

He looked at her in consternation. "I'm afraid I don't." A low chuckle sounded in his chest.

Smiling and laughing. She could count the number of times she'd seen him do that on one hand. "Up the stairs and through the drawing room, first room on the left."

He stared at her a moment, making her mildly uncomfortable, but not for the reasons she would have expected. He looked at her with something he never had before—curiosity. "I want to be sure you understand that I don't expect our marriage to resume as it once was."

As it once was... Was he trying to say he was going to be a better man? She couldn't bring herself to ask. What he'd put her through, that horrid, dark time—it wasn't something she talked about. It wasn't something she *thought* about. And, as he'd indicated about his time away, she preferred to leave it in the past.

"You seem…changed. Perhaps we should behave as if we just met." She made this offer but wasn't certain she could forget what he'd done, who he was. Or who he'd been, if he truly had changed.

"That seems a wise idea." His head dipped briefly. "Let me know what you want to do regarding the boy. I will await your direction. Until later, then." He inclined his head before stalking toward the stairs and climbing to the upper floor. She watched him disappear into the drawing room and let out a breath she hadn't realized she'd been holding.

Her body wanted to collapse, but she fought the drain of tension and anxiety that threatened to send her into a puddle. Instead, she turned, and made her way from the King's Hall through the Great Hall to the stairs that led to her private quarters in the corner opposite the drawing room.

She went up to the study that adjoined the ducal chamber and strode immediately to her writing desk, where she penned a short letter to her cousin Diana, begging her to come at once.

Verity's hand shook as she finished. She needed her cousin, the person to whom she was closest in the entire world, the person who would help her face what she must.

Rufus was *home.*

Gone were her plans to reclaim her future and forge a path for herself and Beau. A scant hour ago, she'd been filled with hope and excitement as she planned for the changes that would allow her to fully inhabit her role as duchess and ensure her son became the duke she wanted him to be.

Now she had to answer to her husband once more. A man filled with more cruelty and anger than ought to be possible for a person to feel. And yet, the man who'd arrived today was not him. He was perhaps something worse. An unknown who could take away every freedom she currently enjoyed. Or more terrible still: her son.

No, she wouldn't fall to pieces. She would hold strong—for Beau. She stood to take the letter downstairs and vowed that she wouldn't let Rufus ruin their lives. She'd protect herself and Beau at any cost.

Chapter Three
❦

THE STEAM FROM the bath had long since ebbed, and the water had gone tepid. He stood, sluicing water over the edge of the tub, and reached for the towel that sat on a nearby table.

Stepping from the tub, he dried off, then deposited the towel over the back of a chair pushed under a wide oak desk. He padded into the small dressing chamber adjoining the bedroom and found his meager belongings tucked away.

There wasn't much to choose from, but he found something suitable to wear. Tomorrow, he would need to find a tailor to come and measure him and make new clothing. Unless... Had the duchess saved any of his clothing? Should he ask?

Damn, she'd been skittish. But what did he expect after a nearly seven-year absence.

He turned to the glass to tie his cravat and paused at the reflection staring back at him. He didn't look like a duke.

Probably because he wasn't one.

Christopher Powell blinked. What the hell was he doing? If he went through with this... He snorted. Too late. He'd already committed.

The cravat almost tied itself as his fingers threaded the silk. It wasn't the same as knotting rope on his ship, but he was as good at either. He supposed a duke needed a valet, but he didn't.

Satisfied with his handiwork, Kit turned from the

glass and finished buttoning his waistcoat, frowning at the lackluster gray fabric. Yes, new clothing would be necessary since the fire had claimed most everything he'd owned, including his finery.

He reached for his dark blue coat and shrugged it on before smoothing his hair back from his forehead. And now what? He couldn't leave his room for fear he'd run into the boy.

Good Lord, he had a son. Or had to pretend he did anyway. When the duchess had mentioned him, he'd tried to cover for not asking about him straightaway. But then it had seemed she hadn't expected him to know, so he'd had to cover for that too. Hell, he was going to have to be on his toes.

At least the boy hadn't known him—Kit could perhaps relax with him. No, he couldn't do that. Hell, he didn't even know what to say to him. Perhaps he should consider that first.

He turned back to the glass and smiled. "Beau, I'm your father."

He winced and tried again. "Look at what a big boy you are. I'm pleased to meet you, I'm your father."

Scowling he turned away from the glass and chastised himself once more. This hadn't been his plan. He'd *planned* to find his way onto the estate and into the castle from which he'd steal something valuable but of little import that would scarcely be missed. The place had to be full of costly artifacts that would provide the remaining funds he needed to replace his ship and hire a new crew. He doubted he'd be able to recruit any of his old hands, but he'd try. They'd had to move on after Kit's ship had gone down.

No, becoming a duke hadn't been his plan, but faced with the opportunity, he'd been loath to pass it up. So he hadn't.

And here he was, the Duke of Blackburn, and he'd be damned if he'd regret it.

A knock on his door took him from his thoughts. Grateful for the interruption, he stalked through the chamber and found Kirwin standing in the hall. He remembered Kirwin and had suffered a moment's apprehension as he waited for the butler to recognize him in return. But he hadn't. What had Kit expected? He'd met the man nearly two decades ago.

"Your Grace," the butler began. He still carried the glimmer of surprise in his light blue eyes. "Her Grace has requested you meet her and his lordship in the drawing room in a quarter hour."

A burst of anxiety broke over Kit, and sweat dappled his neck. "Thank you, Kirwin."

"May I say, sir, that you seem a bit different, but then you've been gone a long time. Her Grace explained what happened, and I must offer my condolences for what you've surely endured."

Kit felt a bit horrible for lying to this kind man, but it was necessary to achieve his ends—ends that would not adversely affect any of these people. "I appreciate that, Kirwin."

The butler offered a slight bow before adding. "Dinner is served at six in the small dining room." Then he took himself off.

Kit closed the door, and pushed out a pent-up breath. What the bloody hell was he thinking? Of course this could adversely affect these people. He was about to tell a boy who wasn't his son that he was his father.

Fuck.

He should go. Immediately. Before any damage

could be done.

Except, if they were to meet in a quarter hour, she'd probably already told the boy.

Get a hold of yourself. The voice in the back of his head was stern and insistent. He was only taking that which should have been his. And judging from the duchess's reaction, she wouldn't miss him when he left. On the contrary, he'd be willing to bet his new ship that she'd be glad to see him go.

He took a deep breath and reined in control of his senses. He could manage this. He'd faced and defeated far worse than… Christ, he didn't even know her name. *The Duchess of Blackburn.* He wouldn't *have* to call her by name, for he had no plans to be that familiar.

Smoothing his palms over the lapels of his coat, he walked to the door and left the room. The drawing room was to his immediate right. He remembered it well, as it was the primary living space of the castle. Some of the other rooms—such as the small dining room—would take some effort to find. If caught as he wandered about, he would easily explain that he was simply relearning his home by exploring every room.

Yes, the drawing room looked much the same, though the furniture had been replaced. There was still a case stuffed with books in the corner, the wide hearth surmounted by a painting of a long-ago duke and duchess seated in the King's Hall as they granted an audience to their serfs, and a framed map of the estate from the medieval period hung opposite the fireplace.

Kit had studied that map endlessly during his single visit and had traversed every inch he'd seen. He crossed to it, and his gaze fell on a table beneath. Scattered across the top was a collection of toy soldiers, reminding him of what he'd consigned himself to…

"Papa!"

The cry startled him as he turned back toward the corridor leading to his bedchamber. A small, dark-haired boy rushed to him and threw his arms around Kit's legs. He'd expected the lad to be reticent and wary, as his mother had been. He'd never imagined this warm reception—or the burst of warmth he felt in return.

Kit patted the boy's head, then took a step backward. "Let me look at you."

Beau—he looked like a Beau, if anyone could really look like a name, because he was a rather handsome child with bright eyes and a strong chin—stood tall and puffed out his chest. "I'm six."

"Of course you are. Although you could easily pass for seven."

A grin spread over the boy's features, lighting his green eyes. *Green.* Like his. Well, that was something, he supposed.

Beau took Kit's hand, and though it was a small, simple gesture, he felt it all the way to his toes as the boy dragged him toward the settee. "Tell me all about where you were, Papa. Mama said it was a terrible ordeal and that you wouldn't want to speak of it, but I said you'd tell me." He let go of Kit's hand and sat on the settee. As soon as Kit dropped down beside him, he scooted as close as he could. "I told Mama you'd been kidnapped and held captive. Why else wouldn't you have come home?"

Why else indeed. "Did she tell you I spent much of my time aboard a ship?"

He glanced toward the doorway where the duchess still lingered. She was tall with a lithe, graceful frame. Nearly black hair framed her heart-shaped face, which was punctuated with a small, slender nose and pert, pink lips. Her eyes were dark and long-lashed and, he suspected, seductive if she chose. Her arms were folded across her chest, and she wore the same look of guarded skepticism she'd had since his arrival. That was a long way from seduction, and he had to wonder why he'd even thought of that.

"No," Beau said. "Can you sail a ship, Papa?"

Kit turned his attention to Beau. "Yes. Maybe someday I'll teach you." He winced inwardly knowing that would never come to pass. Damnation, this was a terrible idea.

Beau's green eyes glowed with excitement. "Oh yes! But first you much teach me to shoot and wield a sword. I've already learned to ride, though Mama says I need much more practice."

"You should always listen to your mother." He looked over at her again and caught the flash of surprise in her gaze. Christ almighty, what kind of bastard had the duke been? Given her demeanor, Kit could only imagine a right despicable one.

"That's what Thomas told me today too," Beau said. Who was Thomas? "Mama knows everything."

Kit couldn't contain his laugh. His mother, though she'd died when he was only eight, had known everything too. She'd managed their household with strict precision and a wealth of love for both him and his father. Her death had decimated their tiny family, and it had spawned the end of Kit's innocence. "Yes, mothers usually do," he said.

Beau's gaze turned pleading as he stared up at Kit. "Tell me about the bad men who took you, Papa. Did you have to kill them?"

"Beau!" The duchess's sharp, feminine tone sounded

through the room, drawing both him and the child to whip their heads in her direction. She'd left the doorway and now came toward them, her brows pitched low on her forehead. "That's an awful question. He didn't kill anyone. And even if he had, you're far too young to hear such gruesome stories."

In truth, Kit had killed many men. His livelihood—which had led him into war—had demanded it. But he wouldn't say so. He couldn't disagree that Beau shouldn't hear of such horrors.

Kit angled himself toward the boy and looked him in the eye. "When you are old enough, I will tell you about my journeys, all right? But for now, I would like to concentrate on being home with you. And your mother."

He darted a look toward her again and caught the bewildered expression in her eyes just before she masked it. Yes, the duke had been a deplorable prick, and he wanted to know in what way and why. For some unknown reason, he felt a fierce urge to protect the child beside him and the woman hovering nearby.

And he protected nothing but himself and his ship. The last at which he'd failed. Disgust rose in his throat, but he swallowed it back. He'd soon have a new ship. A *better* ship. In the meantime, he would play duke. And father. And husband. His gaze slid toward her again and saw her thinly veiled contempt. Not husband, then.

Which was fine. He hadn't come here to woo a wife or coddle a son. He'd do what he needed to regain what he'd lost, and he'd do it with what he deserved. What he'd been promised.

Beau slipped his arms around Kit's waist and squeezed. "I'm so glad you're home. I knew this day would happen, even if Mama didn't."

Kit's gut clenched, and he fought to banish the guilt wrought by the boy's adoration. He looked over at the duchess once more. Her lips were pursed, her brows angled. She really didn't care for this entire situation.

Extricating himself from the hug with a pat to the boy's back, Kit gave the lad a half smile. "What should you be doing now? Surely I've created havoc on your routine."

"He finished lessons early," the duchess said. "But he should go and ready himself for dinner."

Kit blinked at her. "Does he dine with you?" That wasn't typical in houses like this, at least from what little he knew.

"Yes. It's just the two of us, after all. Or was, anyway." The edge of bitterness in her tone was unmistakable. She positively detested this situation. Kit's guilt doubled.

"Must I go, Mama?" Beau asked pleadingly. "Can't I stay with Papa?"

Kit ruffled the boy's hair. "Your mother and I have things to discuss. Things that will surely bore you. Remember how I said you should always listen to your mother?" Along with that Thomas person, whoever he was.

"Yes, Papa." Beau slid from the settee. "After dinner, I will show you all my soldiers."

"I would like that," Kit said. He'd never had toy soldiers. What he'd had was a mountain of books. And absent much else, he'd utterly devoured them. Over and over and over again.

Beau threw his arms around Kit's neck and hugged him one more time. Kit held him close as the scent of grass and boy washed over him. When Beau stood back, he put his hands on Kit's face. "You look like me."

Kit made himself laugh. "Who else should I look like?"

Beau grinned. "No one, just me. Because you're *my* papa." He turned and skipped from the room, turning at the doorway and looking at his mother in alarm. "Where is Papa sleeping?"

The duchess gestured toward the wall that separated the drawing room from Kit's chamber. "In the Blue Room."

"Can't he move next to me? I should like it if he slept close by." He looked to Kit. "You could even sleep in my room, if you want."

Kit suppressed a smile and waited for the duchess to handle this.

"The Blue Room is much larger and more comfortable," she said.

"Is that where you slept before, Papa?"

"Ah…" He looked at the duchess in question.

She turned a smile on her son. "Let me talk to your father about where he wants to sleep."

Kit didn't care so long as there was a bed and not a swinging hammock belowdeck.

"Yes, Mama. But make sure it's next to me." He grinned at both of them before turning and disappearing down the corridor.

The duchess faced him and let out a breath, as if she'd just completed a difficult task. He supposed she had.

"I don't really care where I sleep," he said.

"Then perhaps you should take the room next to Beau. If that's all right?" She looked at him in wary expectation despite the fact that he'd just said he didn't care. He had to get to the bottom of what was wrong with her. Or him. Or both of them.

He gestured to a chair opposite the settee. "Sit. Please."

She dropped onto the seat with alacrity, then blinked as her mouth pulled into a frown. He thought she might say something, but she only clasped her hands in her lap. Her tension was palpable.

He searched for the right words to say. "I sense your discomfort, and I'd like to allay your…" He'd been about to say fears, but decided that was too harsh, "concerns. Please, I ask that you be completely honest."

Her brows shot up, and he could almost see her mind churning as her hands squeezed together and she sucked in her cheeks. It took her another moment to gather her thoughts—or so it seemed. "Truly? You want my honesty."

He offered a placid smile. "Without reservation."

"I don't recognize you at all."

It was a hard punch to the gut, but not unexpected. While he knew he looked similar to the duke, their likenesses were not identical. "I've been gone a long time," he said carefully.

"Yes." She flattened her hands against her skirts and flexed her fingers. "It's not that you look different—though you do. A bit anyway." She blinked at him. "Are your eyes green?"

"Yes. Like Beau's." He'd no idea what color eyes the duke possessed.

"I recall them being hazel."

"Sometimes, depending on the light, there's a bit of brown in them." It was another outright lie, but he'd have to become accustomed to telling those.

She tipped her head to the side and narrowed her

eyes slightly. Straightening, she continued, "As I was saying, it's not just that you look a bit different. Your behavior is… Well, it's completely foreign. Quite simply, you aren't the Rufus I married."

Here was his chance. If not to peel back the layers of her apprehension about him, then to perhaps assuage her concerns. "Is that a bad thing?"

She froze for the briefest moment. "No," she said quietly. "And therein lies the problem. It's quite a good thing, actually. But is it…real?" The words fell from her mouth like petals floating to the earth—soft and halting before settling around him with finality.

"I'm real." That was all he could say. All he wanted to say just then.

"You asked me to be honest. I need to know that I can trust you to be this different person."

How he wanted to ask what kind of person he'd been before! It wasn't good, that much was clear. How much of a prick was his bloody relative? Kit would find out. Someone would tell him.

"I've endured a harrowing experience," he said. "And I've been gone a long time—long enough to have changed significantly." That much was true. He'd left England a fifteen-year-old lad and returned a lifetime later.

"I can trust you to be…kind?"

He inwardly groaned and pledged to smack the duke if they ever crossed paths. Which seemed highly unlikely. "On my honor." He realized his honor was an unknown commodity to her. "How about this: You shall have the power to say and do whatever you feel necessary. I will sleep where you tell me, interact with Beau however you direct, and communicate with you however you prefer. The only thing I require is autonomy to deal with the estate as is my duty."

His duty.

His mind went back to that summer seventeen years ago, when his father—his real father—had brought him here and showed him the life that should have been his. *If* he'd been legitimate. He'd loved every moment, had hungered for the impossible that would allow him to inherit the dukedom some day. But it had been, or so he'd thought, unattainable.

Until now.

He needed money—which his father had promised him—to purchase a new ship. But he *wanted* this position and this place, at least for a little while.

"That's rather generous of you, thank you." She still looked as if she didn't believe him.

He leaned forward and winced as she shrank back against the chair. God, *he* wasn't a monster, but he wanted to throttle the man who'd done this to her. "You don't need to trust me yet. You'll see that things will be…better than they were before." He hated what she must think of him, but it wasn't as if he could tell her the truth. Hell, he could take any number of things from the house and be on his way tomorrow. Maybe that was what he should do…

"As it happens, you *could* help me with something."

He snapped his gaze to hers. "You have only to name it."

"You promise I can trust you? That you won't get angry?" The trepidation in her eyes made his chest burn.

"I promise both of those things. Please tell me how I can help."

"After you disappeared, my father came here to *help* me." The way she said help suggested it was the opposite. "He worked closely with Cuddy, which I thought made sense since he'd encouraged you to hire him. Their relationship seems to have remained close. Despite my being the duchess, I believe Cuddy still answers to him." The bridge of her nose wrinkled as she spoke of them in obvious distaste. Hell, were there any men in her life worth a damn save Beau? "Today I'd decided to dismiss him. I want to replace him with Whist's grandson."

Kit remembered Whist, the former steward, from that brief time he'd stayed here. He'd been relieved to learn Whist was no longer serving in that capacity in case he recalled the bastard who'd spent a summer on the estate. But that was so long ago, and Kit looked, of course, much different now. He also looked rather like his cousin, which was why this charade was even marginally successful. So far.

"Is there anything wrong with this Cuddy fellow? Or is it just that he answers to your father instead of you?" That ought to be enough to discredit Cuddy, and to Kit, it was.

Her shoulder lifted as she looked away from him. "Yes, that's it. He doesn't welcome my participation in the management of the estate. In your absence, I thought it was important for me to take more of a role, especially as Beau grows older."

He couldn't argue with that. "Well, he'll do whatever I tell him to now. I'm sorry he's been difficult."

Her gaze shifted back to his, and the dark irises of her eyes bored into him with their intensity. "You're going to keep him on, then?"

"Doubtful. I don't like people who don't give respect where it's due, and the duchess of the estate deserves that and more. Where does this fellow reside?"

Her disbelief had once again been replaced with bewilderment, but this time, it was no longer fleeting. Perhaps he was finally making progress. "In the southeast tower," she said. "His office is on the ground level, and his living quarters above it."

"Excellent. I'll meet with him on the morrow. Would you care to join me?"

Her eyes widened. "I, ah, yes. If you don't mind."

"I wouldn't have invited you if I minded. When I said I wanted autonomy, I didn't mean to suggest that you would be excluded. I shall involve you in whatever you desire." That word evoked something within him. Not just the word, but speaking the word in her presence. She was, much to his misfortune, a stunningly beautiful woman.

Misfortune?

Yes, because while she was his "wife," he wouldn't presume to approach her in any sort of intimate fashion. Their marriage, short as it must be, would be entirely platonic.

She stood, and he sensed that she needed a reprieve from his presence. "Thank you. I keep saying that, but I am incredibly grateful for this change in your demeanor. I hope it lasts."

He nearly laughed at his thoughts of a moment ago. Intimacy with the duchess wasn't something he would need to worry about. He doubted she'd ever touch her husband again, at least not willingly. And that was just as well. It was also just as well that he didn't know her name. Still, he'd like to.

He rose. "I am at your service. Should I join you and Beau for dinner, then?"

"I think you must. He's over the moon that you've returned. I beg of you, whatever you do, please don't disappoint him."

Kit's resolve wavered. When he'd seized this opportunity, he hadn't known about the boy. And he knew from experience what it was like to be young and suffer loss and disappointment.

Fuck.

A voice in his head yelled at him to knock it off. Beau had never known a father, and from what Kit could tell, that man had been a right son of a bitch. Kit would show Beau what a good father could be, and if he only had one for a short time, well, that was better than to have never had one at all, wasn't it?

"I'll take the room next to his," Kit said. "I'll speak to Kirwin."

"Thank you. Again." She didn't smile, and he didn't expect her to. That didn't mean he didn't want to see it. He imagined her face lighting up with joy and decided that would be worth working for.

Chapter Four

WHEN VERITY WOKE the next morning, she wondered if Rufus's return had been a dream. But then the rapturous face of her son crowded her mind, and she knew it hadn't. Beau was simply enthralled with his father, and so far, Verity couldn't blame him. Rufus was charming, attentive, and exactly the kind of father she would want for Beau.

Which made absolutely no sense.

She longed to ask him why he'd changed. Had he simply suffered enough over the past six and a half years that he'd transformed from the monster he'd been? She supposed that was possible, but it also gave her pause. If he could change so much once, surely he could change back. It would be quite some time until she could relax with him, if she truly ever could.

She and Beau had taken breakfast at the table in her study that morning, as they usually did. Beau had asked why his father wasn't there, and Verity had simply said they would need time to learn a new routine. In truth, she hadn't invited him. It wasn't that she hadn't thought of it, rather that she hadn't wanted to.

And that made her feel terrible.

She thought of Beau, off to the Guinea Room with his nurse already, and her heart squeezed. While she was glad to see him so happy to have his father, a part of her didn't want to share him. Particularly with Rufus.

Oh, she was being awful. Rufus was back, for better or for worse, and those were, in fact, part of the terms of their marriage. She should support him—or at least tolerate him—for Beau's sake.

Last night, he had been rather wonderful, playing soldiers with Beau after dinner and promising to get him a toy ship. He'd said a boy needed a ship. He'd been so passionate about it, in fact, that Verity wondered if he'd come to like sailing while he was gone. Would it be difficult for him to be back here on land? He'd changed so much in other ways that she wouldn't be surprised to find he didn't like it here. Or perhaps that was merely what she was hoping for.

Self-disgust flashed through her again, and she stalked down the stairs to the hallway next to the kitchen before going out into the upper courtyard. Rufus stood near the upper gate, where they'd arranged to meet before going to see Cuddy.

He turned, perhaps hearing her close the door before she descended the steps to the courtyard. As she approached, he looked up at the clock mounted high on the brick. "How long has that been broken?" he asked.

She joined him and squinted at the unmoving hands. "About two years, I think. Cuddy keeps meaning to have it repaired."

"And why hasn't he?"

"When I ask, he says he hasn't found someone to fix it."

"I can probably repair it," Rufus said, surprising her.

She'd never known him to be mechanically inclined. He was good at riding, hunting, and drinking and little else. She supposed he was also good at being horrid. Or *had* been good at that, anyway.

She looked over at him, her gaze lingering on his profile before taking in his costume. He wore the same clothing he had yesterday, and she wondered if that was all he had. His garments were stored around here somewhere—she'd ask Kirwin to bring them out.

"Shall we go see the steward?" Rufus asked.

"Yes." Her pulse quickened. Was it because she worried Rufus would offer his arm? Or was she simply nervous to meet with Cuddy?

Thankfully, Rufus didn't offer. He only gestured for her to join him as they walked through the upper gate.

"The gardens are beautiful. Are there more roses?" he asked. "Or is my memory faulty?"

His attempts at idle conversation still perplexed Verity, but she preferred them to who he'd been before. "No, your memory is fine. I've added more roses over the years. I've taken a special interest in the gardens."

"I look forward to investigating the others."

She almost believed him. She had yet to determine if he was being nice for a purpose or if this was simply the new and improved Rufus. Either alternative made her head spin.

They took the path through the garden that led down to the lower courtyard where she'd met him yesterday upon his miraculous return. Yes, that was an accurate description. To have him home after so much time had passed—never mind how vastly improved he was—was nothing short of a miracle. And one she hadn't prayed for.

They cut across the courtyard at an angle to reach Cuddy's office. After dinner last night, he'd said that he'd sent a note to Cuddy to set the interview. Verity wondered what the steward thought. He'd successfully kept her at bay, which now grated horribly, but he wouldn't be able to do the same to Rufus.

The door to Cuddy's office was ajar, but Rufus rapped on the wood before pushing it wider. "Good morning," he said, indicating that Verity should precede him.

She went into the dim interior. Bright gray spring light filtered through the high-set windows and was supplemented by two lanterns burning—one on the wall and another on Cuddy's wide desk.

The steward stood and came around the piece of furniture. He bowed to Rufus. "Good morning, Your Grace. You look very well." He then bowed to Verity. "Your Grace."

"Shall we sit?" Rufus asked.

"Whatever you prefer," Cuddy said.

As Cuddy walked back behind his desk, Rufus waited for Verity to sit. She took one of the pair of chairs facing the steward. Rufus sat down beside her and didn't waste a moment before launching into their business.

"I'd like to see the account books."

Cuddy nodded. "Of course. I shall have them delivered to the house later today."

"Actually, I'd like to see them now, if you please." Rufus's tone was pleasant but firm. The old Rufus would've yelled, *Give me the goddamn ledger!*

"Certainly." Cuddy hesitated a moment, his gaze locked with Rufus's, before he opened a drawer in the desk. He removed a leather-bound book and slid it across the wood to Rufus. "That is this year and last. I can have the rest sent up to the house. They're in my storage room." His head turned slightly, and his gaze shot to the right. The small storage room was behind the office.

"Thank you," Rufus said. He opened the ledger and

scanned a few pages before snapping it closed with a mild smile. "I look forward to reading this in depth. I must ask why you haven't shared these with Her Grace."

Cuddy's eyes widened briefly as he darted a look toward Verity. A flash of malice darkened the already dark brown irises before he returned his focus to Rufus. "She hasn't asked for them."

Rufus didn't so much as look at her before saying. "She's requested to speak with you and to be more involved in the management of the estate. As the duchess, that is her right. I would argue it's her duty, particularly in my absence. I don't like that you ignored her requests. For that reason, I've decided to terminate your employment, effective immediately."

Cuddy's eyes now widened so much that Verity feared they might fall from his head. He was a large, beefy man, but his features had always seemed small to her—from heavy-lidded eyes to a thin-lipped mouth to a chin that was practically nonexistent. "Your Grace, please, allow me to rectify this mistake."

"I'm afraid that won't be acceptable, Cuddy. We've already found a replacement and would like to have him begin as soon as possible."

"But you only arrived yesterday," he sputtered.

Verity watched the malevolent smile that curled Rufus's mouth. "I work very efficiently. Some may even say I'm ruthless."

A chill dashed up Verity's spine. That was the Rufus she knew. And yet…not. He'd never been so elegant in his abuse. Not that what he was currently doing could be called abuse. No, what he was doing was called justice and fitting, and she couldn't have been happier.

And that caused her to question everything.

How could she find joy in this man? Because he'd done what she'd asked by terminating Cuddy? It wasn't just that he'd dismissed the man. He'd done so by clearly stating the reason—that his treatment of her wasn't to be borne. Furthermore, he wouldn't give the man a chance to rectify his ways.

Verity stared at her husband and tried to dredge up her feelings of anger and resentment. But for now, she could only find gratitude and maybe a glimmer of admiration.

Irritation rose in her throat. No, she wouldn't admire him.

Cuddy laid his hands flat on the desk, and Verity could see a slight tremor in his fingers. "But, Your Grace, I've nowhere to go."

"You may stay for a few days, and I'll give you three months' wages and a recommendation—provided I find the accounts in order. I suggest you begin searching for a new position. I presume you'll land on your feet. Men like you usually do." He smiled that bland, slightly sinister smile again before turning his head to Verity. "Shall we go?"

She stared at him in continued bemusement. "Yes." Rising, she looked at Cuddy, who took a moment to stand. The muscles in his jaw were tense, and lines fanned from his mouth.

The steward inclined his head toward Rufus. "Thank you for your *generosity*, Your Grace." He said the word generosity as if he'd had a pistol pointed at his head threatening him to employ the word or die.

Rufus scooped the book up from the desk. "One of our vehicles will take you wherever you need to go, should you require it. Do send word as to when you plan to leave. Thank you for your service, Cuddy." He turned to Verity and held out his hand toward the door.

She left without saying anything to the steward and preceded Rufus into the bright gray sunlight. Well, not entirely gray, she realized as she squinted up at the sky. A few of the clouds were breaking.

Rufus fell into step beside her, and they walked back across the lower courtyard, reaching the stairs before she dared to speak. She glanced back at the tower and saw Cuddy standing in the doorway, staring at them. "He's watching us," she said.

"I'm not surprised. Plotting murder, perhaps," he said softly.

She snapped her gaze to his profile. "You don't really think that?"

"No, no. He's far too cowardly for that."

"How do you know?" Verity recalled what he'd said in the office, that men like Cuddy usually landed on their feet. "You seem to know a great deal about him, yet he'd scarcely started here before you disappeared."

"I don't really, but I can guess. I didn't care for his hesitation with the account book, and given what you told me of his treatment of you, I have reason to question his authenticity."

They walked through the upper gate, out of Cuddy's line of sight, and Verity relaxed a bit. "You're sure he won't really do something awful?"

"Not entirely, but I plan to keep an eye on him. That's why I offered one of our vehicles to take him to his destination." He paused in the upper courtyard and turned toward her. "We have enough vehicles to do that, don't we? I suppose I should've verified that first."

Verity blinked at the shadow of vulnerability in his

gaze. "Yes, we have several vehicles—a coach, a brougham, a cart, and a chaise. Our stock of horses, on the other hand, will probably not impress you. I haven't kept up on the stables." She'd thought of this last night as she'd fought to find sleep, mentally cataloguing all the things he could find fault with—and for which he might blame her and exact a punishment.

"I wouldn't expect you to. Why would that be necessary anyway? Do you have sufficient horseflesh for the vehicles? Beau told me all about his pony—and your mare. It sounds as if you've managed things fine."

"We sold your horse," she blurted, immediately horrified for telling him in that fashion. She'd dreaded it, but the animal had been difficult for anyone else to ride, so they hadn't. And he'd become even more difficult, so Cuddy had sold him. "It was Cuddy's idea." She hated how that sounded, like she was shifting blame, but it was the truth.

He cocked his head to the side, his gaze boring into hers. "You thought I'd be angry."

"Yes. He was your favorite...creature." She'd been about to say person, but that made no sense, of course. And yet, he'd treated the animal better than anyone else on the estate. His dogs had come in a close second. Verity had found homes for them with tenants within the first year of his disappearance. All but the smallest hound—Falstaff—who'd clung to her skirts the moment Rufus had left for London. They'd forged a strong bond until Beau was born, and then the dog had shared his adoration with the baby too. He'd died last year, much to her and Beau's sadness. But now they had his offspring, who nearly had their run of the castle. Along with the cats, the rabbits, and the squirrel. And soon to be goats.

"Speaking of creatures," she said. "I told Beau yesterday that I would see about moving a goat herd closer to the castle. He was quite taken with Whist's baby goat."

"Baby goats are incredibly endearing. Are there several herds on the estate?"

"Yes, but I was thinking of asking Mr. Maynard. His flock is largest, and he may not mind sparing a few."

"I shall ask him this afternoon, when I begin my tour of the estate," Rufus said. "Would you care to join me? In the absence of a steward, I should be eager for a guide."

She blinked at him, once more at a loss for words in the face of another thoughtful invitation.

"I've made you speechless again," he said. "I seem to do that quite a bit. You think about it and let me know at luncheon." He'd promised Beau he'd take the midday meal with him.

"It's fine. I mean, I can tell you now. Yes, I'll go with you." She took a deep breath to calm her suddenly racing heart. "This is all very strange."

"I'm afraid I wasn't a very nice person before." He said this almost as if he didn't remember the horrible way in which he'd treated her. "I do hope I'm behaving better since my return."

He was, but that didn't mean she was ready to embrace him. "I meant what I said yesterday," she said cautiously, afraid to poke the bear. "I don't want to go back to the way things were."

"Nor do I. I thought we were going to behave as if we'd just met."

"I'm not sure I can behave any other way. After all this time, I scarcely know you. In fact, I feel as if I don't know you at all. And yet, I can't forget who you were before. I'm not sure I want to." Her strong sense of self-preservation wouldn't let her.

"That makes perfect sense to me. Please know that I have no expectations. And I want you to have none of me either." He gave his head a small shake. "Actually, that's not quite accurate. I want you to expect kindness, respect, and gratitude for all you've done in my absence. You deserve nothing less."

"I'll…try." She didn't mean to hesitate, but she couldn't help it. "It's going to take me some time."

"I understand completely. And I'm delighted you'll be joining me for the tour. Should we invite Beau?"

Probably—he'd love it so. But Verity wasn't ready to expose him to Rufus quite that extensively yet. She wanted time alone with him first, to ensure he really wasn't a threat to her son. "He has lessons, and I hate to disturb his routine. And don't tell him, because he'll try to wheedle his way along."

Rufus chuckled softly. "To be a young boy again when we think anything is possible, even changing our mother's mind."

Verity found his sentiment strange. Rufus had rarely spoken of his childhood, and when he had, it was only to curse his father, who'd been cold and autocratic. She had to assume Rufus had taken after him. That made her wonder how his father and his uncle, the former duke, had been so different. Augustus had been warm and kind, though she supposed he'd also possessed an underlying sadness due to the loss of his young son at the very house party where she'd met Rufus.

"Where is this Entwhistle fellow currently employed?" Rufus asked, drawing her back from her reverie.

"Bleven House."

"Is that far?"

She looked at him in surprise. Surely he would remember who their neighbors were. "It borders Beaumont Tower to the south."

"Right." He nodded as his mouth split into a self-deprecating smile. "I've forgotten so much, I fear."

But he remembered his youth. A youth she didn't necessarily recognize. Did she still think there was a chance he wasn't actually Rufus? That couldn't be. The likeness was too strong, and he did know certain things.

"I shouldn't visit Entwhistle at Bleven House, but I'd like to speak with him before making a final decision regarding his employment."

She's already hired him, and it was possible Thomas had already informed his employer. "But you told Cuddy we already had a replacement."

"I wanted him to be sure my decision was final."

His decision. He'd discharged Cuddy, and he'd be the one to hire Thomas. He hadn't said as much, but she understood what he meant. "I've already offered Thomas—Entwhistle," she corrected herself, "the job."

"Oh, *he's* Thomas?" When Verity gave him a quizzical look, he said, "Beau mentioned him a few times yesterday. I wondered who he was." He transferred the account book to his other hand. "Entwhistle is just going to have to understand that I will make the final decision."

Verity bristled. "He's expecting to work here."

"And he probably will," Rufus said evenly. "I can sense your…indignation, and I would remind you that you gave me full autonomy to run the estate."

She had. So far, he'd done an excellent job, if firing Cuddy was any indication. Granted, it had only been one day.

It wasn't as if she could argue with him. He'd been nothing but deferential and thoughtful since his arrival. Things could be so much worse.

"My apologies. This is an adjustment."

"I understand. And I appreciate your trust."

She nearly laughed. *That* he didn't have.

And he likely never would.

Chapter Five

⋯⋅ई⋅३⋅⋯

LUNCHEON HAD BEEN a lively occasion with Beau introducing Kit to his new pet squirrel, Mr. Cheeks. His name was, of course, due to the amount of food he could stuff into the pouches in his mouth. Apparently, Beau had spent the last several weeks coaxing the animal ever closer to the house until the creature had finally come inside. Now he visited each day around midday, much to the chagrin of the three dogs who were also present. The two cats weren't amused either as they kept their distance and glared at the squirrel— and the dogs, truth be told—with cool dismay.

The menagerie reminded Kit of his own childhood at the vicarage. His mother had loved cats, and his father's best friend had been a scrappy terrier who was never more content than on his master's lap. Which didn't mean he also didn't appreciate frolicking with Kit in the yard.

Those had been happy times. Before his mother had died in yet another failed childbirth. Before darkness had descended upon them and stolen his father's joy.

Kit looked over at Verity riding nearby. She was a very handsome woman, and her seat was excellent. She looked as though she'd been born on a horse, the earth-brown skirt of her riding habit nearly blending with the flank of her horse.

She'd been nervous to have him see the stable, but then she was almost always nervous around him. If she wasn't, she was confused. Or bemused. Or just outright confounded.

He still didn't know what sort of beast he'd been, but he planned to find out. In fact, he'd hoped to do so today, thinking the tenants might shed some light; however, he'd surprised himself by inviting her to join him. That would make things a little more difficult.

She moved closer to him and gestured to the cottage just ahead. This would be their first stop, apparently. He didn't expect to see the entire fifty thousand acres in one day, of course, but hoped they would visit a handful of tenants. First on their agenda was visiting Mr. Maynard and his goat herd.

As they rode into the yard, a woman came from the cottage, wiping her hands on her apron. A girl, not as young as Beau, trailed her down the steps.

Kit pulled his horse to a stop and dismounted, then turned his attention to helping Verity down. He hadn't helped her mount—one of the grooms had done that—and wondered what it would be like for him to touch her. Would she flinch? He half expected her to.

He reached up and gently clasped her waist, helping her to the ground in a fluid motion. He withdrew from her immediately, but the connection had told him several things: her waist was quite trim, she possessed a fair amount of muscle, and she really, really didn't like him touching her.

As soon as her feet hit the earth, she moved away from him. She was also careful not to make eye contact. He didn't blame her. He blamed her rotten excuse of a husband.

Kit turned his attention to the cottage. The girl who'd followed her mother outside was now heading toward a lean-to shed, while the woman strode toward them. She wasn't wearing a bonnet, so she held her hand to her forehead to shade her eyes.

The duchess—whose name he *still* didn't know—smiled at the woman. "Good afternoon, Mrs. Maynard."

"Good afternoon, Your Grace." Mrs. Maynard executed a fine curtsey. Her gaze dashed over to Kit, while her mouth twitched with perhaps a bit of nerves.

"Mrs. Maynard, may I present His Grace, the Duke of Blackburn."

A short, sharp burst of pride bloomed in Kit's chest. Would he tire of being introduced like that? Probably not, since he didn't plan to be here that long.

Mrs. Maynard's gaze flashed with surprise before she sank into a deep curtsey. She didn't quite lift her eyes to his as she rose. "It's a miracle you're home, Your Grace. We prayed for your safe return every day."

"Did you? Well, I appreciate that. My fortune is undoubtedly due to your thoughtfulness and grace."

A pretty blush stained the woman's cheeks as she finally looked at Kit's face. But it was only a fleeting moment before she turned her head. He followed the direction of her attention and saw the girl coming back around the house. She was preceded by a man dressed in work clothing. A wide-brimmed hat shielded his face as he strode purposefully toward them.

Mrs. Maynard rushed to meet him and spoke to him briefly before he continued toward Kit and the duchess. It became clear that Mrs. Maynard had warned her husband as to the identity of their guest.

He bowed sharply. "Your Grace, we're honored to have you visit." He also bowed to the duchess. "Your Grace."

"You're my first stop on a tour of the estate," Kit said. "I understand you keep an impressive goat herd.

Would you mind showing me?"

"It would be my privilege. Come." He led them past the shed from whence he'd come toward a large fenced area. "This is just one of the pens," he said over his shoulder as he approached the gate. "There are four others of similar size."

Kit looked out at the goats grazing about. He caught sight of a handful of kids, and turned to ask the duchess, "Beau wanted a baby goat, is that right?"

"He was taken with a baby goat, but he'll love all of them the same."

Mr. Maynard opened the gate and held it while Kit and the duchess went into the pen. Mrs. Maynard and their daughter hadn't followed them.

When they were all inside, Mr. Maynard closed the gate and led them toward a group standing nearby. "We've had four births in the past fortnight, and we're expecting a half-dozen more in the next fortnight. Spring's a busy time!" He laughed as he looked toward Kit.

"I can imagine," Kit said. "As it happens, we'd like to have a small herd nearer the castle. My son would like to learn to tend goats."

Mr. Maynard's brows climbed. "Would he now? That seems an odd education for a future duke, but a right noble one."

Kit knew the man meant no offense, and in truth, he would have agreed. He wondered if the real duke would have allowed Beau to tend goats. From what he knew of his cousin, he would wager not. "I agree. You will find I am not your typical duke." He smiled and couldn't help darting a look toward the duchess.

She was staring at him with something akin to amazement. Someday, he would stop shocking her.

Maybe. Again, he might leave before that happened. In this case, he hoped not. He wanted her to trust him. He just wasn't sure why. Maybe because he thought it would be good for her. She needed to know that her current husband wasn't the horrid beast she remembered.

Until he left her, and then he really would be that horrid beast.

Except she wouldn't care. She'd be relieved to have her life back the way she wanted it—he saw resentment buried beneath the alternating waves of apprehension, shock, and bemusement.

"Do you think we could have a small herd?" the duchess asked Mr. Maynard.

"Oh, certainly. And I'd be happy to come build a pen. You'll need a shed for shelter too."

"I can help with those," Kit offered. When both the duchess and Mr. Maynard looked at him in surprise, he realized he'd once again stepped outside the normal bounds of his role. "As I said, I'm not your typical duke. Let me know the size and specifications, and I'll see that we have the lumber. We're keen to have the goats up at the castle as soon as possible."

"I look forward to helping, Your Grace." Mr. Maynard's gaze shifted to a spot over Kit's right shoulder. "Blast! Racer's found his way out of the gate again. I thought I'd fixed that latch!" He dashed toward the perimeter of the pen, and Kit followed, quickly realizing that he would be able to catch the wayward goat faster than Mr. Maynard.

Kit easily leapt the fence and broke into a hard run. He caught up to the animal and swept him up off the ground. A loud bleat filled his ears as he slowed and pivoted back toward the pen. "Aren't you a noisy thing? Disappointed to be snatched so quickly, eh? I bet you've given Mr. Maynard a great deal of trouble. Perhaps you should come to the castle. I think Beau might like chasing you about."

Mr. Maynard and the duchess waited for him just outside the pen as Kit deposited the goat over the fence. "I thank you kindly, Your Grace. I'd still be after the louse."

"Glad to be of assistance, Maynard. Perhaps you'd better send—Racer, is it? A fine and accurate name, it seems—to the castle if he's causing you difficulty."

Maynard looked at him with doubt. "He's a bit contrary. Are you certain you want to have him there?"

"I'll trust you to decide what's best. I only wanted to make the offer if it would be helpful to your herd management."

They walked back to the cottage, where Maynard offered them refreshment. Kit declined, saying they had several other tenants to visit. Maynard promised to send specifications for the pen and shed to the castle by the following morning.

When Kit and the duchess returned to the horses, he offered to help her up. She didn't respond, only nodded slightly. He did his best to touch her in only the most perfunctory of ways and terminate the connection as quickly as possible.

When she was settled in her saddle, she looked down at him in question. "It appeared as if you were speaking to that goat. What did you say?"

"I told him he was noisy and asked if he was upset that I caught him so quickly. Then I asked if he wanted to come and be Beau's pet."

She stared at him and then the most beautiful thing happened: she laughed. Her lips curved up, and a sound akin to the birdsongs he'd heard in the tropics wrapped around him. He stood below her, basking in the glow of her humor and decided it was the warmest, brightest place in the world.

"You should do that more often," he said softly, then immediately wanted to take it back as the joy leached from her face. The carefree woman with the enticing smile faded into the guarded and distant duchess.

"My apologies," he said. "I didn't mean to overstep. Let us continue."

He climbed onto his horse, and they rode to the next tenant, who showed them his cow herd. Kit had little experience with cattle and was excited by the prospect to learn more. As he asked dozens of questions, he could hear the voice of his father saying, *"Kit, you can't mean to know everything in the world, but by God you will try."* He also realized he could spend the rest of the afternoon here, but they needed to move on. He promised the tenant he'd return soon. All during the conversation, the duchess had watched him with something between bafflement and awe. She'd also asked questions, which Kit had found admirable.

The third tenant was a farmer, and by now, Kit was heated enough that he accepted the man's offer of ale. He refused, however, to sit, instead preferring to tour the fields, tankard in hand. The duchess had gone inside with the farmer's wife, and Kit wondered if they should return to the castle. The afternoon had grown quite warm. Perhaps they could visit just one more tenant. He'd expected to find this tour interesting, but now felt something far deeper—he was invested.

Kit finished his ale and handed the empty tankard to Mr. Dooley. "Thank you for your kind hospitality."

"Thank you for coming, Your Grace. Are you

heading back to the castle now?"

"I think we'll visit one more tenant."

Dooley nodded. "I'm on my way to my neighbor to help him repair his roof if you'd care to come along. Not to fix the roof, of course, but I can introduce you. Bricker is a bit brusque, but he possesses a good soul, and he needs help from time to time. He lost his sons in France and Spain."

Kit's chest squeezed. It seemed hardly fair for people like his cousin—noblemen with wealth and prestige— to be exempt from such horrors while young country boys gave their lives, often leaving their families much the poorer for it.

"Does he do all right?" Kit asked.

"Well enough. We help each other out, Your Grace. That's why I'll go and fix his roof."

"I'm coming with you—to help," he said firmly, making his intention clear.

Dooley appeared momentarily aghast, but seemed to accept that Kit's offer was genuine. It was also not open to negotiation. Although, he was quickly realizing that a duke was never questioned. "That's too kind of you. I'll just go and fetch my tools. I'd planned to walk if you want to go on ahead."

"The duchess and I will meet you there."

After Dooley provided directions to Bricker's house, Kit went to the cottage and knocked on the door. Mrs. Dooley answered with a smile, and the duchess appeared behind her.

"Ready?" the duchess asked as she tied her riding hat beneath her chin. It was a jaunty piece with a peacock feather, set at an attractive angle atop her dark locks.

"Yes." He thanked Mrs. Dooley for her hospitality, and the duchess did the same. Outside, he explained they were going to make one more stop. "I hope that's all right with you," he said.

"Certainly."

"You're not too warm or too fatigued?" he asked.

She narrowed her eyes at him briefly. "I am not the typical duchess."

Whether she was trying to be charming or not, he was utterly captivated, and he couldn't keep a chuckle from escaping. "I will remember that."

She arched a brow at him in the shade of her saucy hat. "How about you? Are you overheated or tired?"

It was a fair question, and he had to revise his earlier sentiment. It seemed there was *one* person brave enough to question a duke, and, given her behavior, he'd never imagined it would be her. Perhaps he was making a positive impression. *Perhaps* she was letting down her guard.

"I'm fine, thank you." He helped her onto her mount, again with all due haste, and they were quickly on their way to Mr. Bricker's. They passed Dooley a short way down the track, and he waved as they trotted by.

"Is Mr. Dooley going to Mr. Bricker's too?" she asked.

"We're going to fix his roof. If it looks as though it will take a long time, I can see about finding an escort for you back to the house."

"That won't be necessary. As I said, I'm not too tired to continue." She shot him a quick glance as he happened to do the same toward her. "First you say you'll help build the goat pen and shed, then you catch a goat, and now you mean to fix a roof? Did you learn all these things while you were away?" She sounded rather incredulous, and now Kit wondered what her husband had done to pass his days. Riding, he'd seemed to enjoy riding. How…dull. Unless one had a specific destination or an engaging companion. He sent another glance in her direction.

"Are you aware of Mr. Bricker's situation?" he asked.

"No. Should I be?"

"He lost his sons in the war and requires help to keep up his home. I plan to assess his circumstances and see what I can do to improve them."

"I can do that while you repair the roof," she said as they rode off the track toward his cottage.

He brought his horse to a halt and dismounted. As he went to her horse to help her down, he said, "An excellent idea. We'll work together to ensure Mr. Bricker's comfort."

She set her hands on his shoulders as he swept her to the ground, and since they'd already done this several times, he was aware that this time, they rested upon his coat a fraction of a moment longer than they had previously. "I'm afraid I wasn't aware he was alone, and I should have been. I allowed Cuddy to keep me out of things. I should have ridden out here myself and done what you're doing."

He heard the self-derision in her tone and wanted to allay her remorse. "Don't admonish yourself. It's not as if you've been idle. You've had Beau and the management of the castle, which is more than enough to keep you busy. From what I can tell, you've acquitted yourself quite well in my absence."

"How can you tell? You've scarcely been back a day."

Perhaps he couldn't really, but his intuition told him he was right. "The staff clearly revere you, and your son absolutely adores you. I'd say that's pretty damn successful." He winced as he realized his transgression with his language—and he'd been working so hard. "My apologies. It's a bit difficult to leave the life of a sailor behind."

"So I'm beginning to see," she murmured. Her gaze moved past him, and she inclined her head toward the cottage. "Here comes Mr. Bricker."

Kit pivoted to face the man as he ambled toward them. He moved slowly and possessed a bit of a hunch. Kit wanted to offer the man retirement right then and there.

"Good afternoon, Mr. Bricker," Kit greeted. "I'm Blackburn."

Bricker cocked his head to the side and studied him a moment. The longer the man waited before he spoke, the more Kit's anxiety kicked up. Did he see something? Could he tell Kit wasn't Rufus Beaumont? "You look different, Your Grace. In fact, if you hadn't introduced yourself, I wouldn't have thought it was you. I'll admit there's a small resemblance, so I might've wondered." He looked over at the duchess. "You sure this is him?"

Kit's breath stalled in his chest as Bricker moved his scrutiny back to Kit. He dared to look at the duchess, who'd turned her head toward him.

"As sure as I can be," she said.

It wasn't exactly a resounding endorsement, but it was the best he could hope for. He sought to move past the awkwardness as quickly as possible. "I understand you're in need of roof repair. Mr. Dooley is on his way, and I'd like to help. What seems to be the problem?"

"You're going to fix my roof?" There was a note of admiration mixed in with the man's surprise.

"I'd like to, yes." He glanced back toward the track

and saw Dooley approaching. Good, the man would be here in a few minutes, and they could get to work. Kit turned his focus to the thatched roof of the cottage. "Do you have a leak?"

"A bit in the corner. I'll show you." He led Kit to the edge of the small cottage and pointed at the watermarks on the exterior. It's worse out here, but there's some drip inside if you care to take a look."

"Of course. That's why I'm here. Tell us, Mr. Bricker, what is it you do here?"

"I keep a few sheep, Your Grace. I've a small farm too, but Dooley and Wallace—he's to the north of me—do most of the work nowadays."

"Well, that doesn't seem quite right, Mr. Bricker." Kit realized his error as the man's bushy gray eyebrows pitched low over his eyes. "Not that you aren't doing the work, but that you don't have adequate help."

"I do have adequate help," Bricker said hotly. "Dooley and Wallace help me just fine."

Before Kit could respond, the duchess moved closer to the older man and gave him a warm smile. "I'm sure they do, Mr. Bricker. Would you mind escorting me inside where it's likely a bit cooler? I'd love to hear all about your sheep." She gave Kit a pointed look and tucked her arm around the older man's. Bricker seemed to stand straighter as he turned from Kit and walked her into his house.

It wasn't lost on Kit that Bricker hadn't treated him with any of the deference that every other person had so far. Probably because he didn't think Kit was actually the duke.

Well, it had been bound to happen, he supposed. But would the man question him? Kit would've doubted it, but Bricker seemed immune to ducal decorum.

That made Kit smile.

Dooley strolled toward the cottage. "You met Bricker, then?"

"I did. I'm afraid I might have given him the wrong impression, that he should perhaps not require assistance." Kit shrugged out of his coat and set it on the stoop. He didn't much care if it got dirty or ruined, or if the same happened to any of the clothes he was wearing, for that matter. Tomorrow, the tailor would come to measure him for a new wardrobe. He didn't plan to procure anything extravagant, but he was in dire need of at least *some* garments that befitted his new station. Hell, he just wanted a few extra things that weren't old and worn.

Dooley set his tools down, and his mouth quirked into a smile. "I expect he was crotchety about it. He's a curmudgeon, but don't let that get to you. As I said, he's a kind soul. Underneath all that," he said with a chuckle. "I'll just go and fetch his ladder." He moved around to the side of the cottage, and Kit rushed to help.

An hour later, they'd repaired the thatching. Kit had removed his waistcoat too and had practically soaked his shirt with sweat. The labor felt good, and he looked forward to building the goat pen.

Bricker came outside and immediately stepped directly on Kit's coat, not that he seemed to notice, as he walked into the yard to survey their work.

The duchess closed the door behind her as she came out into the sunlight. She nearly stepped on Kit's clothing too, but bent to pick it up with a slight frown. Her gaze came up and traveled around until landing on Kit. From the widening of her eyes and the faint streaks of pink on her cheeks, he assumed she was scandalized by his state of undress.

He glanced toward Dooley, who was also in shirtsleeves. But his was a work shirt, and he was expected to toil, while Kit was apparently supposed to supervise and refrain from activity. *Well, fuck that.*

"His Grace did a fine job," Dooley said. "I was grateful to have his help today." He nodded toward Kit. "Thank you."

"It was my pleasure." Truly, he'd enjoyed every moment. "Please let me know if I can be of assistance again." He decided to shake both men's hands, first Dooley to show Bricker what he meant to do and then the older man, who still looked at him with a dose of skepticism but also a scant bit of something that might have been admiration.

"I appreciate it, Your Grace," Bricker said. He turned a fond look toward the duchess. "Her Grace said you'd like to offer me a retirement cottage. I'm much obliged, but I'd still like my sheep."

"We'd be delighted for you to keep your sheep, Mr. Bricker," he said. "I'm sure there is no one better."

They said their good-byes, and Kit unrolled his sleeves as he walked toward the duchess. She held up his waistcoat with an arched brow—a favored expression of hers, he was beginning to learn.

He pulled the garment on, then took his coat from her as they walked to their horses. "Thank you," he said simply.

"I didn't want to say so, but your clothing is a bit of a disgrace. Your old garments are somewhere in the castle—I'll have Kirwin dig them out."

"He already did," Kit said as he pulled on his coat, then set to buttoning his waistcoat. He'd have given anything to pull off his cravat, but decided a duke shouldn't go that far.

"Already?" She shook her head. "I shouldn't be surprised. Kirwin is exceedingly efficient. You said I ran the castle well, but the truth is he and Mrs. Hunsacker manage everything so ably that I hardly need to do a thing."

"I find that hard to believe." He detected a penchant for her to discount herself and wondered if her lousy husband was to blame.

She waved him off as they reached their horses. "Well, it's true." She looked at his costume. "If Kirwin brought your clothing, why are you still wearing this?"

Because none of it had fit. He was, apparently, a couple of inches taller than his cousin and far wider in the shoulders. His legs were also a bit more muscular, which had made the breeches impossible to wear. He decided to seize on that excuse. "It seems my years at sea have increased the breadth of my shoulders and the circumference of my thighs." He laughed, hoping she wouldn't recall what Bricker had said earlier.

Her gaze dipped over him very briefly, and that enticing bit of color returned to her cheeks. "I can see that. I suppose you'll need to summon a tailor. Or has Kirwin already taken care of that?"

"He has. The tailor will come to the castle tomorrow."

She nodded with a half smile. It wasn't as splendid as the one she'd given him earlier, but he'd take it like a child grasping a sweet at Yuletide.

Kit helped her onto her horse once more, and they waved to Bricker and Dooley as they rode onto the track back toward the castle.

The moment they rode into the stable yard, Kit sensed the air of tension. He swung off his horse as

Kirwin strode toward them with purpose.

A groom helped the duchess dismount while Kit addressed the butler. "Is something amiss?"

Clearly it was, given Kirwin's pitched brows and slightly gray color. "It's his lordship." He turned his primary focus to the duchess, which Kit understood. His heart started to race, and he could only imagine what she must be feeling. "Please come at once—to the east garden."

Kit would've broken into a hard sprint if he remembered where the bloody hell that was located. Instead, he moved beside the duchess as she picked up her skirts and ran as quickly as she could. All the while, he prayed Beau was all right.

Chapter Six

❦

As THEY HURRIED to the east garden, Verity tried not to panic. "What is wrong with Beau?" she asked Kirwin.

"He followed Whiskers up into the oak tree—farther than he's ever gone before—and I'm afraid he can't get down."

They crossed the lower courtyard to the entrance tower and dashed around the side of the castle to the east garden. The oak tree was about thirty feet tall with a jumble of limbs to climb and stood at the far corner of the garden.

"He's climbed this tree before?" Rufus asked as they hastened along the path.

"Several times, but he knows not to go too high." Even so, he often tried as temptation overcame him. Which was why he required supervision. "Where is his nurse?" Verity asked just as she saw the woman wringing her hands beneath the tree.

Kirwin gestured with his hand. "There, Your Grace."

Verity rushed forward. "What happened?"

The nurse began to cry. "Oh, Your Grace, I told him not to go any higher, but he was insistent that Whiskers needed help."

Clearly the cat did not, since the gray animal was now seated beneath the tree, staring up the trunk.

"Mama?"

Verity went to the trunk and looked up into the branches until she found Beau. He was quite far up.

"I'm here, Beau."

"Excuse me." Rufus's deep voice sounded near her ear. He'd shed his coat, and she turned her head to see Kirwin held the garment.

"Are you going to get him?" she asked.

"Of course." He started up the trunk and climbed to Beau with speed and ease, as if he climbed trees all the time.

She saw him talking to Beau, who clutched the branch with both arms. His little face was drawn and pale, and Verity longed to hold him close and tell him everything would be all right. Then she'd scold him for not listening to her or to Nurse.

It took several minutes of what looked like cajoling, but then Rufus moved. He seemed to dangle from the tree, and Verity's breath caught. He put his back to Beau, and a moment later, one of her son's arms wrapped around his neck. It took another moment, during which Verity still didn't breathe, but Beau's other arm joined the first, clasping Rufus tightly. Beau's eyes were tightly closed, and Verity fought to keep hers open. If he dropped her son...

Rufus said something, and Beau's eyes came open. Then Rufus began to descend, far more slowly than he'd gone up. Verity had the sense he could've made it down in half the time it had taken to ascend but didn't because of his precious cargo.

When he reached the main trunk and was just a few feet from the ground, she finally exhaled. Rufus's boots hit the dirt, and Verity stepped forward to take Beau from his back. Beau transferred his arms to her and squeezed his legs around her middle.

"I'm sorry, Mama." He whimpered against her neck for a moment, and she held him close as she pressed her lips to his dark head.

"You're safe now," she said. Her gaze drifted to Rufus as Kirwin helped him don his coat. The butler brushed at something on Rufus's sleeve and looked at him with something akin to admiration.

She understood because she felt that too, and she had no idea what to do about that. She'd loathed and despised him for so long.

Beau lifted his head from her shoulder and turned to look at Rufus. "Did you see what Papa did? He's the best climber ever!"

"I did see," Verity murmured.

"Because of all the rigging on the ships. He said the first time he had to climb up, he was terrified, but that he had to do it."

"Just as you had to come down," Rufus said with a half smile. "We have to learn to conquer our fears. You did that today, and I'm proud of you."

Beau seemed to swell in her arms so that she could practically feel the joy his father's words gave him. Verity wasn't immune either. "Thank you," she said, though it was a far too simple expression of her appreciation. It wasn't just that he'd saved Beau but that he'd taught the boy a valuable lesson.

She would have expected him to punish Beau. In fact, even now, she waited for him to address the fact that Beau had ignored his nurse. When he didn't, she set her son down and squatted to look him in the eye.

"Beau, I am very glad you're safe, and it sounds as if you learned a lesson about being brave. However, you also need to learn a lesson about listening to Nurse. What if Papa hadn't been here to save the day?" She practically choked on those words, never imagining she would say them.

Beau's gaze dropped to the ground. "I would still be up in that tree," he muttered. "I'm sorry, Mama. I should have listened to Nurse." He lifted his green eyes to hers. "Should I have a punishment?"

Verity acknowledged that she was perhaps too lenient with Beau, but he was a good boy overall. She looked up at Rufus, who was watching them. He gave a slight shrug, clearly leaving the matter up to her. He was doing precisely what he'd said and not meddling in things beyond the management of the estate.

"You probably should," she said, looking back to Beau. "No tree climbing for three days."

Beau opened his mouth, likely to protest, but he glanced at his father and nodded. "Yes, Mama. But then can Papa teach me how to get up and down by myself? He promised me."

He had? That must have been one of the things they'd been discussing up in the tree. Along with Rufus's own fear at having to climb the rigging of a ship. She found herself intrigued by the experiences that had changed this man, and more than a trifle curious. Too bad he'd said he wouldn't speak of them. Except, it seemed, when he needed to persuade his son to come down from a tree.

Would there be a reason he'd need to confide in her about the past six and a half years? She couldn't see one, but right now, she accepted that her life had turned completely upside down.

"I'll talk to him about it," Verity said, rising. Part of her still feared to entrust Beau to Rufus, but so far, he'd proven himself up to the task. "But now I'd like you to go upstairs and change out of your dirty clothes."

"Yes, Mama." Beau gave her a quick hug, then went to Rufus and hugged him too—albeit for just a

THE DUKE OF LIES

moment longer. Or so it seemed.

Jealousy needled through Verity as she watched Beau take Nurse's hand and walk back toward the house. She turned to Rufus. "I suppose we must be grateful for your time aboard ship."

He shrugged. "I would've rescued him anyway, just perhaps a bit more slowly."

"I guess you did conquer your fear," she said, thinking how it was common knowledge that he hadn't liked to climb to the tops of the towers.

"Yes." Had that been a flash of uncertainty in his gaze? "I think I'll go inside and change as well," he said. "And perhaps take a bath before dinner."

Kirwin turned toward the castle. "I'll go and arrange that, Your Grace."

Rufus smiled and held up his hand. "That's not necessary. I can direct a footman." He inclined his head toward them and returned to the castle, leaving Verity alone with the butler.

They were quiet watching Rufus disappear from view as he went back through the entrance gate.

It was Kirwin who spoke first. "He's quite changed, Your Grace. If it's not too forward of me to say."

"It's not, and I agree." Verity narrowed her eyes and looked back toward the tree before starting toward the house. Kirwin fell into step beside her. "He said you found his clothes—from before. Thank you for thinking of that."

"They didn't fit."

"So he said. He also told me you arranged for a tailor to visit tomorrow."

"I did. It was absolutely necessary." He fell quiet for a few steps before saying, "I didn't see him try on the clothes, but I did watch him hold a coat up and realized straightaway that it would never fit."

"Yes, he's bigger after his time away." More muscular, which had been readily demonstrated by all the activities he'd undertaken that day. Now, as she thought of him climbing the tree, she had to admit he was remarkably well formed. She didn't recall him having muscles like that, but then she'd endeavored to touch as little of him as possible.

"Actually, he seems a bit taller as well," Kirwin said. "And I noticed he didn't wear the boots, which were practically new when he disappeared. I don't think those fit either."

"My feet changed size after I had Beau," Verity said. Not that Rufus had borne a child, obviously, but the point was that changes could happen. Was she trying to make excuses against the possibility that he wasn't actually Rufus? And yet, how could that be? He looked so much like him, and he knew things that a stranger wouldn't.

He'd known Kirwin, and he'd asked why Beau's name wasn't Archibald. She suddenly wanted to probe further and see what else he knew—or didn't.

"I don't know what prompted him to change so much, but I'm quite glad," Kirwin said. "For his lordship's sake as well as yours."

Verity agreed but didn't say so.

As they moved across the lower courtyard, Kirwin looked over at her. "Mrs. Hunsacker and I wanted to apologize for our behavior after you first came here. We knew he wasn't treating you very well, but we were too afraid to say anything. I like to think I would have, if he hadn't disappeared."

She stopped at the base of the stairs leading to the path that went to the upper gatehouse. "I'm sure you would have."

Looking back, she'd no idea how she would have survived being married to him. The abuse had started with insults and progressed to degradation. Then he'd started to touch her more roughly, which echoed his brash treatment of her in the bedchamber. Those pinches and grabs had become pushing and then hitting, but that hadn't been his preferred method of torture. No, that was refusing her things—her finest undergarments, food and drink, and finally sleep.

Two days before he'd disappeared, she'd disappointed him in bed, and he'd made her stand in the corner for the remainder of the night, saying that if he awoke and found her sleeping or moved, he'd make her spend the night outside. It had been pouring rain. And since he tended to wake once or twice in the night to use the chamber pot, she'd stayed there, too terrified to move.

"When I first saw him yesterday, I was distressed," she said softly.

"We were too." Kirwin's support meant more to her than he could know. "We immediately pledged to keep you and his lordship safe—at any cost."

"It seems as though you won't have to take any drastic measures. He does seem rather different." She only prayed he stayed that way.

Kirwin perhaps shared her reservations. "If we have the slightest inclination that he's reverting to his old ways, we will protect you."

She touched his arm and gave him an affectionate smile. "Thank you, Kirwin, and please thank Mrs. Hunsacker. But I caution you to be careful. He is a duke after all, and next to him, we are all nothing." Rufus had reminded her of that so many times. In fact, this entire conversation only served to remind her of how awful he'd been. She suddenly wanted a bath too, to wash away the complacency that had settled around her that afternoon. She would scrub off his kindness, his care, and his touch—even that had been drastically altered. When he'd helped her to mount and dismount all afternoon, she'd almost imagined him touching her with affection.

Almost.

She couldn't allow herself to believe he was anything other than the devil she knew him to be.

⤙𝓔•3⤚

TWO DAYS PASSED in a blur as Kit spent considerable time planning the new goat pen and shed, visiting more tenants, and reviewing the account books following the departure of Cuddy late the day before. Kit looked down at the open book, which included entries through last week, and frowned. He didn't understand why repairs hadn't been made, such as to the clock in the courtyard, or why horses had been sold. The estate seemed to be doing well, and yet there was no surplus.

He'd have to read them a second time. Thankfully, he was a very fast reader.

A knock on the office door drew Kit to stand. Anxiety coursed through him, and he rolled his shoulders to shake it off. He'd asked for this meeting, had invited the Entwhistles here. Would Whist recognize him…

"Come in," Kit called, sounding far more calm and collected than he felt.

The door pushed open, and the former steward came inside. He pulled his hat from his head to reveal a thinning patch of gray hair. A man of average height and build, Whist barely looked older than when Kit had seen him last, some seventeen years ago. There were, however, a few more lines around his eyes, and his frame seemed a bit less robust.

He was followed by a taller man with wider shoulders and bright blue eyes. This must be his grandson, the seemingly popular Thomas Entwhistle, who had charmed both the duchess and Beau.

And whom Kit wasn't entirely sure he wanted to hire. He well understood the duchess's desire to employ her own choice, and he meant to exercise the same right.

Kit came around the desk and extended his hand. "Whist, it's good to see you again."

The older man stared at his hand a moment before cautiously shaking it. "Good morning, Your Grace. Allow me to present my grandson, Mr. Thomas Entwhistle."

Entwhistle bowed and seemed even more reluctant to shake Kit's hand. It was then that Kit finally understood that a duke shouldn't be shaking his inferiors' hands. Hell, he'd been doing it with the tenants since his arrival, and while they'd also hesitated, he hadn't put it together.

Eager to put the awkward, and perhaps telling, moment behind them, he circled back around the desk and gestured for them to sit. "Thank you both for coming today. As you know, we are looking to employ a new steward."

"Looking?" Whist said with surprise, his brows climbing. "Her Grace offered the position to Thomas."

"I'm aware, but that was before I returned home. Now that I'm here, I will make the final decision."

"But you dismissed Cuddy?" Entwhistle asked.

Kit's invitation to this meeting had included the information that Cuddy was no longer serving as steward. He hadn't indicated why, but imagined that sort of gossip traveled quickly across the estate. And Whist resided on the estate in a retirement cottage. This prompted Kit to say, "Whist, I've a tenant who needs to retire to a cottage where he can keep a small flock of sheep. Where he lives now is too much of a burden."

"Bricker? He likely should've moved to a smaller place a few years ago." Whist shook his head. "I offered my assistance to Cuddy from time to time—when he was new to the position—but I gave up when he never wanted it. I should've just checked on things myself."

This was, of course, similar to the duchess's regret. "Cuddy gave the appearance of doing an efficient job, and if the account books are to be believed at their face value, things are in excellent order."

Entwhistle leaned slightly forward in his chair. "You don't sound convinced."

"Because I'm not. There should be a surplus based on what I'm hearing from tenants, but when I reviewed the books last night and this morning, I'm not seeing evidence of that."

Whist eyed Kit skeptically, making Kit tense. "Forgive me for saying so, Your Grace, but your estate management experience isn't very extensive. Thomas and I could review things and provide an expert opinion. But perhaps that's why you summoned us here."

Relief poured through Kit. So far, the man seemed not to recognize him for anything other than what he was—the Duke of Blackburn, Kit's handshaking faux pas notwithstanding. With that fear somewhat laid to rest, Kit now found himself mildly annoyed by Whist's judgment. Which was ludicrous because everything he'd learned about estate management had come seventeen years ago, and he'd never imagined he'd have occasion to put it to use. "Not primarily." He'd invited them before his suspicions had taken root. "But now that I've reviewed the accounts, I find I have some questions. It seems the former duke—Augustus— spent outside his means. Is that an accurate assessment?"

Whist looked pained. "I'm afraid so. He liked to host parties and demonstrate his power and wealth. He also donated quite a bit of money to various charitable causes, particularly orphaned boys."

Kit had seen entries in the journals to support that, but hearing Whist say it made his spine chill. He'd given money to other boys but, after a point, not to his own son. And now that Kit needed it, there seemed to be none to have. Or at least not as much as he'd hoped. And here he was spending money on a goat pen and shed. What the hell was wrong with him? He should've taken that money and gone. He needed a new ship and a new crew, not to build lodgings for goats.

And yet here he was with no intent to leave. At least not yet, not when there were things to be done and an opportunity to leave Beaumont Tower—and its denizens—better than he'd found them.

"I can see the duchess doesn't spend like that. In fact, she runs a rather frugal household."

"They've no need for extravagance," Whist said a bit defensively.

"I didn't say they did. However, if the estate is

running similarly and the expenses have decreased, why is there no surplus?"

Whist and his grandson exchanged a look of concern.

"As it happens," Kit said, "I would like you to review the accounts. Perhaps you can help me discover what's gone wrong."

Now Whist registered the surprise Kit had come to expect from damn near everybody on the bloody estate. The duke had been a right prick. Whist answered carefully. "We would be happy to, Your Grace. However, such a review would require us to interview every tenant and audit the information recorded in the journals. I must point out that Thomas is still, for a spell anyway, employed at Bleven House. He doesn't have an excess of time to conduct an overview of Beaumont Tower in addition to his duties, particularly if you don't plan to hire him."

Meaning, if Kit would just hire him outright, everyone's needs—and desires—could be met. Kit ought to just hire the man. Whist had been a damned good steward from everything Kit had heard, and he had to imagine the man's grandson was no different.

Why was Kit hesitating? He'd be leaving soon. Or would he? He honestly didn't know. He wasn't going to take money to fund his ship—not until he was certain the estate wouldn't suffer.

Kit turned his focus to Entwhistle. "When can you start?"

The man, who was perhaps five years Kit's junior, straightened. "In a fortnight or so. I could come Sunday—it's my day off—to begin the review, if that's acceptable."

"That is, thank you," Kit said.

"I can start now, if you'd like," Whist offered.

"That would be helpful." Kit indicated a small stack of journals on the corner of the desk. "Those are the accounts since you retired."

"Do you mind if I sit here and review them?" Whist asked.

"Not at all. I have other matters that require my attention. I'm to begin construction on a goat pen and shed not far from the stables."

Whist's mouth turned up. "For Beau?" He winced. "I'm sorry, for his lordship?"

The man's familiarity didn't bother Kit. What he wondered was how familiar the younger Entwhistle had become with Beau—and with the duchess.

"Yes. I believe I have you to thank for igniting his goat obsession."

Whist chuckled. "That boy loves animals of all kinds."

"I should return to Bleven House," Entwhistle said, rising. He gave Kit an earnest look. "Thank you for the opportunity. I look forward to serving you and Beaumont Tower to the best of my ability."

Kit rose and inclined his head toward the younger man. "I'm confident you will."

Entwhistle departed, leaving Kit alone with Whist, who was now watching him with a dubious look. The anxiety returned, and Kit wondered if now would be the moment when someone would pierce his ruse. He sat down, but only perched on the chair in case he felt the need to flee at a moment's notice.

"You're quite changed, if I may say so," Whist said.

"Everyone says so." Kit saw no reason to pretend otherwise. He knew people discussed it. Several times now, he entered a room or the stables to have the staff grow instantly quiet. He supposed it could just be because he was the duke, but he knew better. They looked at him with a mix of fear and distrust. He was desperate to change that. Sooner or later, Beau would hear what kind of man his father had been. Maybe, in the time he had here, he could lessen that blow by being a man Beau could be proud of.

"How?" Whist asked, drawing Kit back to his question. "Where have you been all this time?"

"Sailing. I was impressed."

Whist's brows arched. "Indeed? Can't imagine you on a ship. Did you enjoy it?" He waved his hand as his mouth tipped into a self-deprecating smile. "Of course you didn't. You're a duke and were pressed into hard service." His eyes narrowed as he scrutinized Kit a moment. "I guess that's why you changed. Or so it seems."

A tremor of anxiety rattled Kit's frame. "Are you suggesting I'm somehow dishonest?"

Whist shrugged. "The changes are great. What's to say you won't revert to the man you were? I don't mind saying I worried about the estate under your care. But then, you never would've sat for a meeting like this, let alone invited me and my grandson to come."

Kit winced inwardly. This was nothing he hadn't already surmised, but hearing it over and over again was beginning to weigh on him. Perhaps that was why he was so committed to ensuring things were set to rights before he left.

The air in the room seemed to thin a bit as Kit's discomfort grew. He stood once more, anxious to escape the small space. "I am an entirely different person than I was before I disappeared. One might even say *that* Rufus is dead."

Whist stared up at him, his eyes dark and flinty in the light filtering from the windows high in the stone wall. "I hope so, because there are many of us who will ensure the duchess and her son are safe from the man we thought we knew."

Kit sensed the man's guilt along with his righteous conviction. "No one wants that more than I." He stepped around the desk and looked pointedly at the old man. "No *one*. Take as much time as you need here. If you're up for it, we'll visit with some of the tenants this afternoon."

Without waiting for a response, Kit left the office, closing the door behind him as he stepped into the cloudy spring morning.

He expelled the breath he'd been holding. One of these days, someone was going to call him out on this charade. He'd do well to be gone before that could happen. Perhaps he should go now.

Without the money he needed?

Not only did he have nowhere else to go—and going to work on someone else's ship was out of the question—he couldn't turn his back now, not when he suspected Cuddy had been a less than honest steward. If the man had been stealing from the estate, and Kit wouldn't be surprised to learn he had, Kit would find him and make him return what he'd stolen.

A voice in the back of Kit's mind asked, *but hadn't you planned to steal from the estate?*

It wasn't stealing if your father promised it to you and reneged.

And he would do his best to leave a positive mark on Beaumont Tower and everyone here. He'd be a duke to remember, for himself as well as them, if only for a short time.

Chapter Seven
❧❦❧

OVER THE PAST ten days, Verity had lived with a stranger. Rufus looked like her husband and sounded like him—as far as she could remember; it was difficult to tell since he spoke to her in an entirely different manner. However, his actions and behavior continued to make her question whether he really was Rufus.

Yet with each day that passed, she came to a sinking realization: she wanted him to be.

Not for her. No, she had no interest in him. But for Beau, he'd turned out to be warm and caring and quite engaged in his son's upbringing. He'd procured a toy boat, had taught Beau about the Caribbean and its islands as well as the coast of America. Beau had hung on his father's every word, and to watch the relationship develop between them was more than Verity could have ever wanted.

While making her jealous at the same time.

It was difficult to be angry with Rufus since he was so helpful and so unassuming, but at the same time, Verity missed her independence. Not that Rufus seemed to care what she did. In fact, while they shared a home and a son, their relationship was strictly... What was it exactly?

She watched him standing at the gate of the new goat pen, Beau anxiously hopping from foot to foot at his side as the goats arrived. Mr. Maynard led them into the pen. There were eleven, including a very small baby who was only a week old. Beau went directly to that kid, and Verity smiled as he petted the animal while the goat bleated softly in return.

Verity stood outside the pen and surveyed the enclosure Rufus had built along with the impressive shed. Mr. Dooley had offered his assistance, as had Mr. Maynard. The three of them, along with help from a couple of the grooms, had assembled the entire thing over the past handful of days. That Rufus was capable of the manual labor, let alone managing the project, was nothing short of stunning. Verity still couldn't quite believe it.

And therein lay her singular problem with him. She just couldn't quite believe him. She *wanted* to believe him. Who would prefer what he was before to who he was now?

But preference wasn't the issue. She just couldn't be sure he was really Rufus. And if he wasn't, who was he? An imposter who appeared more ducal than the real duke.

In his new wardrobe, he looked important and approachable, and most of all, terribly, terribly handsome. When she'd first met him at the house party, she'd found him attractive. They'd danced and sat together at a dinner. He'd been charming and pleasant, even after the tragic death of Augustus's son, who'd fallen into the pond and drowned. In fact, Rufus had been the one to find him and had taken the boy's death quite hard. He'd also been supportive and comforting to Augustus—behavior that impressed Verity and was the reason she'd accepted his marriage proposal before she and her father had left.

Six months later, they'd returned so she could wed Rufus, and that very night, she met the real man behind the façade. After that, she'd realized outward looks meant nothing.

Which was why he was far more attractive to her now that his character had improved so drastically. But had he changed enough? For what? In what way would she want or expect their marriage to change? She shuddered at the thought.

She blinked as she realized he was coming toward her, his hat pulled low over his brow against the sun.

"Aren't you coming in to see the goats?" he asked.

"I plan to, yes. I was just watching Beau." *And you.* But she didn't say that.

His green eyes—she still couldn't remember them ever being that color—sparkled in the afternoon light. "He's quite enthralled."

"He is indeed. Thank you for this." She genuinely meant it. His return had meant so much for Beau, and for him to take such an active role in his son's life was astonishing. And more than most fathers would do.

Rufus's gaze fixed somewhere beyond her. "Ah, here come the Entwhistles."

Verity looked over her shoulder and saw Thomas driving a cart. His grandfather sat beside him. "Did you invite them?"

"I did. This is, after all, indirectly Whist's fault."

Verity smiled. She was growing used to his sense of humor, but it still took her by surprise sometimes. "I suppose it is. It's kind of you to include them."

"I had to, really. Whist spends a great deal of time here, and I fear he would've invited himself if I hadn't."

"Would you have minded?"

"Goodness no, he's more than welcome. He's practically family."

Verity noticed he'd changed his speech a bit since arriving. That first few days he would have said "hell no," but now hell had been replaced with goodness. It seemed he'd had to relearn being a duke. Or actually learn in the first place, because she didn't think he'd mastered it very well before he'd disappeared. "It certainly feels like it, given the amount of time he's been spending here for the audit."

"True. But that will decrease when Thomas takes over in a few days."

Thomas had helped his employer find a new steward and was currently helping him get settled. "I'm surprised he found time to be here today," she said. "I would think he'd be too busy at Bleven House."

"It is Sunday, his day off," Rufus noted.

Thomas and Whist approached them, and while Whist went directly into the goat pen to see Beau, Thomas walked to where Verity stood outside the fence. He looked toward Rufus and offered a slight bow. "Thank you for including us today, Your Grace."

"It seemed fitting since Beau became enamored of your grandfather's goat."

"That's true," Thomas said with a laugh. "And do you know, I think he's going to offer Beau that goat since he has a place to keep her."

"That is too generous of him," Verity said. "I thought he was rather fond of his goats."

"He is, but you should know he's fonder of Beau."

"Papa! Papa!" Beau's gleeful voice carried to them.

With a grin, Rufus pivoted. "It sounds as though that offer may just have been made."

Verity couldn't suppress her smile as she watched Beau take his father's hand and excitedly talk while he gestured toward Whist.

"You look happy," Thomas said, drawing her attention.

She considered herself a happy person—generally. But the way he made the observation made it sound as though it was an oddity. "I am."

"I wasn't sure you would be, but Grandfather says His Grace is kind and thoughtful, and that everyone seems to like him, especially the tenants."

"Yes, I think they do." They ought to since he spent most of his time with them. And when he wasn't meeting them and helping them and soliciting their assistance with the audit, he spent his time with Beau. Or building this goat pen for Beau.

Thomas put his hand on the top of the fence and angled himself toward the pen instead of her. "I'm glad for you." The note of regret in his tone said something different, but she wasn't sure what to say to that.

She thought back to when Rufus had returned. That same day she'd offered Thomas the steward position, and she'd begun to consider him as maybe something other than someone who would manage the estate. Since her cousin Diana had visited last December—and married her husband—Verity had begun to look at men in a different way, a way she never had before. Only, she didn't meet very many that were unmarried or the appropriate age. Thomas, however, was near her age, attractive, intelligent, and unmarried. Furthermore, her son liked him, and he was good with Beau.

She hadn't really considered a courtship, but the possibility *had* entered her mind. But then Rufus had returned, and now all that was moot. Thomas's behavior seemed to indicate the possibility may have entered his mind too.

"Are you still looking forward to working here?" she asked, wondering if this would be awkward now.

He looked toward her. "Of course. It's an

extraordinary opportunity, and I think I'll enjoy working for His Grace." He said this with a bit of the surprise she still felt on a daily basis. One would think she'd be used to Rufus's alteration over the past fortnight, but the change was just so very drastic.

"Mama, Thomas!" Beau called. "Why are you standing out there?"

"I've no idea," Thomas murmured with a grin. "I'm going in." He glanced toward her. "Are you coming?"

"How can I refuse?"

He held the gate open for her with a grand gesture. She curtsied to him and laughed as she moved past him. Her gaze moved to Beau and caught a different pair of green eyes watching her closely.

Rufus's gaze was inscrutable before he withdrew it from her, but not before she felt a flash of heat along her spine. Confused, she ascribed it to the warm afternoon.

Beau excitedly told her about Whist offering his baby goat, and Verity thanked him profusely for his generosity.

"It's my pleasure to see the boy so delighted. And he's promised me I can visit whenever I like. Because I'm family, you see." He winked at Beau, who laughed before taking off running after Racer. It seemed the goat liked to be chased, and Beau was more than eager to oblige.

The sound of a coach arriving in the stable yard drew everyone's attention. Verity sucked in a breath as soon as the door opened and out stepped her dear cousin. "Diana!" She felt as giddy as Beau with his goats as she hurried from the pen.

By the time Verity reached the yard, Diana and Simon had stepped away from the coach. And Verity instantly knew something was different. Something wonderful. But she didn't say a word. Not yet. There would be time for them to gossip like magpies.

They wrapped each other in a tight embrace and then Verity hugged Simon next. "I'm so glad you came," she said.

"As soon as we could." Diana looked past Verity at the goat pen. "Is that him?"

Verity turned. Though there were three men standing together, it was clear who "him" was. "Yes."

"And you say he just rode up on a horse after six and a half years?" Simon shook his head. "I hope he had a good reason for staying away." He said this with humor.

"He was kidnapped and pressed into naval service," Verity said. "But he won't say much beyond that. He's an entirely different person from the man I married."

"You don't mean that literally?" Diana asked.

Did she? Sometimes she was certain he had to be someone else. And other times, she convinced herself that he was Rufus. How could he not be? "No." She didn't sound convinced because she wasn't. Yet, she couldn't quite bring herself to voice her fear. Because if he wasn't Rufus...

Simon looked slightly alarmed. "Is that a bad thing?"

"On the contrary, it's a very good thing. He's much improved."

Diana smiled at her. "I'm so glad."

"I suppose we should meet him," Simon said. "That is why we've come all this way."

Diana elbowed him gently and gave him a look of loving exasperation. "And to see Verity and Beau. And to share our news in person." She turned her glowing expression to Verity, confirming her suspicions.

"Simon and I are expecting a child in the fall. I do hope you'll be his godmother."

"*Her* godmother," Simon corrected.

Diana rolled her eyes with a chuckle. "I've already told you it's a boy."

"How can you possibly know?" Simon looked at Verity. "Did you?"

Verity thought back. She'd been so terrified that Rufus might return and that he'd be as horrid to their child as he was to her. She just prayed her child would be safe from harm and hadn't given a thought to its sex.

That wasn't entirely true. When she'd first realized she was expecting, she'd hoped for a boy because it would make Rufus happy. He'd made it clear he expected her to become pregnant as soon as possible and that her primary role in their marriage was to provide an heir and at least one spare.

"I didn't know," Verity said softly. "But that doesn't mean Diana doesn't." And she truly believed that. Diana's situation was vastly different from Verity's. Just watching them together, their love was palpable. Simon's hand hadn't left Diana's back, and they stood close enough that her shoulder touched his chest.

"Well, we shall see," Simon said, sounding quite skeptical. "Now let's go meet this husband of yours."

Verity tensed. She'd told Diana about Rufus, but only in general terms. No one knew the specifics of her marriage, and she wasn't sure she'd ever reveal them. Especially not now when he was so…likeable. Anyone who hadn't known him before would never believe he was capable of such cruelty.

They walked to the goat pen, Verity a bit ahead as Diana and Simon followed arm in arm. Verity had told

Rufus that her cousin and cousin-in-law would be visiting soon.

Rufus met them at the gate and opened it. "Welcome, Duke, Duchess." He inclined his head to both of them.

Simon offered his hand. "Call me Romsey, if you please."

"Very well. I hope you'll call me Blackburn."

"Blackburn… Such a dastardly name. Sounds like a pirate."

Rufus laughed. And laughed. And then laughed some more. He wiped a hand beneath his eye as he sought to gain control. "I beg your pardon. I'm not entirely certain why, but that's incredibly amusing. Don't you think?"

Verity stifled a smile. Because he'd been on a privateering vessel, no doubt.

Beau skipped toward them. "Think what, Papa?" Before waiting for an answer, he hugged Diana. "I'm so pleased you're here, Auntie Diana. Do you want to see my goats?"

"I most certainly do," she said with a smile. "You remember Uncle Simon?"

"Yes, but he wasn't my uncle then." He wasn't really his uncle now, nor was Diana his aunt, but those seemed the best titles for him to use, particularly since Diana felt like a sister to Verity. Beau bowed formally to Simon and said, "How do you do," in a tone deeper than his usual voice.

Verity couldn't withhold a giggle at her son's performance. It was quite good, and, if the sparkle in his green eyes was any indication, he knew it.

"Well done, Beau," Rufus said with a wink. It seemed he'd been coaching their son. While it didn't surprise her given the interest he'd taken in Beau, it was heartwarming nonetheless.

"Thank you, Papa," Beau said with pride. "Now you all need to come meet my goats. I wanted to call the baby Sailor because Papa was a sailor, but since Whist gave me *another* baby goat, I think I should maybe name the first one after him instead."

"Why not call the goat Whist gave you after him?" Simon asked.

"She's a girl!" Beau said with a giggle. "Besides she already has a name—Agnes."

"I see," Simon said thoughtfully. "You'd like us to help you decide between Sailor and, Whist is it?"

Beau nodded.

"We'll need to meet this fine animal before we can decide. Lead the way, my boy."

They all trailed Beau, who had them neatly in hand, just the way he liked them. For the first time in her life, Verity was aware of the feeling of family around her. And that didn't mean just people who were related to her by blood or marriage. It was far more than that. It was a feeling of belonging, of connection. Surely that was due to having Beau, Diana, and Simon here together.

Then her gaze fell on Rufus's back. He walked in front of her next to their son. *Their* son. Whether she liked it or not, Rufus was her family, and because of Beau, they were irrevocably linked.

While she might not like it, she realized she no longer hated it. Which was a terrifying prospect.

❧

AFTER A QUARTER hour of visiting with the goats, the

Duchess of Romsey turned to her cousin with a weary smile. "Verity, would you mind if I went in for a respite before dinner?"

Verity! At last he knew her name!

Kit tried not to laugh at the irony since her name meant truth. It was an amusing antithesis to the utter lie of Kit's entire presence there. But also sobering.

It was also a very fitting name because to him, truth meant beauty, and as far and wide as he'd traveled, he'd never met a woman more beautiful than her.

Verity.

He might just repeat her name over and over in his mind for the rest of the day. Hell, he was smitten with her. And who could blame him? Beyond her beauty, she was an excellent mother, a respected duchess, and possessed a wealth of intelligence he'd been pleased to tap. She'd proven herself an accomplished assistant with the auditing project, accompanying him to visit tenants on days when Whist had needed to rest. She was precisely the kind of helpmate a man could hope for.

If he were looking for a helpmate, which Kit never had.

Privateers rarely married because few women wanted to join them on the sea. And the alternative meant a marriage of living separately for the most part, which didn't appeal to Kit at all. Wait, something about marriage appealed to him? He'd never given it a second thought.

Lately, he'd given it third and fourth thoughts. How could he not when he was, albeit falsely, in possession of a wife?

Possession... That word stirred something inside him, something that intensified when he looked at

Verity. He didn't think he could possess her, nor would he want to. No. He rather preferred the idea of her possessing him. He'd been alone and untethered for so long that the idea of someone wanting him and taking him, and not just in a purely sexual sense, was extraordinarily appealing. Christ, he had to stop thinking about this, because the sexual sense was beginning to take over, and if he wasn't careful, he was going to grow hard.

As he'd done the past several nights thinking of her. Verity.

Verity.

In the midst of his daydreams, he'd completely missed the ensuing conversation, but somehow, the women were headed toward the house with Beau, and Thomas and Whist were taking their leave.

"See you tomorrow," Whist said with a wave.

Kit waved back. "Yes, tomorrow."

"And I'll be here Wednesday," Thomas said with a nod.

"I look forward to it." Kit watched them turn and walk toward their cart and recalled watching Thomas with Verity earlier. There had seemed to be something between them, but Kit wasn't entirely certain, and he couldn't very well ask. How would that go, exactly? *Say, if you two are romantically inclined, I'll be leaving in a few weeks so don't let me stand in your way.*

So many things about that drove Kit mad. One, he didn't know when he was leaving and he didn't really want to contemplate it. Two, he couldn't say anything like that, of course, not without revealing the depths of his dishonesty. Three, the idea of Verity and Thomas— hell, of Verity and *anyone*—romantically inclined toward each other made him irritable.

Yes, he was bloody well smitten, and that was a damn shame. For there was nothing to be done about it.

"Something wrong?" Romsey asked, prodding Kit from his jealousy.

"No, no," Kit said, shaking his head. "Shall we go in?"

"Yes, I want to check on Diana. She's expecting our first child in the fall." It sounded blithe but wasn't necessarily something men discussed, especially men who'd just met. But the pride and excitement in the man's voice were unmistakable. He was thrilled, and he wanted everyone to know it.

Kit could respect that. And envy it, if he were to be honest. Just as he'd never considered marriage, he'd never thought about fatherhood either. But from the moment Beau had sidled up to him on the settee that first day, he'd been lost. In fact, the thought of leaving made his chest ache and his stomach turn. Never mind Verity and his affection for her, he wasn't sure he could leave Beau.

"Congratulations to you," Kit said, wondering if his voice sounded as thin as it felt. As much as he cared for Beau, the boy didn't belong to him and never would. And he'd likely never have a son to call his own. Was it selfish of him to want to claim Beau? Especially when the boy was clearly elated to have his father at last?

Kit went to the gate and held it open for Romsey. Racer made a dash for the opening, but Kit snapped it closed before he could make it through. With a disappointed bleat, Racer rejoined his group. Kit checked the latch to make sure it would hold. He'd built it to be extra strong given Racer's penchant for breaking free.

"Seems like you expected him to try to escape," Romsey observed.

"Always. But he's got a good personality."

Romsey swung his head to look at Kit in disbelief. "A goat has a personality?"

"As much as a dog or a cat or a horse."

"I suppose that makes sense, although I'm not entirely convinced about cats. They *have* personalities, but they're enigmatic as hell."

"They can be," Kit agreed. "Whiskers is quite fun. He even plays fetch with Beau."

"Indeed? I'll need to see that to believe it. That boy has quite a menagerie. Are you sure there's room for guests?"

Kit laughed. "For now, but he does seem to collect animals at an alarming rate. He has a very kind and inquisitive heart. He's learning how to care for the goats. Tomorrow, I'll show him how to milk one."

"*You'll* show him?" Romsey asked. "You know how to milk a goat?"

As they entered the lower courtyard, Kit nodded.

Romsey narrowed his eyes at him. "And you built that pen and shed." Whist had told the duke and duchess about that earlier.

"I did." Kit was well used to people's shock, although the tenants no longer demonstrated any surprise. They'd quite accepted him for who he was. Rather, who he was pretending to be. Except that person—at least his character—was really who he was.

What a bloody tangle.

"Did you know all that before you disappeared, or did you spend the last six years herding goats?"

Kit looked over at him, trying to ascertain if he was speaking in jest. He wasn't entirely sure. "I spent most of the last six and a half years on a boat."

"So I heard. I was joking about the goats. I presume you were active in the management of the estate before you went missing."

"Actually, I've learned about goats since returning. Beau took an interest in them." Kit didn't feel the need to defend himself, but neither did he want Romsey asking awkward questions. Best to allay the man's curiosity, and Kit hoped that was all this was, straightaway.

"Well, it's damned impressive," Romsey said as they walked up the steps toward the upper gatehouse. "I imagine it's been strange being back."

Strange, challenging, wonderful. "It's been an adjustment."

"Were you surprised to come home to find a son? Diana said you disappeared before you knew Verity was expecting."

Kit shot a quick look toward Romsey. He called her Verity? Kit wanted to call her Verity. Now that he knew her name. But he wouldn't ask. The parameters of their relationship were clear, and such familiarity wasn't part of it. Instead, he focused his mind on the relationship that had no limits and that had completely overwhelmed him in ways he'd never expected. "Coming home to Beau has been a true joy," he said, meaning every word.

Romsey peered over at him as they moved through the upper gate. "Is it painful to think of the years you missed with him? I imagine it would be." He said this with an understanding that led Kit to believe this man knew something of loss.

"I try not to think about that," Kit said. In truth, what he tried not to think of were the years he'd miss after he was gone. In scarcely a fortnight, he'd become rather attached to the boy, and he wasn't ready to contemplate leaving him.

"Probably for the best. It doesn't help to focus on the past. Still, six and a half years is a long time. Verity says you were pressed onto a ship. How did you manage to survive that? Not just survive it, but come out seemingly the better for it."

He already knew that Kit's behavior was different? Had Verity written to them about him or told them in the stable yard? Kit had watched them talking, aware they were discussing him from the way they kept looking in his direction.

Kit resisted the urge to ignore Romsey's question as they walked through the upper courtyard to the back of the castle. "You just…survive."

They paused in front of the wide door that led into the King's Hall, and Romsey nodded in understanding. "You do. And maybe, if you're lucky, you come out better on the other side. Seems as though that's what happened to you. That's certainly what happened to me—and I credit Diana for that."

Kit seized on the opportunity to shift the focus of their conversation. "What did you survive?" He opened the door and gestured for Romsey to precede him.

Romsey grimaced. "It's a fairly depressing topic. I was married before, and she died. It was a tragedy, and I feared I would never recover."

"Yet you did." Kit had also noted how close Romsey stood to his wife, and how he touched her with care and frequency and…love.

"Because of Diana. She saved me in every way a person can be saved." He inclined his head toward Kit. "I can only imagine what holes may linger in your soul after such a harrowing experience, but perhaps Verity will help patch them up. And now I must go check on my wife. See you at dinner." With a nod, he turned and climbed the stairs.

Kit intended to go up as well but didn't immediately follow. Romsey's words cloaked him in discomfort. Holes in his soul? Harrowing experience? He'd chosen to get on a ship at the age of fifteen, and he'd never looked back. Certainly he'd missed his father from time to time, but the life he'd led had been exciting and rewarding, if a bit lonely. Any holes he might possess came from the time before he'd gone to sea, left by the death of his mother, the pervasive sadness of his father, and the truth of who he really was—as well as who he could never be.

Except he was precisely that person now. At least for a short time.

Or forever.

If he wanted it.

No, he couldn't continue this ruse indefinitely. Someone was bound to discover the truth. He'd need to be long gone before that happened.

Chapter Eight

❦

"YOU ARE A VERY tired boy, I think," Verity said as she perched on the edge of Beau's bed that night.

He yawned widely even as he tried to shake his head. "I'm not *that* tired, Mama. Papa is going to read *Robinson Crusoe*." Despite his obvious exhaustion, his eyes were alight with excitement.

"I didn't realize we had that book." The collection of books in the library downstairs didn't include many novels, and the ones that Verity had procured over the past few years were in her study.

"We didn't. Papa told me about it last week, and the copy he ordered arrived today."

"Indeed it did," Rufus said, mildly startling Verity as he came into Beau's room.

"He's awfully tired," she said, looking up at Rufus. "Perhaps you should postpone this to tomorrow."

"No, Mama! I can listen with my eyes closed if I must."

"We'll just read a half chapter." Rufus eyed her carefully. "If it's all right with you." He looked down at Beau nestled beneath his covers. "Remember that we always listen to your mother."

Beau exhaled. "Yes, Papa." His expression didn't seem to agree.

Verity patted her son's chest and let her hand lie on him for a moment. "I see nothing wrong with you listening, and if you fall asleep, your father will simply have to reread it tomorrow."

With a grin toward his father, Beau said, "He won't mind. It's his favorite story!"

Verity glanced at Rufus. "Is it really? I'd no idea." She didn't expect him to respond, and he didn't. While he'd demonstrated kindness and charm, he was often closemouthed so that he seemed even more of a mystery to her. He wasn't the man she remembered, and she found herself wanting to know just *who* he was.

She leaned over and kissed Beau's cheek. "Sleep well, my sweet boy."

He kissed her cheek and squeezed his arms around her neck. "Sleep well, Mama."

She stood and moved past Rufus with a murmured "Good night."

He inclined his head and responded in kind, his deep voice sliding over her like the drape of a silken chemise. She went to the door and turned before leaving. Rufus had sat next to Beau with his back propped against the headboard of the bed. He opened the book and began to read. She lingered a moment, allowing the rich baritone of his voice to lull her into a sense of warmth and peace and…rightness.

With a start, she pushed away from the door and went into the corridor. Before she could turn toward her chamber, she saw Diana come around the corner toward her. They'd planned to meet in Verity's study tonight to talk in private.

Verity waited while Diana traversed the length of the corridor. "I was just saying good night to Beau."

Diana glanced into Beau's room as she passed, and Verity saw her face soften.

Leading the way to her bedchamber, Verity paused, then closed the door behind her cousin after she came inside.

"Does he read to Beau every night?" Diana asked. "It's very sweet."

"Nearly. Tonight, he's starting *Robinson Crusoe*. Apparently it's his favorite." Verity arched a dubious brow before walking across the chamber and into the study that adjoined the room. This was her private space where she could fully withdraw. Two years after Rufus's disappearance, she'd taken over this room as well as the bedchamber and over time had banished his presence entirely. Decorated in warm gold and pale pink, the room was bright and feminine and reminded her of how happy she'd been for him to simply vanish.

"You sound skeptical," Diana said, depositing herself on a chaise near the windows. She propped her feet up and rearranged her dressing gown to cover her legs.

Verity sat in her favorite wingbacked chair situated between one of the windows and the hearth and put her feet on a footstool. "I had no idea he even had a favorite book. In the months I knew him before he disappeared, I'd never known him to read anything."

"Not even an estate ledger?"

"Goodness, no."

"*Could* he read?" Diana asked.

Verity thought for a moment, then laughter bubbled from her chest. "I honestly don't know. He must have."

"I know you didn't care for him," Diana said slowly. "But I have to say he seems rather charming. I think Simon likes him."

"Everyone likes him." Verity couldn't keep the bemusement from her tone. "It's beyond peculiar, Diana. He simply isn't the same man I married. It's as if his entire personality was swept away by the ocean and replaced with someone else's."

Diana cocked her head to the side as she folded her arms in her lap. "How is he different?"

Verity leaned back against the chair and tried to categorize the ways. "That's difficult because it really is in every single way. He's much kinder, gentler, more patient, much more involved in the estate, and he knows things he didn't before, such as how to build things, or is eager to learn them. Honestly, his thirst for knowledge is astounding. He's absolutely thrown himself into the estate since his return."

"That all sounds very good and positive. Are you unhappy about it?"

"No, it's just strange." Verity surrendered to the need to share all the suspicions that had crowded her mind over the past fortnight. "There are other things too. None of his clothes from before fit. He said it was because he'd changed physically after working on a ship, but Kirwin thinks he's a bit taller, and I have to agree."

Diana's brow creased. "You don't know for sure? I could tell you Simon's exact height using my hand above my head."

"Yes, well, your and Simon's marriage is far different from mine."

Diana winced. "I know, and I'm sorry. I shouldn't have said that."

Verity sat forward and gave her an earnest look. "Please don't feel badly. It's not your fault. It pleases me so much to see you so happy."

"Thank you." Diana blushed. "I-I am happy. More than I ever thought I could possibly be."

"And you deserve it after everything you've been through." They'd been raised by awful men, brothers with a penchant for disparagement and other abuse, though Diana's father was far worse than Verity's. Both men presented a pleasant and affable face to the world, but to their families, they were ruthless.

"So do you. I sometimes think your time with Rufus, though short, was more terrible than the abuses I suffered with my father. But you've never revealed specific details." Diana's gaze was full of compassion. "And I am not asking you to."

Verity appreciated that. Diana was the one person she could tell, but to share her shame wasn't something she was sure she could do. Instead, she returned to the ways in which Rufus was different. "His boots didn't fit either. I would guess his feet are too big." She'd stared at his feet countless times since Kirwin had told her about him not wearing the nearly new boots.

"That is odd. You can explain gaining muscle while working on a ship, but a change in height or foot size seems inexplicable."

"I will say that my feet did grow a bit after I had Beau. I feel I should share that with you given your condition."

Diana stroked a hand over her belly. "Fascinating. My body will change in many ways, I suppose. I only hope Simon will still find me attractive."

"I think you could turn into a weathered old hag, and he would only adore you more."

Diana laughed. "Perhaps. He does seem enamored of me, but no more than I am of him. Goodness, it's a bit revolting, isn't it?"

No, it was wonderful. Envy burned Verity's chest as she struggled to respond. "Not at all."

Sobering, Diana knitted her hands together and settled them on her stomach. "So what do you think all this means? Could it simply be that he has changed?

Simon asked him about it this afternoon."

"He did?" Verity said sharply.

"Yes, is that bad? He only asked what had happened to improve his disposition. Or something like that."

"Rufus doesn't like discussing his time away."

"Are you afraid he'd be angry? He didn't seem to be. He told Simon it had been a harrowing experience and that such a thing was bound to change a man. Or something like that." She shook her head. "Since I've been with child, my memory for details is just not what it once was."

Verity smiled knowingly. "That won't last. You'll require all your wits when the baby comes, and your body will realize that. Or so it did for me." Beau's birth had been an awakening from the months of uncertainty and anxiety precipitated by Rufus's disappearance. Beau had given her everything she'd been missing—a purpose and love.

"I'm glad he wasn't angry," Verity added, then frowned. "Actually, he doesn't seem to get angry. Not anymore."

"He really does sound like a different person," Diana said.

"I think he might be," Verity said quietly, finally giving voice to the suspicion that had haunted her mind since he'd returned.

Diana sat forward, her blue eyes wide. "You think he's an imposter?"

"I don't know. I just don't think he's the man I married."

"But he looks like him, doesn't he?"

"For the most part. I would say his appearance is different, but I suspect much of that is his demeanor. He is far more relaxed. He smiles and laughs. All that changes the texture of his face." She looked down at her lap and smoothed away a piece of lint from her dressing gown. She snapped her attention back to Diana. "And his eyes are green."

"What color were they before?"

"Hazel. When I pointed out the difference, he said they look different depending on the light. I've yet to see them any hue but green since his return."

"Aren't Beau's eyes green?" Diana asked, settling back against the chaise.

"Yes. In fact, I would say their eyes are very much alike." Verity shook her head briskly and stared out the window into the darkness. "That's what's very strange. I would wager he isn't Rufus, and yet he has to be." She turned her gaze back toward Diana. "Who else would he be?"

Diana blew out a breath. "That is a very good question. Since there is a resemblance, could he be a relative?"

"I'm not aware of any. Rufus was the only remaining male offspring in the line when Augustus—the former duke—died. The duke's only son died when he was seven or eight."

"Which left his younger brother's son as the heir. And Rufus has no siblings."

"He had a brother and a sister, but his brother died in Spain in 1809, and his sister of an ague when she was twelve." She knew so few details about her husband, and what she did know were things Augustus had told her. Otherwise, she might not have known Rufus had siblings at all. She hadn't thought to ask him about them. Perhaps she should.

Except that was tantamount to saying she thought he was an imposter, and she didn't want to do that. If he *wasn't* Rufus, then her real husband could be out there somewhere. A slight shudder racked her frame.

Did she really believe that? She'd long thought him dead. No, she'd *hoped* him dead. There was a distinction, and it had been brought into sharp relief the moment Rufus had returned. Anything was possible, and she would take nothing for granted. For now, this version of Rufus was far better than the last, and she didn't want to provoke a disturbance.

Was she still afraid of him? Yes, though her apprehension had diminished. Which scared her more than anything. She must remain vigilant and be prepared for when he returned to his former self.

Only she didn't think he was his former self, did she? Verity propped her elbow on the arm of the chair and dropped her forehead into her palm.

The touch of Diana's hand on Verity's head drew her to look up at her cousin. Diana gazed down at her in sympathy. "What can I do?"

Verity lifted her head and pulled her feet from the stool so Diana could sit. "I don't know that there's anything anyone can do. He's my husband."

"Or not. You could question him, force him to go to London to be recognized as the duke."

"I could do that?"

Diana shrugged. "I'm not sure, but wouldn't he be summoned with a writ if he didn't appear?"

"That would be upon his inheritance, which happened seven years ago, and which he answered. I have no idea what to expect in this instance."

"I can talk to Simon. He might know."

That would mean sharing her suspicions with another person. She wasn't sure she wanted to do that. Her hesitation must have been apparent, because Diana said, "He can be trusted as implicitly as I can. I should have told you this before you confided in me, but Simon and I don't keep secrets. I wouldn't feel right not telling him."

Verity both understood and envied that. "Your marriage is truly something to aspire to."

"Is there a chance you could have that—or something close to it—with Rufus? Rather, whoever is reading to your son?"

Verity's eyes widened, and her spine stiffened. Put like that, a stranger was alone with her child. What kind of mother was she to allow that?

Again, reading her expression, Diana reached over to take Verity's hand. "He's *fine*. He's been caring for Beau the last fortnight, and that's gone well, hasn't it?"

"Better than I could have imagined." Emotion welled up in Verity's chest. Her throat tightened, and she had to wait a moment to speak. "I was always so happy he was gone, that Beau would never have to know——" She stopped short of saying what a monster his father had been. But if this wasn't Rufus, if this was really someone else, someone kind and caring and who seemed to love her son… Maybe she could find peace again.

With a stranger claiming the title and usurping her position as head of the estate.

"If he's not Rufus, I should want him to leave," Verity said. "I'm the steward of the estate, and I'm Beau's guardian. That means my word is law here, not his." Yet, so far, he'd allowed her word to *be* the law, and he gave no indication that would change. Perhaps it was time to push him a bit, to test the honor of his word.

Diana's eyes narrowed slightly. "You seem to be

thinking something."

Verity's mouth curved into a small smile. "You know me too well. I was just thinking that I want to get to know the man a little better, to determine if he's actually Rufus."

"And if he's not?"

"If he's better than Rufus and will allow me to retain control of the estate, perhaps I should let him stay. Then if Rufus did return, he couldn't easily claim the title—provided the man claiming to be Rufus is recognized as the Duke of Blackburn in the House of Lords." That prospect gave her the first moment of true relief since Rufus—or whoever he was—had arrived.

"It sounds as if you have a plan. While we're here, we'll do our best to ascertain the man's true character. There's no way Simon and I will leave you with anyone dangerous." Her gaze turned sad. "Am I correct in gathering that Rufus—the old Rufus—caused you harm?"

"Yes, but please don't ask me to explain. It was a mercifully brief chapter that I'd prefer remain in the past."

"I understand. Do you want me to stay with you tonight? Simon would understand."

Verity laughed softly. "That's not necessary. I've been managing quite well."

"Is his chamber really just on the other side of Beau's?" Diana asked.

"Yes, at Beau's request. It's fine. We've established a pleasant working relationship with regard to the estate and to Beau."

"So there's no chance your marriage could be something more?" Diana took a deep breath and shook her head. "Forget I asked that. I'm trying to be romantic. I only want you to be as happy as I am." She squeezed Verity's hand before letting it go. "But if you could remain married to him as you are now, there are worse things."

Yes, such as the marriage she'd already endured. "Thank you for coming tonight. I feel much better having unburdened myself." Verity rose, and Diana stood with her.

Diana smiled. "That's what we do for each other. Without you, Simon and I might not be married."

"Nonsense. You would've found your way to the altar. I merely gave you a nudge. Time, if you recall, was an important factor." Because Diana's father had been on his way to rescue Diana from her "kidnapper."

"Indeed it was," Diana said, with a glint of relief in her eyes. They embraced, and Diana left.

As Verity lay in bed a short time later, she realized she really did feel better. Acknowledging her doubt about his identity had energized her. If he was Rufus, could they find their way to a real marriage? She didn't expect what Diana and Simon had, but couldn't stop herself from fantasizing.

This Rufus was very charming. And kind. And helpful. And a wonderful father to Beau. She thought of them cozied up together while he read *Robinson Crusoe* and couldn't help but smile. If he wasn't Rufus and she asked him to go away, Beau would be devastated.

She turned to her side and closed her eyes. As she drifted off to sleep, she dreamed of a faceless man aboard a ship. The ocean breeze lifted her hair as he swept her into his strong arms. She felt safe and happy. Content.

Until sometime later when she awoke with a jolt. The man had gained a face—the ruthless visage of Rufus, who looked somehow different from the man who'd returned. The angry lines on his forehead and the rough set of his mouth gave him away, and she was never more certain that they were two different men.

That was easy to believe in the middle of the dark night as her heart pounded in her chest. But maybe it was only a dream—all of it. Maybe this man really was Rufus, and maybe he would revert to the monster he'd been.

No, she wouldn't let that happen. She'd kill him first.

***

THOUGH IT HAD rained the last few days, Simon had accompanied Kit on his visits with the tenants. They'd formed a friendship of sorts, but there was still a sense of disconnection. Or maybe that was just for Kit since he had to be so careful about what he revealed.

Today was Thomas's first day as steward. He'd arrived last night and moved into his new lodgings in the tower. This morning, they'd all—Verity, Kit, Diana, Simon, Thomas, and Beau—shared a breakfast, and as they left the dining room, Beau bid everyone a reluctant farewell as he went upstairs for his lessons. Verity and Diana planned to go into Blackburn to purchase linens for Diana and Simon's baby from a particular weaver.

Kit wished he could accompany them into the town and look at a few of the spinning mills. While there were individual weavers on the estate, there were no spinning mills. He was planning to change that.

They all exited the castle into the upper courtyard, and Simon kissed his wife's cheek as she and Verity prepared to leave. Kit felt a moment's awkwardness, as if there were an expectation that he should do the same. He wouldn't, of course, but he found himself wondering what that would feel like. A jolt of heat raced through him, and he decided he should stop wondering.

"Have a good trip," Thomas said with a smile as they took themselves off, leaving the trio of men in the courtyard. He turned to Kit. "Where shall I begin?"

"Romsey and I nearly finished the audit. We have just a few more tenants to speak with today." Kit glanced up at the darkening sky. "In the rain, it would seem."

"You could postpone," Thomas said.

Kit started toward the upper gate, and the other two men followed. "I'd just as soon get it finished. We're very close. I would invite you to come along, but I'd prefer you review the latest accounting. I left it on your desk before breakfast."

"Thank you, Your Grace. I'll read it immediately."

Kit nodded. "We can discuss it later. Until then." He pulled his hat more firmly onto his head and led Simon toward the stable yard.

Once they were on their horses, it began to drizzle. Kit was glad the tenants they had left to visit were relatively close.

"You're certain of your new steward?" Simon asked as they rode.

"I know his grandfather was well respected, and I expect he'll do a fair job. Bleven had nothing but high praise for him and was sorry to lose him."

Simon grimaced. "Was that awkward?"

"Not particularly. Bleven understood that this was an improvement for Entwhistle and didn't begrudge him the advancement."

They were quiet a moment, but Kit had the sense Simon wanted to say something else. Kit looked over at him. "Last night at dinner, you said you were in the process of searching for a new steward as yours wants to retire. Are you thinking to poach mine?"

"God, no," Simon said vehemently. "I'm not that uncouth, never mind that horrid nickname people call me."

Kit had no idea what he was talking about. "What's that?"

"Of course you wouldn't know. How pleasant. Some gentlemen in the ton are given descriptive nicknames."

"Descriptive how?"

"They're meant to describe their personality or their notoriety. I've been called the Duke of Ruin since my wife died. It's a rather long and lurid story, but suffice it to say that I'd earned that nickname until recently. Until I married Diana. My best friend is the Duke of Ice. He's a bit, er, cold. Or he was until he married the love of his life."

"I'm sensing a theme here—wives fix everything?"

Simon shouted with laughter. "In our cases, yes."

Kit instantly thought of Verity, though she wasn't really his wife. If given the chance, would she be able to fix his woes? And what would those be? He wasn't in need of fixing as far as he could tell. He was only in need of money and a ship.

Nothing was that simple anymore, however, and he knew it. The moment he'd assumed the mantle of duke, he'd taken on responsibilities he'd be loath to walk away from. The estate. The tenants. Beau. His chest tightened. Verity.

"Back to your question," Simon said. "I'm not

poaching Entwhistle. On the contrary, I wanted to know if he was up to the task or if there was some other reason he'd wanted this position."

Kit frowned. "What does that mean?"

"I, ah, perhaps I shouldn't say anything. Forgive me." Simon increased his speed, but Kit easily came abreast of him again.

"Say what you were going to say."

"Entwhistle looks at your wife in a certain way."

"What way is that?" Kit wasn't obtuse; he wanted his suspicions confirmed.

"A way that I wouldn't allow him to look at Diana," Simon said wryly.

The day the goats had come to the castle, Kit had wondered if there might be something between Verity and the steward. She had wanted to hire him rather badly. And yes, he had noticed the way Thomas looked at his wife—at Verity.

"You think he has a tendre for the duchess."

Simon shrugged. "Maybe. Maybe not. I'd keep an eye on things, if I were you." He slid a glance toward Kit. "If it bothers you. If it doesn't, forget I said anything. Another man's marriage is none of my business."

"And yet here you are meddling," Kit murmured.

"Sorry."

"Don't be. I appreciate your confidence." Yes, it was rather like they were friends. It reminded Kit of the camaraderie he enjoyed aboard ship and found himself missing, only it was slightly different. Men on a ship could come and go. Here, on land, it was easier to maintain relationships. Or so he thought. He couldn't say since he'd spent half his life on the sea.

"Well then, I may as well meddle," Simon said. "I know your marriage is in name only at present. Again, my apologies, but Diana and I don't have secrets."

"It isn't much of a secret. We keep separate rooms." Separate lives, for the most part. If not for Beau, Kit had the sense he could leave at any moment and not be missed.

"I imagine it's difficult to start back up again after six and a half years away."

Particularly when you'd been an absolute beast.

Simon winced again. "My apologies. This is really none of my affair. It's just that I care deeply for Verity. She is my wife's favorite person—aside from me, I think—and she was a good friend and support to us when we needed one most."

"She's a good woman," Kit said. The finest he'd met.

"You sound as if you'd maybe like to change the circumstances of your marriage." Simon said this slowly, as if he were testing to see if he might be saying something he should apologize for again.

"As you said, it's difficult to readjust. We don't spend much time together outside of estate management or Beau."

"Perhaps you should."

It was a simple statement, but so very powerful. It repeated in Kit's head until it neared a crescendo of clarity. Yes, perhaps he should.

Maybe she'd go to town to look at a spinning mill with him. Or to the Eanam Brewery. Hell, anywhere. Or maybe he should start simple and just find a way to spend time with her here. It wasn't as if they didn't share common interests—the estate, Beau. If Kit could let down his guard a bit, he might find they shared even more.

They arrived at the first tenant and conducted their business in under an hour. The second tenant took slightly longer, and the third offered them lunch, which they gratefully accepted.

As they rode back to the castle, Kit definitively stated what he'd known for a while now. "Cuddy was stealing. Every single tenant reports different payment amounts from what the ledgers show."

"What do you plan to do?"

"I'm not certain. I think he's still in Blackburn." One of the grooms had delivered him to a lodging near the edge of town.

"Diana and I had planned to leave day after tomorrow, but if you'd like me to stay, I will."

"I appreciate that, but it's not necessary," Kit said. "I know you need to return to London."

"Do you plan to go? When word of your return reached the House of Lords, it caused quite a stir." Simon had mentioned this at dinner on their first night at Beaumont Tower, but Kit had artfully diverted the conversation. He didn't want to go to London. He wanted to return to the sea before someone discerned the truth. He wasn't entirely sure what happened to someone who impersonated a duke, nor did he want to find out.

"Not right now, and maybe not during this session."

"It's only the end of April. It may go until July, which is bloody hellish. I have to admit, I haven't fulfilled my duties very well the past few years. I'm trying to make up for it now." Simon peered over at him as they neared the castle. "They may send you a writ, and then you'll have to go."

"Do me a favor and prevent that."

Simon chuckled. "I will try."

They rode into the stable yard, where a groom took their mounts, and they returned to the castle. The women had returned, and Simon was clearly anxious to see his wife. He hurried inside while Kit went to see if he could find Thomas.

The man who perhaps coveted his wife.

His not-wife. Verity. The woman Kit wanted.

Did he?

Yes.

The realization hit him hard, and he slowed in the middle of the courtyard on his way to Thomas's tower. He couldn't think about that. He needed to focus on Cuddy and keeping himself out of the House of bloody Lords.

Except he was supposedly the Duke of Blackburn, and it was his duty to sit in the damned thing. If they summoned him, he would have to go. Or disappear immediately. And though that was his ultimate goal, the thought pained him more than he could say.

Cuddy. Focus on that thieving blackguard.

What did Kit plan to do? He wanted to know how Verity's father had come to encourage Cuddy for the position. But since Kit—as Rufus—was supposed to have been here at the time and had presumably done the actual hiring, he had to tread carefully.

She'd said that Cuddy and her father had maintained a close relationship over the past six and a half years. Did that include direct oversight of Cuddy? If it did, surely Verity's father should have realized the man was embezzling. Except the differences had been small enough to avoid notice but large enough to accumulate quite a sum over time.

Where was that sum now? If Kit recovered it—and he planned to—he'd have enough to get his ship and still restore a portion to the estate. Only, that made him no better than Cuddy. Stealing from a thief was still stealing, especially when Kit knew where the money belonged.

He needed to talk to Verity about Cuddy and about her father's role. This was the perfect opportunity to take Romsey's advice. Yes, he'd ask to meet with her and see if he could turn the occasion into something pleasant and engaging for both of them.

Anticipation coursed through him as he strode toward Thomas's tower until another realization smacked him in the face. If he had a nickname, it would be the Duke of Lies. He was lying to everyone. How could he possibly hope to build a relationship on that?

Chapter Nine

⊷ℰ•3⊷

VERITY STOOD OUTSIDE Beau's room and listened to Rufus read the end of a chapter of *Robinson Crusoe*. Every night, she wanted to ask if she could join them, and every night, the words stuck in her throat. The more she found herself relaxing around Rufus and accepting him, the more annoyed she became. He deserved her scorn or at least her apathy.

But it's to spend time with Beau, she reasoned.

Except she was enchanted by Rufus's voice. The way he read the story was warm and engaging. It was the voice of a man who'd experienced adventure and would hold you in his thrall if given half the chance. She found herself wanting to give him an entire chance.

But she wouldn't.

Taking a deep breath, she notched up her chin and bustled into the room. "Are you ready for a kiss good night?"

Rufus snapped the book closed and stood from the bed as Beau giggled. "Do you mean me or Papa?"

A blush started to rise up Verity's neck, but she worked to keep her embarrassment at bay. "You, silly."

Beau looked up at her, his green eyes wide and innocent as they flicked over to Rufus and back to her again. "Why don't you kiss like Auntie Diana and Uncle Simon?"

Absolutely robbed of speech, Verity worked not to gape at her son.

Thankfully, Rufus saved the moment. "Some people

don't like to kiss in front of others."

Beau's forehead pleated as he looked between them again. "But you both kiss me all the time in front of other people."

"It's, ah, different with children," Verity said quickly. She leaned down and kissed his head, smoothing his hair down and then pulling his coverlet up to his chin. "Time for dreaming now. Sleep well."

"I love you, Mama."

"I love you too, Beau."

"And I love you, Papa."

"And I love you." Hearing Rufus say those words to Beau turned an already tense moment into something that was nearly excruciating. Standing here, they almost felt like a family. She could imagine Rufus kissing her. Worst of all, she could imagine kissing him back.

"Oh, and Mama? You used to say that the picture of Papa on my wall didn't look very much like him. I think it looks exactly like him." Beau yawned before closing his eyes and snuggling beneath his covers.

Verity glanced toward the picture and murmured, "I have to agree." In it, he wore a half smile, and his eyes, though not as green as those of the man in the room, crinkled with amusement. It gave one the sense that the subject of the portrait was happy and charming. So yes, in that respect, it looked far more like the man in the room than the Rufus she recalled.

"Sleep well, Beau." Rufus blew out the lantern but left the other one burning on the other side of the room because Beau didn't like to be in the dark. That fact had worried Verity—she'd been afraid Rufus would say he was being a coward.

On the contrary, Rufus had understood completely and said light helped guide people in their dreams. At every turn, he'd surprised and impressed her.

Of course you can imagine kissing him.

She hurried from the room, anxious to put some distance between herself and Rufus.

However, once they were in the corridor, he turned to face her. "I was hoping we might share a nightcap and discuss the estate. We've finished our audit, and I'd like to share the results with you as well as ask you about Cuddy."

She blinked at him, caught in a state of surprise and apprehension. She ought to say no, that they could talk tomorrow, but she was also interested to hear what he had to say.

"I suppose we could do that," she said slowly.

He gave her a wry smile that was one of his most attractive varieties. Yes, he had many smiles, and she'd grown to like every single one of them. She'd even begun to anticipate what would make him smile—his favorite cheese on toast for breakfast, Whiskers chasing Mr. Cheeks through the courtyard, and pretty much anything Beau did.

"I'd invite you to my office, but I'm afraid I don't have one," he said.

"That is a problem, isn't it? I'm sorry I didn't think of it before now."

"It's quite all right. I was using the tower office since Cuddy's departure, but now that Thomas is here, I need to find another space."

"How about the antechamber off the Knight's Room? That's seldom used and has a lovely view of the west garden and the hills beyond."

"Why don't we go take a look, and we can talk along the way?" He'd neatly maneuvered that, but Verity didn't feel particularly manipulated. She could refuse him if she wanted and knew he would let her go.

With a nod, she joined him in walking along the corridor. They turned, passing the guest rooms before reaching the drawing room. They crossed the landing at the top of the stairs into the more formal Knight's Room.

Rufus stopped abruptly. "I forgot to stop for our drinks." He gave her a sheepish smile that was also one of her favorites. Innocent with a touch of mischief, it reminded her the most of Beau. "What would you prefer? Sherry, perhaps?"

"Yes, thank you."

"I'll be but a moment." He dashed back into the drawing room, and she brushed her palms down her dressing gown, feeling suddenly nervous.

There was no reason to be, she told herself. So they were alone at night. With spirits. After their son had asked them about kissing.

Heat suffused her body, and she feared the blush she'd avoided in Beau's room was now coloring her cheeks a bright red. She brought her hands to her cheeks and went to the windows, where hopefully cooler air would calm her flesh.

Thankfully, her face felt normal again when he returned and handed her a glass. While the heat was gone, a peculiar tickle remained in her belly.

"You still like whiskey, I see." She took a sip of sherry, hoping to banish that tickle.

"I developed a taste for rum, but absent that, this will do."

"I've never had rum. What is it like?"

"Thick and rich and a bit sweet. Decadent. There are all kinds, but the best taste just like that. In my opinion. Yours may vary. I'll have to see if I can procure some."

He picked up a lantern before turning toward the antechamber. "It looks dark in there."

"We don't keep it lit or heated, but if you want it as an office, that will change, of course."

They went into the rectangular room, and he glanced around. "This is a good size. I looked at it when I returned, but I wasn't seeing it as an office. It's almost too big for that." It sounded as if he were trying to cover for not remembering the room—or perhaps he'd never seen it before his arrival.

If he wasn't really Rufus.

She didn't want to play this game with herself tonight. All she knew, and all that mattered, was that he wasn't a monster. Not anymore. No one who cared for a child the way he did could be.

Verity walked toward the inner wall and turned. "You could put a desk here if you want to be close to the hearth. Or at the opposite end if you prefer to have a seating area near the windows. This room is a bit drafty in the winter, so I might choose the former."

"Then that's what I'll do," he said. "I appreciate your advice." The room contained two seating areas, one in front of the fireplace and one at the other end of the chamber. "Where will the extra furniture go?"

"We'll find a place for it, or we can always give it to a tenant, or several tenants, depending on what you don't want to keep."

"Do you do that often?" he asked. "Give things to tenants?"

"As much as I can." She gestured toward a comfortable armchair near one of the windows. "In fact, that chair over there might be a nice gift for Mr. Bricker's new cottage."

He lifted the lantern toward that side of the room to

better illuminate the space. Then he turned his head and stared at her a moment. "That's very thoughtful of you, but then I've come to expect nothing less."

Something seemed to stretch between them, an invisible pull that she fought with all her being. Then he brought his glass to his lips, and the moment began to fade…until she began to focus on his mouth.

Abruptly turning, she went back into the Knight's Room, where a low fire burned and there was ample illumination.

He set the lantern back down on a table and walked to the settee in front of the hearth. "I'll build some bookshelves so that I may have a small library."

"You seem to like books." She'd seen him reading in the library downstairs several times, and Kirwin had reported that he'd once been found there in the middle of the night, asleep on a settee with a book open facedown on his chest.

"I do. It's one of the few pastimes you can undertake on a ship. But due to space, you're often reading the same things over and over. I'm quite thrilled to have variety again."

"Beau says *Robinson Crusoe* is your favorite. I never knew that." She eyed the settee, wondering if he planned to sit there. But of course he wouldn't sit at all until she did, which meant he could choose to sit by her. She'd take the chair, but he stood between her and it, and doing so would make an already awkward situation fully uncomfortable. Or so she worried.

In the end, she dropped onto the end of the settee, her hip bumping the side and indicating it was as far away as she could sit.

He took the chair, and she instantly relaxed. "I've always loved that story," he said. "I'm sorry we didn't discuss such things before. I'd like us to now. What's your favorite book?"

"Oh, I couldn't name just one," she said. "I like to read plays. Perhaps because I like to see them and don't often have a chance to." Rufus had never taken her to see one, but then they hadn't been married long enough to do much of anything.

Don't think about that time. Stay in this moment where he's not a threat.

"What did your audit find?" She sipped her sherry, then rested the glass on her leg as she held the stem.

"I'm confident Cuddy was stealing, and I'm sorry for it."

She couldn't keep from scowling. "I feel like such a fool."

"Don't chastise yourself. There's no point. He was very smart about it. He stole enough to accumulate a tidy sum after all these years, but it was little bits at a time. You couldn't have known unless you'd acted as steward right alongside him."

"I should have performed an audit, as you've done."

"This is not your fault. I won't allow you to blame yourself."

She arched a brow at him. "You won't allow me?"

He flashed a grin, and she thought *this* might be her favorite. His eyes crinkled at the corners, and his straight white teeth showed for a brief moment. It was an infectious smile, and she found her lips curving up of their own volition.

"Forgive me," he said. "I only meant to demonstrate my strong preference that you *not* castigate yourself. Please."

"I'll try."

"This is entirely on Cuddy. Though I would like to

ask about your father's involvement."

Her gaze snapped to his. "What do you mean?"

"You said it seemed as though Cuddy worked for him. Why did you think that? Was it because he encouraged me to hire him?"

"In part, yes. My father visits at least once a year, and they spend a great deal of time together when he's here."

Rufus nodded slowly. "And do you recall how your father knew of Cuddy? I'm afraid I don't remember the connection or if there was one." He winced apologetically.

"I don't recall. I wasn't invited to participate in estate matters before you disappeared. But it seems you may not recall that either."

He looked away as a bit of color flashed briefly across his cheekbones. She might have attributed it to anger if he were the old Rufus. But this looked more like embarrassment.

"I must apologize profusely for my behavior…before." He looked back at her, his eyes brilliant with candor. "I can't make you forget, but please know that I've worked very hard to. In fact, I've done such a thorough job of it that I sometimes struggle to remember things."

Or you aren't actually Rufus.

That voice in the back of her mind was growing stronger despite her desire to silence it—at least for now. Some day soon, she might not be able to ignore it any longer. However, for now, she was content to keep things as they were, particularly given his devotion to Beau and to taking care of the estate. Which included getting to the bottom of Cuddy's theft.

"Do you think my father was involved with Cuddy's

embezzlement?" Verity asked.

"I don't know. I only want to learn as much as I can about Cuddy."

"Should we invite my father here?" She couldn't think of anyone she wanted to invite less.

Rufus arched a sandy brow at her. "You don't sound as if you want to."

"We don't have a very good relationship, but perhaps you remember that." Apparently, she *was* going to play that game tonight, for she'd decided to push him, to see what he might reveal.

"Vaguely," he said, shifting his gaze to the hearth. "I'm sorry you aren't close."

She wanted to push a little harder. "Really? It never bothered you before. You and my father were quite close. I would even say he preferred you to me, despite only knowing you a handful of months."

Registering the flare of his nostrils and the slight widening of his eyes, she suffered a moment's panic. She'd overstepped. Was now the moment she'd feared? Would he finally reveal the anger he'd kept buried since he'd returned?

"I'm... I don't know what to say." He took a long drink of whiskey, nearly draining the glass. He fixed his gaze on hers with piercing intent. "I know I keep saying this, but I'm not the man I was before. I can't change the past, but I swear that I only want the safety and security of you, Beau, and everyone at Beaumont Tower. I'll make sure your father doesn't meddle. You have my word on it."

His word. Rufus's word had meant nothing. But this man's word—and she was more sure than ever that he was someone else—was something quite different. Rufus would have defended her father. No, he would have gone further than that.

She took a deep gulp of sherry to calm the anxiety that started to swirl in her gut. Would she ever be able to think of him—of the man she'd married—without feeling powerless and afraid?

Maybe if she knew this man—the man she hadn't married—would keep her safe. Which he could if she'd allow it. Or maybe that wasn't even necessary. He didn't seem to require her permission. He would give her his protection whether she wanted it or not.

Warmth spread through her, and she was quick to credit her sherry instead of the man sitting nearby.

"Will you tell the authorities about Cuddy?" she asked.

"If I must, but first I'll give him the chance to return what he stole."

"That has to be quite a bit over six and a half years. Will he be able to do that?"

Rufus shrugged, and his eyes took on a frosty sheen that made her shiver. "I don't care. He'll pay one way or another." He finished his whiskey and redirected his attention to the dying fire.

His statement and the ominous manner in which he'd made it prompted Verity to drink the remainder of her sherry. She was suddenly eager to put an end to this interlude, despite the fact that she'd enjoyed it. For the first time, she glimpsed the possibility that this man might possess a darker nature—or at least the capacity for darkness.

"Fire is so treacherous," he said. "It draws us in with its warmth and beauty, but it can wreak total devastation."

She puzzled at the direction of his thoughts but didn't question him.

"Water is more beautiful, though. The ocean has a quiet cadence and a serenity that can calm even the wildest of things." One corner of his mouth ticked up. "The *most* beautiful is when the fire meets the water—a perfect burning sun setting into a wide, cool sea." He turned his gaze to hers, and the intensity in the green depths of his eyes captivated her. "None of that compares to you, however. You're beyond beautiful. You exist in that space near perfection—for nothing is truly perfect—where wonder and joy convene."

His words enthralled her, obliterating her discomfort of a moment before. No one had ever spoken to her like that. "You should write that down." Her words came out low and soft, and it was a silly thing to say, but she meant it.

"Maybe I will." His lips curved up again in that charming half smile, and she was confident *that* was her favorite.

They were all her favorite.

"Papa?"

They both turned at the sound of Beau's voice.

Verity leapt up and crossed the room to him. "What is it, my sweet boy?"

Rufus joined them, sweeping Beau up into his arms. "Can't sleep?"

Beau shook his head. "My tummy hurts."

Verity wanted to take him from Rufus, but Beau had laid his head on his father's shoulder. She moved around behind him and smoothed Beau's hair from his forehead. His temperature felt fine, and she exhaled with relief. "Do you want to sleep with me?"

"Can I sleep with Papa?" His lids were heavy, and though she wanted him with her, she wouldn't say no.

"Of course." Her heart clenched, and she wished she

shared a bed with Rufus. Then Beau wouldn't have to choose. Not that it had seemed much of a choice. She hated the feeling of being usurped by this man who probably wasn't even Beau's blood. But what could she say?

In truth, she didn't want to say anything. She couldn't bring herself to diminish the bond that had sprung up between them, not when Beau was so happy. His happiness was everything.

Beau's eyes closed, and Rufus's gaze found hers. "I can bring him to your room if you prefer," he whispered. "He won't know. He's already asleep."

She shook her head. "No. You take him." She smiled softly, appreciating his thoughtfulness so much. "Thank you." For caring for her son. For being gracious. For abdicating to her wishes.

For being exactly what they needed.

He returned her smile, then carried Beau from the room.

As she collected their glasses and put them on the sideboard in the drawing room, she began to believe their future wasn't in jeopardy. She wanted so badly to believe that. So right now, in this moment, she would.

❖❖❖

KIT STOOD WITH Verity just outside the entrance tower and waved to the departing coach, which carried the Duke and Duchess of Romsey. The past week had been far more enjoyable than Kit had imagined. Indeed, it had given him a sense of connection and belonging, which was making it damn hard to contemplate his escape plan. That had become especially daunting after the evening they'd spent two nights ago, sharing drinks and planning his office. They'd both dropped their guards, and he'd felt as if he'd come to know her much better.

At the same time, he couldn't ignore the disaster that would likely come if he stayed. He'd come precariously close to revealing his own secrets when the topic of her father had arisen. He'd nearly cocked everything up by not knowing a thing about the relationships between her and him, as well as him and her father. Apparently they'd been close, which was a bloody nuisance and would likely cause a problem if the man decided to show up. Hopefully, he wouldn't, at least not while Kit was still here. Kit did find himself wondering, however, why the man hadn't at least written, if not shown up— if they were as close as Verity thought them to be.

Over the past couple of days, Kit had worked to uncover as much information as he could using strategic discourse with various members of the staff. He'd learned that Verity's mother had died at least a decade ago, that her father lived in London, and that the prior duke—Kit's real father—had died a month after the nuptials. He'd been in decline after the death of his *legitimate* son the previous fall and had taken a turn for the worse. Finally, Kit had ascertained that Verity and his father had become close despite the brevity of their acquaintance. He longed to ask her about him, but since he—as Rufus—had supposedly been there, he could not. In some ways, this ruse was growing quite tiresome.

Verity expelled a small sound, something between a sigh and an expression of regret. Tiny lines crossed her forehead, and her lips were twisted into a slight frown.

"You're going to miss them," he said, perhaps unnecessarily. Her disappointment was evident and possibly something she preferred not to discuss.

"So much. I love Beaumont Tower, but sometimes I wish we lived somewhere farther south."

They'd made a promise to visit Lyndhurst later this summer, a pledge Kit knew he wouldn't keep. It stuck in his chest, making him mildly uncomfortable. He really was the Duke of Lies. They fell from his mouth like blossoms drifting from the trees, only they weren't pretty. With each one, he felt a sinking sense of defeat, as if he were losing a battle. But for what? Morality? Self-respect? Decency?

All those things and much more. This was beyond difficult because he liked Verity and Beau. No, he *loved* Beau. That much he could admit to himself. The boy had entrusted him with his care so effortlessly and so completely. The love of a child was truly unconditional. However, Kit knew that he could break the boy's heart in a moment, and the day would come when he would.

Pain pierced his chest, and he sought to find a way to ease the ache. Perhaps he could ease her melancholy too. He turned to her. "Come with me into Blackburn. I want to tour a spinning mill, and then we can stop at a pub. One of the grooms told me that Cuddy frequents the Sheep's Head, and I want to see if he's still in the vicinity." Because one of the grooms had taken him into town, Kit knew precisely where Cuddy was lodging—assuming he was still there.

He suddenly regretted inviting her. What if Cuddy was there? He couldn't very well confront him in front of Verity. If things turned sour, he didn't want her anywhere in the vicinity. But it was too late to rescind his offer, and what's more, he didn't want to.

She pivoted, her dark gaze reflecting surprise and just a touch of wariness. She'd all but become used to him—or so it seemed. Two nights ago, he'd glimpsed what their relationship might have been like. *If* he'd been the duke and married her. He'd wanted the title for so long, had been bitterly disappointed to know it would never be his, and now he found himself wanting it for an entirely different reason. For her.

"That sounds delightful," she said. "I'll just go and get ready. Shall I meet you in the stable yard?"

"I'll be waiting." He gave her a smile that faded from his mouth as soon as she turned her back and went into the courtyard.

Oh, this was going to end in disaster. He should leave now. But no, first he had to find Cuddy and recover what he'd stolen. Then he'd go.

Who the hell was he fooling? That would be a disaster too. There was just no way this would end well, at least not for him. Verity and Beau would continue on as they had before he'd come. This would be a brief interlude that would fade from their memory, especially for Beau since he was so young. Kit wasn't entirely sure he believed that, but he would cling to it nonetheless. He didn't have any other choice. This was never going to be a permanent situation. Even now, his body ached for the rhythm of the sea.

Perhaps he should go there instead of Blackburn. The coast was a day's ride, and he'd have to spend the night. He feared he wouldn't want to come back, and he had to. There was business to be finished. In Blackburn, he would work to track down Cuddy as well as investigate the spinning mill. He was going to leave the estate better than he found it—that was one pledge he would keep.

A quarter hour later, they set out in the chaise toward town. Kit hadn't spent much time driving vehicles, but he'd tried his hand in recent days, asking Simon to drive so that he could watch and learn. It had been an effective scheme, for now he was able to drive the chaise with enough confidence so as not to attract attention.

It wasn't easy pretending to be a duke.

They arrived at the spinning mill and were given a tour. It might not be easy being a duke, but it was damn convenient. People gave you whatever you wanted and treated you with reverence. It was a bit like being captain of a ship, which Kit missed. In this way, he appreciated his current role. He also found the workings of the mill fascinating and was inspired to build one on the estate.

They left the mill, and he escorted Verity into the chaise, where she climbed in easily. He regretted his choice of vehicle since it didn't require him to assist her. He rarely had occasion to touch her, and he found himself starving for the next time.

The other night, he'd wanted to sit next to her on the settee, but had seen the hesitation in her eyes and decided it best not to make her uncomfortable.

He settled into the chaise beside her and drove into the center of town. The pub he wanted to visit was just ahead, but he now wondered if it was perhaps a shade too disreputable for Verity. "I'd planned to go to The Sheep's Head, but I don't think that's the best place for a duchess."

"Is that the place Cuddy visits?" she asked, studying the run-down pub as they approached.

"Yes." Damn, he should have brought a coach so that he could leave her. "I can return another day."

"No, that's silly. I'll go to the draper. It's just around the corner." She gestured to the side of the street opposite the Sheep's Head. "Drop me off there, and you can fetch me when you're finished."

He hesitated to leave her alone but admitted to himself that this was a matter of propriety with which he had no experience. "Are you certain?"

"Of course," she said blithely, with a wave of her hand.

He turned the corner and, when he saw the draper, brought the chaise to a halt in front of the store. "I'll be back as soon as I can."

"Take as long as you need." She climbed out of the chaise. "It's important to track down Cuddy. I look forward to your report." Her mouth lifted in a faint smile before she turned and disappeared into the store.

Kit didn't leave immediately as he still pondered the wisdom in leaving her here. But perhaps he was being foolish. She'd said it was fine, and really, what did he know?

He drove the chaise back around the street to the pub. He found a place to leave the chaise that was somewhat equidistant from the pub and the draper. After informing the horse, unnecessarily, that he'd be back shortly, he walked briskly into the pub.

Scanning the dim interior, he registered ten or twelve patrons scattered about. The bar was at the back of the establishment, and a barkeep stood behind the scuffed plank of wood.

Kit went to the bar and greeted the man with a firm nod. "I'm in search of Mr. Strader. I understand he patronizes your establishment."

"He does. Bit early for him, though."

Withdrawing a coin from his pocket, Kit slid it across the wood to the barkeep. "Is he still lodging at the east end of town?"

The man picked up the coin and stashed it in his pocket. "As far as I know." His gaze dipped over Kit. "You want an ale, or are you just being nosy?"

Kit flashed a smile and offered two more coins. "Does he come in every night?"

"Aye, for dinner. Then stays until I throw him out, usually." He shrugged. "Always has plenty of blunt, so I don't mind."

"Thank you for your help." Kit turned and walked out into the dappled sunlight filtering through the clouds, making his way toward the draper. He didn't dare chance driving by Cuddy's lodging, not with Verity. He'd come back one night soon. Knowing Cuddy spent his nights at the Sheep's Head gave Kit the idea to go to the man's lodging and search it while he was out. Perhaps he could recover some of the money he'd stolen. Kit doubted he'd get the lot, not after all this time, particularly since it sounded as though Cuddy liked to spend it.

Kit walked into the draper, his heart beating faster than it ought, and searched for Verity. It wasn't a terribly large store, and when he didn't see her, his pulse picked up more speed. The storekeeper, a slender fellow with a broad smile, came to greet him. "Good afternoon." His gaze flickered with surprise and then recognition. "Your Grace, you must be looking for Her Grace. She's just in the back salon, perusing furniture in *Ackermann's Repository*." He turned, indicating that Kit should follow him.

Why had the man recognized him? Had Verity described him or had he recalled Kit—rather, Rufus—from all those years ago? The latter had happened when he'd arrived in town several weeks ago now to take a room. The innkeeper had instantly identified him as the lost Duke of Blackburn. Kit had simply stared at the man while the denial died on his tongue. It had been a massive gamble to pretend to be the duke, for there'd been every chance that while the innkeeper had recognized him, everyone else would know he was an imposter.

But when Kit hadn't responded, the innkeeper had announced to the common room, which had contained at least a dozen people at the time, that the long-lost duke had returned. Everyone had turned their heads with marked interest, their scrutiny fixed on his person in a most uncomfortable and invasive fashion. Then one gentleman had shouted his agreement and raised his tankard in a toast. It was all Kit had needed to seize the chance to walk into Beaumont Tower with a purpose for being there, and to inhabit the birthright that would be forever beyond his reach.

Kit followed the draper through a doorway into a small chamber decorated like a sitting room but with a long table akin to a dining table. Verity looked up from a color plate depicting a bookcase. "You're back."

"I'm back. What are you looking at?"

"Bookcases. For your office."

She was looking at furniture for his office? They'd found Rufus's old desk in a storage room yesterday, and it was being installed in Kit's new office today. He hated using the prick's desk but saw no reason to buy one, particularly when he wouldn't be using it for very long. He certainly wasn't going to endorse purchasing a bookcase.

"I don't need a bookcase," he said.

Her brow pleated with confusion, making her look impossibly adorable. "You said you did."

He supposed he had. "I can build them, I mean."

"Can you, Your Grace?" the storekeeper asked. "How extraordinary."

Verity stood from the table. "He's quite skilled with his hands." Her gaze dipped to those appendages, which were currently covered in gloves that he longed to throw away so he could slide his bare fingertips along her jaw.

She either read the direction of his mind or perhaps realized the double entendre of what she'd just said. Whatever the reason, a delightful blush highlighted her cheeks.

The storekeeper hovered as Verity came around the table and moved to Kit's side. "Do let us know if you require anything beyond bookcases." He gave them a hopeful look.

"We most certainly will," Kit said with a smile. The touch of Verity's fingers against his arm startled him. He turned his head and saw her watching him expectantly. It took him a moment to realize he should offer her his arm. Hell, he really wasn't very good at this. Or parts of it, anyway. He was once again very grateful he hadn't been summoned to London and hoped Simon would ensure that didn't happen.

He extended his elbow toward her, and she curled her hand around his forearm. Their flesh was separated by gloves and sleeves and just too many damn things, but he relished the connection.

She bid the storekeeper good day, and Kit escorted her from the shop. It was a simple thing, the way she touched him, but it seemed another step forward in whatever was building between them.

Was something building?

He looked at her askance. Her profile was as stunning as she appeared straight on. The line of her nose was a graceful sweep and the jut of her chin both pert and strong, while the curve of her lips was soft and tempting. He doubted he'd ever have occasion to taste them, but a man could dream.

As they walked to the chaise, she asked, "Did you learn what you needed to?"

"I did. I'll visit Cuddy on another day."

She withdrew her arm. "When?"

Kit wanted to snatch her hand back to his but didn't. Instead, he watched her climb into the vehicle. "I haven't decided yet." And when he did, he wasn't sure he wanted to tell her. A man bold enough to steal from a ducal estate was either incredibly foolish or disturbingly dangerous.

He sat beside her in the chaise and drove the horse into the street. "Thank you for coming with me today."

"Thank you for inviting me."

"Shall we go to a pub now?" he asked. "A nicer one, I mean."

"I think I'd like to get back to the castle. I promised Beau we'd visit the goats together. You're more than welcome to join us."

"Thank you, I may do that."

They fell silent as he drove out of town along the road that led to the castle. He lived in a bloody castle. Sometimes, he couldn't quite believe that. Hell, most of the time, he didn't believe that. At thirteen, his eyes had grown wide when the tower had come into view that first time. And when he'd seen it again just a few weeks ago, he'd had that same stirring of anticipation and excitement. It was no wonder he was loath to leave.

But the place was nothing compared to the people. How was he going to find the courage to go? The same way he had all those years ago when he'd chosen the sea. Back then, he hadn't known what he was getting himself into. Now he did. He would be captain of his own ship again, answering to no one. Completely free.

Except he began to see that being tethered to something—or to someone—might not be such a bad thing.

"I thought we might take a picnic on the next sunny day," Verity said.

He glanced over to see her looking at him. Her dark eyes gleamed in the afternoon sun, and for the first time, he noticed a thin band of amber at the edge of the iris. Her black lashes were long and lush, curling against her pale flesh as she blinked. He jolted himself before he became lost like a sailor succumbing to a siren.

He tried not to sound overeager in his response, but he was thrilled that she would invite him to spend time with her. "I would like that very much."

"With Beau, of course."

"Of course." While he wanted to be alone with her again—as they'd been the other night—he couldn't see having a picnic on a nice day without their son.

Their son.

No, he was hers. Beau would never be his, and he'd do well to remember that.

Chapter Ten

❦

AS IT HAPPENED, the next sunny day was the following one. Verity arranged for a basket of food to be ready at midday and asked Rufus to meet her and Beau in the lower courtyard near the well house.

She stopped in the kitchen to pick up the basket and thanked the cook for what looked to be an excellent picnic. Hefting the basket with her right hand and carrying the blanket with her left, she strode out the door and stood at the edge of the rose garden near the well house at the top corner of the lower courtyard.

After a minute, she set the basket on the ground to wait. Had the tutor lost track of time? And where was Rufus? Perhaps he was detained somewhere. Her gaze traveled toward Thomas's tower in the opposite corner. He'd been very busy since his arrival, and she hadn't seen him aside from when he'd joined them for dinner a few times.

The minutes stretched, and she transferred the blanket to her other arm. The day was warm and bright, and she was looking forward to being outside. The door she'd come through suddenly burst open. Beau dashed out, his laughter immediately filling the courtyard.

He was quickly followed by Rufus, who chased him along the edge of the garden to the center path. Beau didn't slow as he rounded the corner, and his feet slipped on the cobblestones. He fell down, landing on his side.

Verity dropped the blanket and ran toward him, but Rufus beat her by quite a bit. It was then that she realized he hadn't been using his top speed to chase the boy. She'd seen that when he'd caught Racer that day at Mr. Maynard's farm.

Rufus picked Beau up and set him on his feet and squatted down in front of him. "All right?"

Verity had expected Beau to cry, and his face had gone slightly pale. She lowered herself next to Rufus. "Did that scare you?" she asked, stroking Beau's arm from shoulder to elbow and back again.

Beau nodded. Then a moment later, he ran to the top of the stairs leading to the courtyard. "Come on, Papa, catch me!"

Rufus stood and offered his hand to Verity to help her rise. She wasn't wearing gloves, and neither was he. It was the first time their flesh had touched, and it was like grabbing lightning. Or how she imagined it to be— electrifying and hot, and it left a lasting impression.

"Please don't chase him down the stairs. He already fell once." She turned to Beau and called, "Please be careful."

"I *am* being careful, Mama. And don't worry about the stairs. I ran down them to the kitchen passage and didn't fall."

She looked over at Rufus. "Is that right?"

His gaze drifted to the side, and he hesitated a moment. "Er, yes. We were playing knights and villains."

"Which one were you?"

"It was my turn to be the knight."

Verity frowned and shifted a glance toward Beau. "I don't like thinking of my boy as a villain."

"It's pretend," Rufus said. "But if it makes you feel

better, he only chooses to be the villain because he likes to be chased."

"Can't the villain chase the knight?"

He mouth tipped into a crooked smile, and her stomach did a flip. It was as if lightning had struck again. "It's pretend. We can do whatever we like." He looked back toward the basket and the blanket on the ground. "I'll get the things for the picnic." He turned and started along the path.

"I can grab the blanket," she offered.

He waved a hand. "I've got it."

Verity went to Beau instead. She took his hand, and they descended into the courtyard, then veered right toward the gateway to the stable yard. "Perhaps I should play knights and villains." She wondered why they hadn't done that before and felt bad. It was a stark reminder of how much he'd missed not having a father.

"But you're a girl." Beau sounded scandalized.

Rufus met them as they approached the gate. "What's wrong with your mother being a girl?"

"She wants to play knights and villains." He made a face that clearly showed what he thought of that idea.

Verity was caught between laughter and disappointment.

"It would be better if she joined us," Rufus said, drawing Beau's sharp attention. "A knight needs a fair maiden to rescue."

"Then I am definitely going to be the villain. I don't wanna rescue a girl." He frowned, then sent his mother an apologetic glance. "Except I do want to save you, Mama."

Verity surrendered to the laughter. "Thank you."

"But Papa should be the one to save you. That's what dukes do, right?"

"That's what *husbands* do," Rufus corrected, "whether they are a duke or not."

Verity nearly tripped as they crossed the stable yard. She was almost completely convinced that this man wasn't her husband, and this was just about all the proof she needed. Rufus—the real Rufus—wouldn't have saved her from a damn thing.

Rufus. She looked at his profile and tried to conjure an image of the man she'd married. She thought his chin had been smaller, weaker, but she wasn't sure she knew anymore. When she thought of her husband, this man, whoever he was, filled her mind. And he did so with increasing frequency.

It was a very confusing and alarming thing to go from despising and fearing someone to admiring and liking them.

He's not the same person, she reminded herself.

Then who was he?

Curiosity burned her chest, but she couldn't ask him now, not in front of Beau. Did that mean she planned to tell him she didn't believe he was Rufus? She wasn't sure she wanted to. To admit that, to bring it out into the open, would bring an end to Beau's joy. She looked down at her son, who'd taken Rufus's hand while Rufus juggled the blanket and basket in his other grip. No, she couldn't do that.

She let go of Beau's hand and stopped. "Here, let me take the blanket."

"I can manage," Rufus insisted as he too paused.

She went around Beau and took the blanket from Rufus with a smile. Then she returned to her spot.

Beau slipped his hand in hers again and swung his arms as he clasped both parents. "I like having a mama and a papa." The glee in his voice was palpable, and

Verity feared her heart might burst. "Where are we having our picnic?" he asked.

"I thought we would go to the pond," Rufus said.

"Oh yes, let's!" Beau agreed.

Verity didn't allow Beau to go to the pond without her. That was where Augustus's son Godwin had drowned during the house party where she'd met Rufus. Her gaze slid to the man who claimed to be Rufus. He'd been charming at that party. But this man was different.

The path pitched downward as they neared the pond. A pair of ducks glided across the surface, and Beau instantly took off toward the water.

"Careful!" Verity called, increasing her pace. "He doesn't swim."

Rufus took off running and set the basket in the grass before catching up to Beau and sweeping him up into his arms and spinning him around. Beau's laughter filled the air as Verity neared the basket. She laid the blanket out over the grass with a smile, then transferred the basket to a corner. "Who's hungry?"

Rufus set Beau down and sat with alacrity, patting the spot next to him. Beau immediately dropped onto the blanket, and they both watched as she laid out the food.

After swallowing a bite of cold roasted duck, which seemed rather rude given their company on the pond, Rufus inclined his head toward the water. "I think I'll get a small boat for us to row about. Which means I should build a dock."

"Can I help?" Beau asked before wolfing a too-large bite of bread.

"Not so much at once," Verity said, eyeing her son.

He gave her a sheepish look, then took a much

smaller bite with far less…vigor.

"Will you teach me to build the dock, Papa? I want to build things like you."

"I think that will be an excellent thing for you to learn. Along with swimming."

"Can you teach him that?" Verity asked. "I would feel better about the boat if he could swim."

"I can," Rufus said.

Beau turned his body toward Rufus. "Are you a good swimmer, Papa? You must be if you were on the ocean."

"Would you believe many sailors don't know how to swim?" Rufus nodded when both Beau and Verity shook their heads.

"That seems rather dangerous. And foolhardy," Verity said before nibbling on her duck. She wasn't enjoying it very much. She felt as though the pair on the pond were staring at her in silent judgment. She noticed Rufus had stopped eating his.

"It can be, which is why I encourage everyone to learn, whether they are on a ship or not," Rufus said. "You never know when the skill will be needed."

Beau turned his head to Verity. "Do you know how to swim?"

"I'm afraid I don't."

Beau's face lit. "Then Papa can teach us both!" He shoved a piece of duck into his mouth, clearly oblivious to the proximity of the very species he was devouring. Which was just as well. Given his love of animals, Verity wondered if he would some day refuse to eat the beef or the fish or the duck that arrived on his plate.

A butterfly flitted past, and Beau jumped up to chase it.

Verity inclined her head toward Rufus's plate. "You

don't like duck anymore?"

He winced as he shot a glance toward the pond. "It seems…wrong."

"I thought the same thing." Their eyes met, and they laughed. It was an astonishing moment she'd never imagined would happen.

When they stopped laughing, Rufus gestured toward Beau's plate. "It didn't seem to bother him."

"No, but I'm not sure he made the connection."

"He should. He needs to understand where food comes from."

"Yes, he should." Again she was reminded of all the things Beau could learn from this man. "I'm glad you returned." She hadn't meant to say it, but it was true.

He took a drink of ale, seeming mildly uncomfortable.

She looked down and brushed at a blade of grass on her skirt. "I'm sorry, I didn't mean to make things awkward."

"You didn't. I'm…glad you're glad."

Beau wandered back. "Can you teach me to swim now, Papa?"

Rufus wiped his palms on his thighs. "We need proper bathing costumes, particularly your mother." His gaze strayed to her, and she heated beneath his quick but pointed regard. Suddenly, she recalled Beau's question about them kissing and wished they could do it right now.

That realization ought to have shocked and shamed her, but it only fanned her desire. Desire? She desired him? Suddenly, a dip in the pond sounded like a perfect diversion.

She smiled at Beau. "We could wade in the water, I think."

Beau beamed as he dropped onto the grass and pulled off his shoes. His stockings were quick to follow.

"Wait for me!" Rufus pulled off his boots as quickly as possible and then his stockings, baring his feet.

Verity tried not to look, but it was hopeless. Her gaze locked on his long toes and the sprinkling of dark hair marching up his calves. They should not have been attractive to her—as far as body parts were concerned, they were rather mundane—but she had to tear her gaze away.

Thankfully, he seemed not to notice, as he was intent on rushing to the water with Beau, which she very much appreciated. He was an incredibly attentive father.

Except he *wasn't* Beau's father.

Her chest burned, and she began to grow irritated with herself. Did it matter? He was a far better father than Rufus ever would have been.

The sounds of splashing and male laughter provoked her to smile as she began to pack up the basket.

"Mama, aren't you coming?"

She stood from the blanket and walked down to the edge of the pond. "My dress would get soaked. Your father is right—I need a bathing costume."

"We don't have bathing costumes, and look, my clothes are already a bit damp," Beau argued.

"Yes, I can see that," Verity said with a smile. "While your father is not."

Beau looked over at him, then, without hesitating, dragged his hand through the water and splashed a fair amount of water across Rufus's legs. "Now he's wet!"

Rufus laughed before narrowing his eyes playfully at Beau. "We'll see who's wet."

Beau trudged through the shallow water seeking to get away, but his efforts were making him wetter, so it was a hopeless endeavor. Verity giggled as she watched them in the silliest chase she'd ever seen.

But suddenly Rufus went down, landing backside first in the water. Verity rushed forward, and Beau looked over his shoulder.

"Are you all right?" she asked with concern.

"Better than your shoes." Rufus looked down at her feet, which were submerged in the edge of the pond.

She hadn't paid attention to where the water started. She'd been too focused on him. Her gaze found his, and she realized he knew it too.

Beau walked to Rufus's side, his little face scrunched up with worry. "What happened, Papa?"

"Well, it wasn't a sea monster," he said with a wink. "I just slipped."

Beau's eyes grew round. "Are there really sea monsters? Why haven't you told me about them before?"

Rufus laughed. "There are no sea monsters. There are very big fish and whales and sharks and octopuses, but they aren't monsters."

"What's an...octo-puss?" Beau dragged out the last letter.

"An eight-legged sea creature."

Beau cocked his head to the side, unsurprisingly interested in anything to do with animals. "Like a spider?"

"No. I'll draw a picture for you. You need a book about sea creatures," Rufus said. "And I need to get out of this pond."

"I'll help you, Papa." Beau took Rufus's hand and pulled. Verity knew Rufus rose of his own accord, but smiled nonetheless when he thanked Beau and complimented his strength.

"Come, let's get your shoes and stockings on," Verity said, taking Beau's hand as he walked from the water. "I'll dry your feet with the blanket."

While she administered to Beau, Rufus took care of himself and finished packing up the basket.

Beau looked Rufus up and down. "I'm sorry you got all wet. I didn't make you fall, did I?"

"How would you have done that?"

"Because you were chasing me. I'm very fast, and you tried to keep up."

Verity saw the slight quirk of Rufus's lip, but he didn't laugh. "You *are* very fast," he said, "but you are not responsible for my clumsiness."

Beau gave him a dubious look. "Are you sure you didn't fall just to make me feel better since I fell earlier?"

Now Rufus laughed. "You're a suspicious lad, aren't you? No, I didn't fall to make you feel better. Should I have?"

"I didn't feel bad at all. I didn't even cry." The pride in his voice made Verity proud too.

Rufus picked up the basket, and when he tried to take the folded blanket from Verity, she shook her head emphatically. "You won't let me carry it because I'm wet?" he asked.

"Not at all. The blanket is damp from drying your and Beau's feet. I'm carrying the blanket because you don't have to do *everything.*"

"I like doing everything. You've done *everything* by yourself for so long. I only want to ease your burden."

"Nothing has been a burden." *Not since you disappeared. And I thought your return would be horrible, and it isn't*. She felt as though she were in an opposite world.

"Good," he murmured, his gaze warm and intense. A cloud moved over the sun, casting a shadow over them, and a shiver shook his frame.

"We need to get you out of those wet clothes," she said firmly. "And into a warm bath."

"Do I need a bath too?" Beau asked, taking both their hands again as they started up the hill.

"At least the parts of you that were in the pond, I think."

Beau exhaled, knowing better than to argue with her about it. Which wasn't to say he wouldn't, but for now, he'd decided not to, and Verity appreciated that.

"As long as I'm taking a bath, you should too," Rufus said. "You can be quick, and do you know how I know that?"

"How?"

"Because we're going to fill one tub and you'll bathe first, and I'll make sure you're fast so the water is still warm enough for me."

Beau looked up at his father. "Shall we race?"

Rufus glanced over at her for approval, and she nodded. "You can use the bathing chamber that adjoins my bedroom," she said. "It's the closest to the kitchen since the stairs go right down next to it—that's where I usually give Beau his bath." She'd be sure to stay very far away until she was sure they were done.

"We'll race to the kitchen," Rufus said. "Go!" He let Beau start, then flashed a grin at Verity before taking off after him, the basket swinging in his hand. She ought to have taken it from him but hadn't even thought to offer. She was too caught up in how normal this felt.

No, not normal. It felt wonderful. It felt like a family.

She'd never had this, not beyond her and Beau.

And they *were* a family. This man treated Beau as his son, playing with him, teaching him, *bathing* him. She'd considered preventing the latter, but she knew he would care for Beau the same as she would. She trusted him—with Beau. With herself? She wasn't ready to address that yet.

She watched them crest the hill and race toward the house. Rufus kept up but didn't overtake Beau. By the time she reached the stable yard, they were gone from view, disappearing into the lower courtyard. She went directly to the kitchen to ask who won. The cook laughingly said Beau did, of course.

Because she couldn't go to her chamber or her study, she went to the library to pass the time. When she thought it had perhaps been long enough, she went upstairs to the Guinea Room, where Beau took afternoon lessons. Finding him there with still-damp hair, he told her they'd finished their baths and Papa was getting dressed. She kissed Beau on the forehead before she went along the corridor toward her room at the end. The middle chamber belonged to Rufus, and since the door was shut, she assumed he was inside.

Was he clothed or still nude?

The thought brought a hot, fast blush to her face, and she hurried to her chamber and then into her study. She was so confused! She was somehow attracted to Rufus—or whoever he was. Not just because he was physically handsome, which he very much was, but because of his behavior and his actions. His character.

Planning to write a letter to Diana in which she could unburden her distressing thoughts, she first poked her head into the bathing chamber. The staff had not yet come to empty the tub. The clothing had all been cleaned up, however. Had Rufus done that? And had he helped Beau to get dressed? She should have asked her son.

Her eye caught a swath of white fabric near the corner on the floor. She went and picked it up—a length of silk. His cravat. Her gaze moved to the hook on the wall above from where it had surely fallen.

The silk was soft and smooth between her fingers. She imagined the flesh of his neck feeling the same way—warm too. Except near the end of the day when his whiskers sprouted. Not quite smooth, then, and maybe not soft. Perhaps rugged and appealing to the touch.

She brought the fabric to her nose and inhaled. It smelled faintly of pine and grass and more strongly of male. Not just any male, of *him*. Not that she'd ever been close enough to smell him. No, this was as close as she'd been, and perhaps as close as she'd ever get.

A gentle cough drew her to turn.

Her heart paused as her eyes met his. His hair was also damp, and she had the disappointing answer to her earlier question—he was dressed.

She abruptly lowered the cravat from her face and knew her embarrassment at being caught was evident. Still, she held her head high and ignored the heat in her cheeks.

"I, ah, left that." He inclined his head toward the cravat in her hand.

"Yes, I just found it on the floor." She walked to the doorway and held it out to him.

His bare fingertips grazed her palm as he took the garment. "Thank you."

"Thank you." She wanted to say more, to expand on

that. *Thank you for looking after the estate. Thank you for taking care of Beau. Thank you for respecting me. Thank you for coming home.*

Only this wasn't his home. And that should've frightened her to pieces.

What frightened her more was that it didn't.

He gave her a faint smile, said, "You're welcome," then turned and left.

Her shoulders sagged as the anticipation of the charged moment fled her body. In its wake, there remained a latent heat, a prurient curiosity she was desperate to explore.

That frightened her most of all.

Chapter Eleven

AFTER TRAVERSING AT least three miles from the castle, Kit crept toward Cuddy's lodging on the edge of town, grateful for the nearly full moon—and the mostly clear night—to light his way. Last night, he'd had to abort the mission because the cloud cover had been too thick. Visibility had been terrible and then it had started to rain. He'd returned to the castle and spent half the night staring at the canopy over his bed, thinking of Verity. Of the way she'd blushed when he'd caught her with his cravat. Of the slight tremble she'd displayed when their hands had touched. Of the fire burning deep in her eyes when she looked at him—so deep that he doubted its presence, but hoped for it just the same.

He banished the thoughts from his mind. He couldn't afford to be distracted.

The building where Cuddy lodged housed a shop on the ground floor. Another building flanked one side while the other side was an open space. Kit prowled to the back and found a locked door. Thankfully, that didn't prove a hindrance as Kit easily picked the lock.

Closing the door softly behind him, Kit adjusted his eyesight to the darker interior. A window to his right let in some of the moonlight, which helped. This appeared to be the back room of the shop, and a flight of stairs rose to his left.

Kit gingerly put his foot on the first stair, testing for noise. The wood gave slightly, but it was fairly quiet.

He ascended slowly as the staircase doubled back on itself, careful not to find a wayward creak. Near the top, he finally found one, freezing as the sound pierced the silence.

With light feet, he hurried up onto the landing and spied two doors—one on the left and one on the right. Recalling that the groom had said Cuddy enjoyed a view of the river, Kit surmised his room was the door on the left, which would afford such a view.

Moving quietly, he went to the door and carefully checked the latch. Also locked and also not a problem. Before he sprang the lock, he took a deep breath and prayed Cuddy was still at the Sheep's Head. He'd thought of trying to verify that first but decided it didn't matter since he couldn't control when the man would show up. This would have been easier with a first mate. He thought of Barkley, who'd served him the past four years and who had opted not to come to England with him after the ship had burned. Barkley would've made an excellent accomplice in this endeavor.

The lock picked, Kit pushed the door open slowly, wincing as it made a low moan. He only opened it as far as necessary to squeeze himself inside. He slipped into the apartment and closed the door with a soft snap. He stood inside a large main room and saw a doorway leading toward another room at the front of the building. Glancing around, he would judge that to be the bedroom, and since the main room was empty, he listened intently for any sign that Cuddy was in the front chamber.

Nothing but silence greeted him.

Exhaling, Kit made his way toward the doorway and peered inside. A lantern from the street below offered meager illumination of the chamber, which contained a narrow bed, a dresser, and a dilapidated chair.

Kit immediately went to the dresser and began searching the drawers. He wasn't entirely sure what he was looking for but would investigate anything of note. There was nothing but clothing and an empty bottle until he reached the bottom drawer. Alone in that space sat a black leather-covered ledger.

Withdrawing the book, Kit went back into the main room where the light was better thanks to the moon. He walked to the window and held the book open. Right away, he saw there were entries. Pages and pages of entries—money coming in and money going out.

Victory surged in his chest, but he wouldn't stop now. Glad he'd left his coat a little ways from the house, Kit tucked the ledger into the back of his breeches beneath his waistcoat. He went back to the front chamber and quickly searched the bed, lifting the mattress and looking beneath the frame. Satisfied that he'd done all he could in there, he moved back into the main room, all while keeping his ears open for the slightest sound. He knew that top stair would creak and the door would moan, both notifying him of Cuddy's arrival.

He glanced out the window and decided the leap to a pile of shrubbery below would likely be his easiest and best escape.

A desk in the corner beckoned Kit. He moved stealthily across the room and saw several papers sitting on top. The bulk of them were to do with seeking a new steward position—advertisements and letters informing Cuddy the position had been filled. The final letter, however, was from one Horatio Kingman, Verity's father.

Before Kit could read the contents, he heard the telltale moan of the door. Somehow he'd missed the stair creaking. Or Cuddy knew to avoid it.

Kit set the letter on the desk and turned to the door, ready to confront the thief. Cuddy stepped over the threshold, his mouth curling into a nasty sneer. "How did you get in here?"

"Helped myself," Kit said pleasantly. "Just as you did with a portion of my estate's profits. I'm here to collect."

The blackguard's eyes widened, and he closed the door as he moved inside. Kit tensed in response.

Cuddy wiped a hand over his mouth. "Careful what you're accusing me of."

"*I* should be careful?" Kit clicked his tongue. "I'm not the criminal in this scenario. I can prove you stole from me." He hadn't studied the ledger in depth yet, but he expected to be able to use it to his advantage. He *hoped* he'd be able to.

He enjoyed watching Cuddy's face turn a dull shade of gray. "I could go to the constable, but I'd prefer you return what you owe me and leave Blackburn. Oh, and tell me whether you're working alone. I suspect not."

"I'm not telling you anything."

Kit shrugged. "Fine. Then you can go to jail. Or perhaps you'll be transported. Where's my money?"

Cuddy's face passed gray and went full white. But only for a moment before scarlet tore over his flesh. "I don't have it. Spent it all."

Kit was well aware of how much the man had grifted over the past six and a half years. He looked around at the ramshackle room with its meager furnishings, all of it damaged or threadbare. If Cuddy had spent the money, it sure as hell hadn't been on his dwelling or comfort. "I hope you have a nice house somewhere. Don't tell me you spent it on drink and women."

Cuddy's dark eyes narrowed as he regarded Kit with disdain. "None of your business how I spent it."

Now Kit was starting to grow irritated. "It's entirely my business. Because it's *my* money. From *my* estate."

The edge of Cuddy's mouth quirked up as he stalked forward. He was a large man with shoulders wider than Kit's and a barrel-shaped abdomen. He was a bit shorter, however, with squat legs that didn't look as if they could run very far—or very fast. But it didn't look as if Cuddy was going to run. And anyway, Kit wasn't going to let him.

Cuddy removed his jacket and tossed it to a chair, then did the same with his cravat, leaving him garbed in a plain waistcoat and wrinkled shirt. His dark hair was matted against his scalp, and from the smell of him, Kit guessed he hadn't bathed in a few days.

"*Your* estate? Is that right?" Cuddy's confident tone and smug expression made Kit's skin prickle with apprehension. "I have it on good authority you aren't really who you say you are."

Fuck. How the hell did this cretin know that? "Someone has been feeding you lies." Kit needed to know who.

"Maybe I puzzled it out all on my own." He tapped his fingertip against his temple. "I'm smart enough to swindle a decent sum of money for a long period of time without getting caught." He chuckled low in his throat. "Seems like we both have things we'd prefer to keep hidden, so why don't you just go on back to *your* castle, and we'll forget this conversation ever took place."

Kit donned the haughty, glacial smile he gave the

captain of an opposing ship just before he seized his goods. "Or, you'll give me the money you stole, and I won't have you transported across the world. That's your only choice, Cuddy, and you're running out of time to make it." Kit lifted his waistcoat to reveal the pistol tucked against his side.

Cuddy launched quickly, aiming straight for Kit, who just managed to pull the gun out and cock the hammer. Cuddy ducked low and shoved his shoulder into Kit's stomach as his hand wrapped around Kit's wrist, squeezing viciously until Kit dropped the pistol.

Kicking the weapon away, Kit focused on the brute, who drove his fist into Kit's cheek. Kit pushed him hard, sending Cuddy flailing backward. But the man didn't fall.

Kit took advantage of the moment's reprieve and reached into his boot for his knife. Cuddy came at him, also wielding a blade. Kit arced his hand out, slicing the blade across Cuddy's chest and catching a bit of flesh as he cut through his clothing.

Cuddy's free hand rose to his chest as he leapt back. "Son of a bitch."

They circled each other a moment before Cuddy lunged again, aiming for Kit's chest and then changing his direction at the last moment. He brought the blade up to slice Kit's face, but Kit managed to correct and pull—mostly—out of the way. The knife scraped into his flesh from his temple to down in front of his ear before he managed to remove himself completely from harm's way.

Blood trickled down his jaw as Cuddy's eyes took on a feral sheen. The man grabbed a bottle from a table and smashed it against the wood. He held up the broken bottle with a taunting sneer and came at Kit swinging both arms, but leading with his knife. Kit met Cuddy's knife with his, and as the blades clashed, Cuddy swiped with the broken bottle. Kit flung up his hand in a defensive gesture, and the glass bit into his palm. He kicked out and hit Cuddy in the thigh instead of his intended target—the groin. Still, Cuddy stumbled back, and Kit pressed his advantage, kicking out again, this time aiming for Cuddy's knife hand. His boot connected with Cuddy's flesh, and the man cried out as the knife fell and spun across the floor.

Cuddy brought his hand up and wrapped it around Kit's wrist, squeezing tight while he brought his jagged bottle up toward Kit's head. Kit chopped his hand into Cuddy's wrist hard enough to make him drop the bottle. All the while, Cuddy twisted Kit's wrist mercilessly until his knife clattered to the floor from his useless grip.

Unarmed, they came together again with fists and fingers and elbows and knees. They crashed into a chair, sending it skidding into the wall. Kit barely managed to keep his balance as Cuddy reached for his leg to try to pull him down.

Kit struggled to draw a breath. "This doesn't have to end badly."

"It doesn't end any other way—for you." Cuddy sneered as he scanned the room, clearly looking for a weapon. His gaze landed on Kit's knife and turned murderous. Kit realized this was a fight he *had* to win.

Kit saw that Cuddy's blade wasn't far. Lunging for the blade, he picked it up and turned it in his hand before sending it flying into Cuddy's chest just as the man turned toward him after plucking up Kit's weapon.

Eyes wide and the color draining from his face,

Cuddy sank to the floor in a heap, falling backward against the edge of a threadbare carpet.

Dammit, Kit hadn't meant to kill the man, just keep himself from being killed. Kit saw Cuddy's coat hanging from a hook by the door and grabbed it before rushing to the man's side. He pressed the garment to the man's chest around the knife. Kit didn't dare remove the weapon.

Cuddy's smile was ghastly, his face pale as blood drained from his body. "Don't have to do that. Won't matter. I'm a dead man. Don't try to tell me you're a duke. Dukes don't fight like that."

"Who told you I'm not Blackburn? Tell me, and I'll fetch you a doctor."

Cuddy's smile widened, and blood leaked through the gaps between his teeth. "You'd like to know, wouldn't you? But no, I think I'll go to my grave thinking of you looking over your shoulder for the rest of your miserable life, wondering who knows your secret. I'll be waiting for you on the other side. Men like us don't get to rest."

Men like us.

Kit wanted to argue that he wasn't like Cuddy, that he wasn't a thief, which was about the most hypocritical thing in the history of hypocrisy. Kit was a liar, and a fucking *paid* and sanctioned thief. No, men like them wouldn't find eternal rest.

Curling his fingers around the bloodied edge of the man's waistcoat, Kit growled, "Tell me!"

Cuddy only smiled again before going limp, his eyes shuttering for the last time.

With an oath, Kit let the man go and sat down hard on the floor, scooting away from the body. What a fucking disaster. He hadn't retrieved the money. He hadn't discovered how Cuddy had known he wasn't the duke. And the man was dead.

And someone was knocking on the door.

"Mr. Strader, are you all right?" The voice was soft and feminine.

Shit. Kit coughed and lowered his tone to a gravelly rasp. "Fine, thank you. 'Night!"

He waited, breathless, for a response. At last came "Good night," and the sound of receding footfalls.

He expelled his breath and looked at the body. Regret coursed through him. He hadn't wanted to kill the man, but Cuddy hadn't given him a choice. In truth, Kit had underestimated him. He'd presumed Cuddy to be a thief, not someone intent on violence. That had been Kit's mistake, and one he wished had turned out quite differently.

Kit considered wrapping the body in the dingy carpet and hide it somewhere, but he wanted the man to be found and to have a decent burial. What he ought to do was inform the constable, but that would draw attention to himself, and he knew his ruse couldn't last much longer. Particularly since there was someone else out there who knew he wasn't the duke.

No, what he ought to do was leave Blackburn immediately. But the thought of abandoning Verity and Beau, of never seeing them again, was more painful than any injury he'd ever sustained.

Wincing, Kit pushed himself up. He hurt just about everywhere from the fight, and at some point he'd lost the ledger from the back of his waistband. The blood on his face had dried, but his hand was still bleeding and hurt like hell. He'd have a variety of bruises come morning and wondered what the devil he'd tell Beau.

Thinking of that innocent boy as a man lay dead in

front of him forced Kit's eyes closed. He took deep breaths and pondered how far he'd come and how different his life was now compared to just a few weeks ago. He'd killed men before, dozens during the war, but this was somehow different.

Because he was different.

Weary and aching, he opened his eyes and pushed himself up. He took his knife from Cuddy's hand and slid it into his boot. Then he located his pistol and the ledger and tucked both into his waistband.

He went back to the desk and stuffed the letter from Kingman into his waistcoat. A quick search of the desk didn't reveal anything else of note.

Rather than risk the landing and the stairway given the presence of others in the building, Kit decided to take the leap to the bushes below. Branches poked into him as he landed, scratching at him and adding to his pains.

After finding his coat, he shrugged into the garment, grimacing. On his way back to the castle, he became even more aware of his injuries. He was also aware that the moon was sinking, and he hoped to make it home before the guiding light disappeared.

Home. Was it really? He'd begun to think so, but Cuddy's words tonight had reminded him that he was an imposter, and this was supposed to be a temporary game.

Hell, he could return to the castle, take any number of items from silver to weapons to Verity's jewelry and be on his way without a backward glance. His chest ached at the thought.

And yet that would be the right thing to do.

No, the right thing would be to take nothing and just leave. In fact, he could divert his path right now and go toward the coast. Just the thought of the ocean lapping the shore, of the salty air coating his skin, of the sound of seabirds calling him… *That* was home.

His feet kept propelling him toward the castle, however.

It took nearly twice as long for him to get back, and the moon had vanished by the time he reached the lower gate of the courtyard. He'd avoided the main gatehouse, which was staffed with a gatekeeper. However, Beaumont Tower had been built as a fortress, and there was only one way into the castle. The underground escape route had apparently collapsed and had never been rebuilt. Perhaps Kit ought to add that to his list of improvements should he require another clandestine trip from the grounds.

Which he might.

He had to find out who else knew—or at the very least, suspected—his secret. Perhaps the ledger would provide a clue.

Praying he wouldn't run into a retainer at this hour, he hurried across the courtyard and into the upper gateway. The door to the stairway that came out next to his bedchamber was still unbolted, just as he'd left it. Once inside, he slid the bolt, then climbed the stairs as quickly as his aching limbs could manage.

Light from the sconce in the corridor made him blink as he adjusted from the darkness. He grazed his shoulder against the doorframe from the stairs with a thud. A moment later, the sound of a door opening made him freeze. It was just ahead. Not his door. Beau's.

Shit.

How was he going to explain the blood all over him to the boy?

But it wasn't Beau. Verity came into the corridor, shutting Beau's door behind her. She came toward him, her brows low. Then her eyes widened as she neared. "Rufus?"

"I'm sorry I disturbed you. Is Beau all right?" He wanted to deflect attention from himself, but even more, he wanted to know why she was in Beau's room at this hour.

"He's fine, just woke up and asked for water. He's asleep now." She edged closer, her gaze fixed on the cut on his face. "What happened to you? Where have you been?"

"It doesn't matter. I'm fine. I'm just going to get cleaned up and go to bed."

"Come with me." She turned and started along the corridor toward her chamber.

"No."

She pivoted slowly and cocked her head at him. "You need help. I'm going to give it to you, and you're not going to argue. I need to get you cleaned up. If Beau wakes up again and sees you like this—"

"He can't." Kit would do anything to keep that from happening. In fact, he should have gone to the kitchen to clean up.

She gestured toward his chamber. "In there, then. Do you have water?"

He nodded and made his way into his room. She followed, closing the door behind her.

The fire had died down to coals, and Kit used a spill to light the lantern he kept on his dresser. Soft, warm light bathed the chamber, and he was suddenly aware that they were alone together with the door closed. With a bed in the same room. And she was barely clothed.

And shortly, he would remove his clothes. No, he wouldn't do that with her here. But God, how he longed to shed his coat. He'd already removed his cravat on the walk back and wrapped it around his injured hand.

"Sit."

"You're very good at giving orders," he said. "Have you thought of commanding a ship?"

She went to the corner where he kept the washbasin and ewer of water on top of a slender cabinet. "Where are your washing cloths?"

He sat in a chair next to the dresser near the light so she could have it to see. "In the top drawer."

She poured water into the basin and withdrew some cloths from the cabinet. "I'd get seasick," she said.

"How do you know?" He bent to remove his boots, his sore body protesting the movements. "Have you been sailing before?"

She came toward him with her supplies and set them on the dresser. "No, but if I ride in a carriage too long, I become ill. I think the motion of a ship on the ocean would be far worse."

"It can be, but you'd grow used to it." He'd vomited for weeks when he'd first walked onto a ship.

She moved the lantern closer to him and surveyed his face.

"I'm guessing I've looked better."

"You look like you've been in a fight."

"I was." He had to tell her about Cuddy. And he would—tomorrow. After he had a chance to review the ledger he'd taken and determine what to do next. It seemed leaving Beaumont Tower might be his only option. "Can I tell you about it tomorrow?"

She stared at him a moment, her dark coffee-colored

eyes narrowing slightly with concern. "Yes."

Pursing her lips, she dabbed a cloth into the water and began to clean the cut along the side of his face. It was just in front of his ear and stretched from his temple to his jaw.

"Will I have a scar?" he asked.

"Perhaps. It's not very deep—you're fortunate." She stopped cleaning when he flinched. "Sorry," she murmured.

"Don't apologize. I appreciate your ministrations."

"You need ointment or unguent. I have something in my room that I use on Beau's cuts and scrapes. You're as bad as a six-year-old," she muttered.

He couldn't suppress a smile. It wasn't what she'd said but the camaraderie between them as she tended his wounds.

She rewetted the cloth, rinsing dried blood off the fabric, then went over the laceration once more. "Does it hurt?"

"Not as much as my hand."

"Your hand?" She looked down at his hands, which rested on his thighs. "Show me."

He unwound the cravat from his left hand and turned it palm-side up to reveal the cut. "It's not terribly deep—I don't think it require sutures."

"I'd ask how you can be the judge of that, but I gather you've been wounded many times." Her gaze searched his face. "So many secrets." The words were soft, but they hit him hard, like a volley sent across the water sending his heart rate toward the sky.

She lowered her eyes to focus on his hand, rewetting the cloth before cradling his hand in hers and wiping away the dried blood. "You won't tell me where you've been the past six years. You won't tell me where you were tonight. You won't tell me who did this to you." She fell silent again as she finished cleaning the wound.

Dropping the cloth into the basin, she didn't remove her hand from beneath his. Her gaze found his once more and in the flickering glow of the lantern he saw concern and vulnerability. And something more he couldn't name.

"I know you aren't Rufus."

His heart tried to leap from his chest and probably would have run away if it could. Instead, it was trapped inside him, pounding a frenzied rhythm and sounding a drumbeat in his head.

He tried to think of a response but there simply wasn't one.

"Are you going to leave?" she asked.

"Now?"

Her gaze found his with dark intensity. "Ever. You aren't my husband. I don't know what you're doing here or what you want."

"I would never hurt you. Or Beau."

"Somehow, I know that. But do you plan to leave?"

He heard what she left unspoken—that leaving *would* hurt them. "No. Not unless you want me to." The words shocked him to his core, but he'd never uttered anything more honest in his life.

Her hand was soft and warm around his. It was barely a touch, something borne from necessity as she'd cleansed his wound. But then she put her free hand to his face, tracing her finger along the edge of the cut.

He waited, breathless, for her to demand to know who he was and why he was there. Instead, she merely stared into his eyes, and it was then that he recognized that unknown emotion buried in her gaze.

Desire.

His body leapt in response, every fiber in him screaming for her. But he did nothing. It was, apparently, enough, because she leaned down and pressed her lips to his.

The contact jolted through him like lightning blazing over the ocean and illuminating everything with a sparkling, wondrous glow. When her mouth moved gently over his, the sensation intensified, heating him to an impossible degree.

Her hand cupped the side of his head as she slanted her lips across his. He tried to hold himself back, to let her direct the kiss. It was, after all, her creation.

Closing his eyes, he longed to clasp her waist, to sit her down on his lap and plunge his tongue into her mouth, to taste her, to claim her, to show her how badly he wanted her. But he did none of those things. He held his breath as she kissed him softly, innocently.

Briefly.

She withdrew, and he opened his eyes to find her staring at him. "I don't really know how to kiss. Was that nice?"

She... What? He'd thought of pummeling her husband many times, and wished he could do so right this very moment. After he railed at him for his stupidity. How could Rufus have been married to this beautiful, graceful, strong creature without wanting to kiss her senseless?

"It was very nice," he said. "In my opinion. More importantly, however, is your opinion since you initiated it. Did you think it was nice?"

Her brows angled down. "Should I not have done that?"

"I'm quite glad you did it, actually. In fact, you have

leave to do so whenever you like."

Faint swaths of pink highlighted her cheeks. "I did think it was nice. But… Is there more? I know there is… I just—" She stopped herself with a shudder.

He wanted to ask what she knew but feared he'd spend the rest of his life hunting her husband down and doing more than pummeling him. "Yes, there's more. If you want me to show you some time, I will."

"Will you show me now?"

His body shouted in response, his fingers itching to hold her and his cock hardening with need.

"I'm not certain that's the best idea. It's late—"

"And you're injured." She averted her gaze. "I shouldn't have asked. I'm sorry."

She started to turn, and he put his hand on her waist, staying her movement.

"Don't. I'm glad you asked." He splayed his hand across the side of her dressing gown, wrapping his fingers along her lower back. "Come here."

She pivoted back toward him, and he used his other hand to guide her down to sit on his left knee. Her hair hung in a single braid, draped over her left shoulder. He touched the plait, running his fingertips and thumb along the soft ridges of her dark locks. Ascending the rope, he reached her face, where he grazed the pad of his thumb along her jawline.

"Do you want me to kiss you? To really kiss you?"

She nodded, her eyes locked with his.

She was so capable, so intelligent, such a fierce woman to raise her son alone and be duchess of such a grand estate. And yet her innocence and naïvete humbled him. He didn't want to mess this up.

Slowly, he wrapped his hand around the back of her neck and guided her head down. He parted his lips slightly as he brought her mouth to his. She closed her eyes, and he closed his. Gently, he kissed her, taking his time to learn her flesh and coax her response.

He kept a low pressure on her back, keeping her secure on his lap while he used his other hand to lightly massage her nape.

He began to move his lips across hers, showing her that kissing could be varied and exploratory. After a moment, he touched his tongue to her flesh, eliciting a soft gasp. She drew back slightly, her eyes opening just after his.

"Perhaps that's enough."

"No, that was nice. I was just…surprised. I'd forgotten about the tongue part."

He could only imagine the awful way in which Rufus had tried to kiss her. Kit battled between drawing a halt to his madness and wanting to show her that not all men were animals, that she could enjoy this.

"I liked that." She wiggled slightly on his lap, making his cock even harder, if that were possible. "I trust you to make sure I like the tongue part."

She trusted him. He couldn't turn her away. And he couldn't screw this up.

"If you want to touch me, you can. With your hands," he clarified.

She put her hands around his neck. "Like this?"

"Whatever you like. I'm fairly certain there isn't a bad way you could touch me."

Her eyes darkened, and in that moment, he knew she was thinking of all the horrible ways in which she'd been touched.

"Oh, Verity, my love." The endearment fell from his lips without thought. "I won't let anything bad happen to you—or Beau. I would protect you with my life."

"Kiss me. I would like to forget every other kiss but yours."

Kit clasped her waist with both hands and eased her from his lap as he stood from the chair. Disappointment flashed across her face. She thought he meant to dismiss her. Nothing could be further from his plan.

He cupped her face, intent on doing precisely what she asked, on banishing every other memory. "From this moment on, you will only think of my lips on yours. Of my tongue in your mouth. Of yours in mine. Of our mouths moving and dancing together and giving each other pleasure. Nothing but pleasure."

He gazed at her intently and drew her flush against his chest as his mouth descended on hers. He moved more purposefully this time, his lips molding to hers, his head tilting to fit himself better to her.

This time when he slid his tongue along the crease of her mouth, she opened slightly. He thrust inside, carefully, reverently, his tongue sweeping against hers. He stroked her back as he held her close, his hands working in concert with his mouth to coax her body into a state of bliss.

She put her arms around his neck, her hands clutching at his bare flesh beneath the collar of his shirt. Need pulsed through him, but he kept himself in check. Everything depended on his control, on his mastery.

He bent her back slightly, and she had to hold on to him tightly. He moved one hand up to cup her nape as he plunged his tongue deep into her mouth. Then he pulled away, giving them a brief respite of air before taking her into another kiss. She moaned softly into his mouth and pressed her body up into his, her breasts warm and soft against his chest.

On and on he kissed her—driving forward and easing back, holding her all the while as if she were the most precious cargo he'd ever possessed.

Her fingers wrapped around his shirt, tugging on the fabric so that it dug into his neck. Her body moved against his, her pelvis stirring beneath his.

The bed was so close…

He eased back one last time and brought her to a straight standing position. He couldn't let this go on. As it was, he was going to have to frig himself the minute she left.

"Was I successful?" He shouldn't have asked, but if he'd failed, he reasoned he'd have to try again. Or so he hoped.

"Very. Perhaps too much." Her lips curled into a faint smile, and his knees went weak. She dropped her hands from his neck and took a tiny step back. "Thank you. I should go to bed." She retreated another step.

"That's probably wise."

Her eyes widened briefly, and she gave her head a shake. "I need to get the ointment. Wait here."

He wanted to tell her they'd apply it in the morning, but knew it was an argument he'd lose. She was the master of this castle, and he liked it that way.

In her absence, his ardor cooled, thanks in part to his brain telling his body to calm the hell down. He slipped the letter and the ledger from his garments and tucked them into a dresser drawer.

When she returned, she applied the ointment, then wrapped a bandage around his hand. "I'll re-dress this tomorrow. We'll tell Beau you had an accident in the lumber room. Some wood splintered and cut your face as well as your hand."

That was a far better excuse than what Kit had come up with. "I was going to say I fell down the stairs. Your tale is less detrimental to my pride."

She laughed, and his ardor stirred again. Everything about her made him want her. Fiercely.

She picked up his basin and the bloody cloth.

"You don't have to take those."

"I don't want the maid to find them tomorrow. It's fine. This is what mothers do—not that I'm your mother."

He winced. "Never that, please."

"No, never that," she agreed softly, her eyes fixed on his mouth.

And suddenly, his cock was at full staff again. "You'd better go," he rasped.

She gave a sharp nod. "Good night. Sleep well." Then she turned and walked to the door, which she'd left ajar when she'd returned with the medicine.

He followed her and held the door for her as she walked over the threshold. "Sleep well, Verity."

She turned to look at him over her shoulder, and he thought she might say something. In the end, she turned her head back and walked toward her room at the end of the corridor. He watched her until her door was closed, then he went into his chamber and shut the door, immediately collapsing against the wood.

Well, this had been an eventful night. He'd been alarmed as hell to learn that someone knew he wasn't the duke.

And now he knew Verity didn't think he was either. He would bet his life she wasn't the person who'd told Cuddy—that made no sense given the timing of Cuddy's departure and the nature of her relationship with her former steward.

Which meant there absolutely was a third person who knew Kit was lying. He had to find that person and make sure they kept the secret. Because he meant what he'd told her—he wasn't going to leave. Not now. Not if she didn't want him to, and maybe that would change once she learned who he really was and why he'd masqueraded as Rufus in the first place. He had to tell her the truth, and probably sooner rather than later. He winced, thinking she might very well toss him out and that he'd deserve it.

But until she did, this was a secret he'd do anything to protect.

Chapter Twelve

❧

NEARLY EVERY MORNING, Beau woke up and came into Verity's chamber. Sometimes it was very early and sometimes it was later, but the routine was the same. He'd come in, and if she was still abed, he'd climb in with her. If she was in the middle of her morning toilet, he would sit with her while her maid helped her prepare for the day. Someday, perhaps soon, that might become awkward for him—to see her in a state of undress. Then he'd probably just wait in her chamber. Until he went off to school. How she dreaded that day.

But today was not that day, and he sat on a chair in her dressing area, his legs dangling as he pumped his feet impatiently. "Can we go on another picnic today?" he asked.

Verity glanced toward the drizzle hitting her window. "I don't think so. It's raining, unfortunately."

Beau exhaled. "We could have it inside."

Yes, she supposed they could. Her maid finished the last touches on her hair, and Verity turned toward her son. "You have a very creative mind. Ready for breakfast?"

He bounded from the chair and dashed through her study to the staircase that led down next to the kitchen. From there, she followed him along the short corridor to the small dining room where they'd begun taking breakfast shortly after Rufus had returned.

The sound of Beau's shriek made her hurry into the room, and she immediately saw the reason for her son's distress. Rufus—or whoever he was—was already present in all his wounded glory. She winced at the dark purple bruise marring his cheek. And of course there was the long cut on the other side of his face, hidden if he held himself at a certain angle.

"Papa, what happened?"

She'd expected to be bothered by hearing Beau call this man—this confirmed stranger—Papa now. Shockingly, she wasn't.

"I'm afraid I had a bit of an accident in the lumber room. But I'm just fine. Come and sit, and I'll tell you about it."

Beau sat in his regular chair at the table, while Rufus took his. Verity went to the sideboard and served her son's plate.

"You're truly fine?" Beau asked, sounding doubtful.

"Quite. It's actually rather humorous." He flashed a self-deprecating smile. "I was trying to cut a piece of wood, and it splintered in a rather spectacular manner. One piece sliced my face here." He indicated the cut on the side of his face. "And another cut my hand." He held up his bandaged left hand.

"That doesn't sound very funny," Beau said.

"Not particularly, but it's what happened next. You see, I was so surprised that I spun about in an effort to avoid further injury. But in doing so, I lost my balance and fell into the wall rather hard. Hence this lovely bruise." He lightly patted his cheek. "I'm glad you and your mother weren't there, for it was my most graceless moment to date."

Beau's eyes were wide, but now they narrowed with laughter as he giggled. "I wish I'd been there so I could have seen it. Also, I would've taken care of you."

Verity set the plate in front of Beau, her heart

swelling at the concern he displayed for the man he thought was his father. As for him... Verity turned her head toward him, in awe of the ease with which he'd told this story she'd concocted and how he'd woven it into something amusing and charming, erasing Beau's apprehension about the event. He was, in a word, wonderful.

"Can I dish up your breakfast?" she asked.

His eyes reflected a flash of surprise. "Thank you. I'll take—"

"I know what you like." She gave him a smile as she served him a meat pie, smoked herring, bacon, and two rolls, one with honey and one with marmalade.

As she put the plate in front of him, he looked from it to her with admiration. "You do know what I like." And then his gaze settled on her mouth, and his meaning was clear—he'd liked kissing her.

Well, good, because she'd more than liked kissing him. She had absolutely nothing to compare it to, but the sensations of joy and pleasure and overwhelming heat had kept her awake nearly until morning. She ought to have been tired and lethargic, but instead, she was excited and energized to meet the day. To meet *him*.

She stared at his mouth another moment, recalling the feel of his lips on hers, of his tongue in her mouth doing all manner of wicked things, of his hands on her, stoking a fire she didn't know resided deep inside herself.

Abruptly, she turned and fetched her own breakfast and quickly returned to the table to eat.

"Papa, I want to have an indoor picnic today because it's raining. Can we?" Beau shoved a roll into his mouth.

"Not so much at once, Beau," Rufus said before Verity could, because she'd been chewing. He effortlessly inhabited the role of caring parent. Who was this man? Did he have other children? It seemed he must, for he was unaccountably excellent at being a father, and yet she couldn't imagine him leaving them. A horrible thought struck her: what if he'd had a family and lost them to tragedy? Her breath caught at the notion. "An indoor picnic is an inspired idea," he said, drawing her back to the present. "However, today I will be busy at the other end of the estate all day. There's a bridge that Thomas and I need to see about repairing."

Verity swallowed a bite of bacon. "Over that gully where the stream runs through?"

Rufus nodded as he speared a piece of herring. "It won't survive another winter, and there are a handful of tenants who use it regularly."

"Will you repair it, Papa?" Beau asked.

"I may, or the tenants might do it themselves. Thomas and I will assess the situation, and I'll provide the materials."

"You take good care of the estate," Beau said. "I'm going to do that too."

"Starting with your goats. Do you need to milk Jane today?" Rufus asked.

"Not today. Every other day is what Mr. Maynard said."

Rufus looked at him with approval, making Beau beam. "You're learning very well."

Verity couldn't quite believe her life right now. This man had stolen in barely a month ago and had become such an integral part of their family. He couldn't leave. And though he'd said he wouldn't, she feared he would. Why was he even here?

Does it matter? a voice in her head asked.

Rufus asked Beau what he and his tutor would be learning today, and they were shortly done with breakfast. Beau was reluctant to go upstairs for lessons, but took himself off, leaving Verity alone with Rufus. Again.

They'd stood from the table, and he reached for his hat, which sat on a long, narrow table in front of the window. "I'm off to meet Thomas."

She rounded the table to where he stood. "Let me see." She lifted her hand but didn't touch him until their eyes connected, and she asked in silent question if it was all right.

He gave a slight nod, and she lightly touched his jaw, turning his head slightly so the light from the window splashed across his bruised cheek.

She winced. "Does it hurt?"

"A bit, yes."

"Some ice would help. I'll have some fetched from the ice house, if you like."

"That's not necessary, but thank you. I did apply a cold compress this morning, and that seemed to improve matters."

"It's rather ghastly. No wonder Beau was so distressed." She removed her hand with some reluctance.

"I regret that immensely."

She shook her head. "Don't. What you told him was wonderful. How do you do that?"

"Do what?"

"Know exactly what to say to him?"

He looked mildly uncomfortable, his gaze darting away briefly as he shrugged. "I don't think about it."

She stared up at him, loving that his eyes were green

and not hazel as they should have been. "And I can't stop." Thinking about it—about *him*.

He looked back at her, and the moment between them stretched until he put his hat on and broke eye contact. "I should go."

"You said you were going to tell me about what happened."

He looked out the window. The rain had stopped, but the sky was gray and dreary. He returned his gaze to hers. "I will, but I can't right now. Tonight?"

"After Beau goes to bed. Come to my study."

The invitation hung between them. They could very easily have met in his office or in the Knight's Room, either of which would be far removed from a bedchamber. Whereas her study was located within her apartments. Where temptation was close.

He nodded, then left, passing by her close enough that she could feel the air move and the heat he left in his wake.

She closed her eyes and suspected this would be the longest day of her entire life.

⬥⊱•⊰⬥

THIS HAD BEEN the longest day Kit could remember. Could it have been the incessant rain that had chilled him to the bone and required him to bathe before dinner? Or the frustration they'd encountered with how to reengineer the bridge? Perhaps it had been the rock his horse had picked up in its shoe that had delayed his trip back to the castle.

No, it was entirely Verity and the fact that she was waiting for him in her study and that she'd *invited* him there.

Next to Kit, Beau sighed in his sleep, having dozed off while Kit was reading *Robinson Crusoe*. They were nearly finished, but the boy just hadn't been able to keep his eyes open.

Kit set the book on the table next to Beau's bed but didn't get up. For when he did, he'd have to go see Verity. Not that he wasn't looking forward to that. On the contrary, he'd been consumed with the coming interview all day. How could he not be after last night?

It was, of course, far more than the kisses they'd shared—and that would have been enough to upset his equilibrium. But what she'd said had occupied his mind just as much, if not more.

She knew he wasn't Rufus. What's more, she didn't seem to *care*. No, what mattered most to her was whether he would leave.

Her question had startled him. Frightened him. Shaken him to his core. Not because she'd asked it— well, a bit because of that—but because of his answer. He'd said he didn't plan to go, which had been an absolute lie.

Until that moment.

Until he'd heard the longing in her voice and the fear of what his leaving would do to Beau. He couldn't do it.

And what the hell did that mean? He'd spent all day asking himself that question, and the answer was always the same: no ship, no privateering, no more Christopher Powell. He'd agreed to be Rufus Beaumont, Duke of Blackburn, husband, father, estate owner, member of the House of Lords.

It was all he'd ever wanted, wasn't it?

Once, it had been. As a thirteen-year-old boy, when his father had brought him here and showed him the life he could have had if not for the circumstances of his birth. It had felt like a taunt—come see what you can never have. He'd gone to sea and never looked back, certainly never imagining he'd be here and be the duke.

With a wife and a son.

He looked over at Beau and felt a surge of love so strong and so sure that he knew his life was forever changed. In just a few short weeks, he'd found something he didn't even know he was looking for— home, family, love.

And not just for this darling boy, but for his mother. He was so unbelievably in love with her, and suspected he had been from almost that very first day. She was an astonishing woman—with grace, strength, and more courage than many of the men he'd met in his travels.

Yet hanging over this joy was the knowledge that someone out there knew he wasn't the duke. That someone could easily bring this idyllic situation crashing down around them. He couldn't let that happen. The only thing he could think to prevent it was to be formally recognized as the duke. Which meant doing what he'd hoped to avoid—going to London and taking his seat in the Lords. He couldn't avoid it now, not if he meant to fully inhabit this role for the rest of his life.

First, however, he had to answer to his wife and make absolutely certain she wanted this too. Even if he meant for the world to believe his lies, she would need to know the truth. She already knew the most important part, and she deserved to hear the rest.

Kit leaned over and brushed a kiss against Beau's head, then eased off the bed. He adjusted the coverlet, and Beau turned to his side, snuggling deeper into the bedclothes.

With a smile, Kit turned and left, closing the door softly behind him. He'd abandoned his coat and his cravat before joining Beau, and briefly considered fetching them before going to see Verity. Why? She'd tended his wounds, she'd kissed him, and now she'd invited him to her private study. Hang the rest of his clothes.

He walked to the end of the corridor, where the door to her room was barely ajar. He rapped softly and waited for a response. Hearing none after a moment, he pushed the door open. The bedchamber appeared to be empty. Rather, devoid of Verity or any other human. One of the cats slept at the end of the massive bed.

The bed dominated the room. Tall, with drapes tied at each post, it was made of ornately carved wood. He recognized the Beaumont crest at the foot. His father had proudly showed him the family emblem during Kit's visit. He'd adopted part of it—the blue and yellow, which wasn't part of the bed carving—into his personal flag on his ship. He'd omitted the lion rampant, which took up the center of the crest.

"I thought I heard you."

He turned at the sound of Verity's voice, pivoting to his right where she stood in the doorway to her study. She wore her floral-patterned dressing gown that hugged her upper torso but left her lower curves a mystery he longed to unravel. He walked toward her. "Forgive my attire. I was reading to Beau."

"I know." Of course she did. She'd left them together after kissing her son good night. "Did you finish the book?"

He shook his head. "He fell asleep after a page and a

half."

She laughed softly, and the gentle sound made the moment feel even more intimate. Because they shared this boy—a love for this boy. He'd never felt more like an usurper. He'd stolen into their lives and forged a place for himself, whether they wanted him or not. All of it was a lie.

And now was the moment of truth. "I went to confront Cuddy last night."

She instantly tensed, her shoulders bunching and her hands coming together in front of her waist. "Please, sit." She gestured toward the chaise in the corner by the windows, and she perched on a chair angled nearby. Concern streaked her face. "You got into a fight?"

"Cuddy attacked me after I accused him of embezzling."

She winced. "Clearly you were able to defend yourself."

"Yes, but I'm afraid Cuddy was intent upon murder. I had no choice but to defend myself."

Her eyes widened as she understood. "Is he dead?"

Kit's gut clenched. "Yes. I'm so sorry."

She lifted her hand to her mouth and turned her head toward the black window. After a moment, she looked back to him. "What did you do? I mean, did you notify the constable?"

He took a deep breath. "I considered it. However, Cuddy indicated that he knew I'm not Rufus."

Her face, after barely settling into a grim acceptance, registered shock once more. "How?"

"I don't know. But he said he's not the only one." He pinned her with a frank stare. "I didn't go to the constable because I didn't want to draw attention to myself. Verity, it's time I told you the truth. All of it."

She nodded slightly. "I know."

He could feel her tension across the space between them but didn't dare move closer. She might throw him out in a few minutes.

"I should start at the beginning," he said. "With my parents—John and Helena Powell. John was a vicar in Poulton. I grew up spending much of my time watching the men who worked at the docks on the River Wyre. And of course the ships that came in bearing goods. That is where I became enamored of ships and the sea."

"Were you actually conscripted?" she asked.

"No. I went of my own accord when I was fifteen."

She gasped softly. "So young."

"Not as young as others."

"Were you in the navy, then?"

His lips curved into a slight smile. "In a manner of speaking. I carried letters of marque."

Her expression reflected surprise again, but along with something else. Perhaps just a glimmer of admiration. "That sounds dangerous. Did you enjoy it?"

"Probably more than a man should. It was so different from the vicarage where I was raised. But I wanted that. Especially after my mother died."

"How old were you?" she asked softly.

"Eight. It wrecked my father. She died in childbirth—it was her fifth attempt to bring a child into the world. All of them failed."

"Except for you."

He shook his head. "I was not their blood. I was given to them to raise."

Another flash of surprise in her gaze. "Why?"

This next revelation would only deepen her shock. Of that he was certain. "Because I was a bastard. Augustus Beaumont's bastard, to be specific."

Verity gasped and lifted her hand to her mouth. "That's why you look so much like Rufus."

"It's a bit more than that, actually. Rufus was my cousin, yes, but he was also my half brother. I am the product of his mother and his uncle—a child conceived in adultery and sent away in shame."

Her jaw dropped. "I'm so sorry."

Kit longed to stand and pace, to release some of the pent-up energy coursing through him. But she was utterly fixed on him, and he didn't want to move. "When I was thirteen, the duke—Augustus—requested my presence. His wife had died several months prior, and he only had three daughters, all of whom had married. He wanted to meet the son he'd sired."

"You came *here*?"

"For a summer." He rubbed his palms along his thighs as he spoke. "The vicar was reluctant to let me come, but one didn't say no to a duke, particularly when that duke was your child's blood father and had provided for his care."

"I'm not surprised to hear Augustus cared for you," she said, allowing a smile to trip across her lips. "He was a kind man."

Kit's muscles tightened and his lip curled. "He was a selfish prick."

Verity started at the vehemence in his tone. "Why do you say that? He was always kind to me."

"I'm glad for you, but he wasn't that way to me. He invited me here and showed me the life I could've had if I'd been born on the right side of the blanket. He promised to send me to school and to secure my future. I asked if I could stay—anywhere—on the estate. I didn't care where or in what capacity, I just wanted to be a part of this place, of this history, of my birthright." He looked toward the window. "He said his new wife would arrive in the fall, and she didn't want his bastard around. I learned from Whist actually that she had two sons of her own and was still of childbearing age. Augustus hoped to sire his own heir, and as you know, he did."

Her jaw dropped. "You met Whist?"

He nodded, returning his gaze to hers. "I worried he would recognize me, but thankfully, my resemblance to Rufus is apparently strong enough."

"It's rather uncanny, really. But now that I know the truth, I see the subtle differences." She shook her head. "I don't understand why Augustus invited you here. Did he mean to taunt you? That doesn't sound like the Augustus I knew."

"Truthfully, I don't know either. I can only guess he was curious about me and hungered desperately for a son. What I do know is that as soon as he had his son the following year, the support to my father stopped. When he wrote to Augustus to ask why and to ensure he still meant to pay for my education, he was ignored. When I turned fifteen, and I went to Liverpool where I boarded a ship and didn't look back. Not for fifteen years."

"Why did you come back now?"

"I needed a ship."

"Were you a captain?"

"I was. Until my ship burned. It's strange to think your ship can catch fire and burn in the water, but that's what happened. Now it's sitting on the bottom of the Caribbean Sea."

"The other night when you spoke of fire and water... Now I understand." She flinched, her eyes turning sad. "You miss that life. You didn't come here to stay."

Agony tore through him at the disappointment in her gaze, but he owed her the truth. "No, I did not. I came here to obtain something of value so that I could purchase a new ship. It was the least Augustus could do for me. But I found that he had died, as had my father." He took a deep breath and plunged onward. "When I learned Augustus had died and the new duke was missing, I decided to come here and take something."

The disappointment in her gaze turned to incredulity. "You were going to steal from the estate. Like Cuddy."

He kept his voice steady even as emotion rioted through him. "Yes. But when I arrived in Blackburn, someone mistook me for Rufus, and I couldn't ignore the opportunity."

"So you pretended to be him." Her scorn burned him. "That's rather arrogant of you to think you could pull it off."

Yes, it was. "I knew enough about Beaumont Tower, and thought I could bluff the rest."

Having sat unmoving for so long, she unclasped her hands and flattened her palms against her knees. "You thought it would be easy to pretend to be my husband?"

He deserved every bit of her anger. "I didn't plan to be here very long, and I thought I could do what I needed to in order to find something of value and take it—something you wouldn't miss. I was actually trying to be a conscientious thief." He tried to inflect a bit of humor to lighten the atmosphere. But he shouldn't have. Her eyes darkened and her brow furrowed.

"You committed fraud." Her eyes were fire and her tone ice. "You pretended to be someone you aren't for personal gain. And you didn't just ensnare me and the staff and the tenants in your lies, you deceived a boy. Explain that to me—if you can."

Chapter Thirteen

VERITY'S HEART THUNDERED in her chest. What had she expected? That he'd masqueraded as Rufus because he'd wanted to help her and the estate? No, that hadn't been his motive, by his own admission, but that was precisely what he'd done. He'd also involved an innocent child.

"I didn't know about Beau," he said softly, his voice laden with regret. "I have no excuse but I will say it gave me pause. I'd intended to be here less than a week at best. However, Beau captured my heart immediately." Warmth heated his gaze, and he leaned forward slightly. "I'm afraid my plans to stay a short time and take what I needed to fund my ship faded into the background as I immersed myself…here. In the estate," he added.

"And in our family." She was torn between anger at his audacity and his self-serving motivation and the joy and contentment he'd brought to Beaumont Tower. "You've put me in a terrible situation. I should despise you." Her voice was low with anger and hurt.

"You should, and I'm sorry for what I've done—to you and to Beau. I never meant to cause you or him to suffer and to think that you might…" He stood and paced across the room. He turned, and his eyes were never a more vivid green, nor his demeanor more open and earnest. "I'm not proud of my motives, but I don't regret a single thing. I can't. Not when it brought me to you and to Beau. I fell in love with both of you, and that it just happens I am in possession of a title that should never be mine but which I desperately wanted is a happy coincidence. I'll do whatever it takes to keep it all." He strode toward her, his face intensely determined. "The dukedom, Beau, *you*. I won't let any of it go."

She refused to be swept up with his words of love, no matter how glorious they sounded. "Even kill a man who knew your secret?"

He swallowed, his throat working as he kept steady and intense eye contact with her. "That's not why I killed Cuddy. It was either him or me, and I have an aversion to dying."

She recalled their conversation last night about his wounds. "It seems as though you've had to defend against that many times. How many men have you killed?" She didn't for a moment think Cuddy had been the only one. Kit had captained a privateering vessel during wartime.

"Too many to count. Nor do I want to. I have generally tried to put them from my mind. But know that each one affected me. It is not something I've done lightly or without remorse." Yet he spoke of it easily, as if it were just a part of who he was. Which she supposed it was.

She was glad to hear his regret, but the matter was far from over. "The constable will likely investigate Cuddy's death. What are we to do about that?"

He paused, his gaze fixed on hers. "You said we."

She had. While she was angry, she wasn't going to cast him out. He said he was in love with her and with Beau. She knew Beau returned that emotion. Did she? She wasn't ready to address that emotion, not when there were so many other things clogging her mind.

"I did. You are a part of this family now. But I don't know that I trust you, and I need to be able to—for Beau."

"Then I shall be as honest as I can. I knew I had to tell you the truth. I just didn't know how. When you said you knew I wasn't Rufus… It was a gift, and I don't refuse gifts."

Because she suspected he'd been given very few of them. Well, neither had she—until Beau.

And until him.

He'd come into their lives with purpose and kindness and an enthusiasm for the estate and, surprisingly, for fatherhood. He'd given Verity space and deference and respect. Those were gifts she'd never been given. She wanted to believe him, to believe *in* him…

"I don't either," she said, moving toward him. "And I won't start now."

His breath caught, and she watched the muscles in his jaw contract. "What do you mean?" The question was low and deep, barely audible.

"You said you'd do whatever it takes to keep the dukedom and Beau and…me. You've already done it by baring yourself completely." His words of love filled her mind. She wanted that too. "I only ask that you be honest and open with me and with Beau."

"Do you want to tell him the truth about me?"

"We must. In time. I don't think he'll care—he loves *you.*" Did it matter that this man was actually his uncle? Or cousin. She truly couldn't have asked for a better father for Beau.

"Not as much as I love him." The ferocity in his statement made her throat ache.

Tears threatened, but she blinked them away. "That's what it feels like to be a parent." That much she knew.

What it felt like to be a wife, someone who was a partner, a friend, and a lover? She wasn't as confident, but she was learning. She moved closer until they almost touched. "Show me what it feels like to be a wife."

Expecting him to touch her, to kiss her, she was surprised when he sank to his knees in a posture of pure supplication. "A wife should be honored." He took her hand and kissed the back. "Worshipped." He turned her hand over and kissed her palm. "Adored."

His words heated her and filled her with hope and passion. "Last night, I asked if you would leave us. If you want to claim your place, I take that to mean you are committed—to the title, to the estate, to Beau, to me."

He stared up at her, his eyes full of emotion. "I am."

She touched his face. "I don't even know your name."

"Kit," he said softly, his lips curving into a smile that made her toes curl. "My name is Kit."

"You look like a Kit." She caressed his cheek and ran her thumb along the rough edge of his jaw where his beard began to sprout. "I want to forget the past and embrace the future you've given me and Beau. I've never experienced anything…pleasant. Last night was a revelation. I'd like you to do more than kiss me. Will you?"

He rose up in front of her and clasped her waist, his touch burning through the meager layers of her dressing gown and night rail. "I will do anything and everything you ask, including stop if you decide you want me to. Verity," he whispered. "Your name means truth, and I want that between us. I promise to go slow and ensure you are satisfied at every turn. Do you trust me to do that?"

"I do." Verity put her arms around Kit's neck and pressed herself into him as his mouth descended on hers.

Last night, he'd taught her that kisses could be beautiful and wondrous, tantalizing and fulfilling. They'd left her wanting so much more. She knew what else could happen—and how awful it had been. But with Kit, it would be different and wonderful, just as everything had been with him.

As with last night, he went slowly, his mouth molding to hers. In fact, she found it was too slow. Something inside her was bursting to be released, and she was more than ready. She angled her head and slid her tongue deep into his mouth, praying she was doing this right.

Apparently she was, for he groaned softly as his hands tightened their grip on her, his fingers pressing with a need that matched her own. She edged backward to the chaise and sat down, taking him with her. The movement broke the kiss briefly, and they exchanged a heated look as she lay back on the chaise.

He followed, settling on top of her. His weight and warmth were delicious. This was a sensation she'd never even realized she was missing. Just to be held and kissed and touched filled her with joy.

He moved his hand along her neck, his palm grazing her flesh followed by his fingertips leaving a trail of breathless desire. His touch continued along her collarbone and lower until he laid his palm over her breast.

She broke the kiss to gasp softly. As she pushed herself up into his hand, he kissed her again, his mouth claiming hers with hot insistence. Need spread from everywhere he touched and pooled low in her belly before sliding down between her thighs. Instinctively, she spread her legs, inviting him between them.

He adjusted his weight, and she was suddenly aware of him down there. His shaft, long and hard, pressed intimately against her. A splinter of fear sliced into her, but she banished the memories of disgust and pain.

Trust him.

She did. She clutched at his hip, holding him tightly to her. With her other hand, she cupped his head and wound her fingers in his hair.

His hand slid beneath the edge of her dressing gown, moving toward her breast until he cupped the flesh. What began as a gentle caress became more firm and demanding as his mouth plundered hers and his hips began to move against her pelvis.

Yes, *this* was what she wanted. She returned his kiss and arched up into him. His hand left her breast, and she felt him working at the tie at her waist. He lifted himself slightly and pushed the gown apart. Then his hand was back on her breast, his fingers teasing her nipple, separated from him now by just a thin, annoying piece of muslin.

He took his mouth from hers and spread kisses along her jaw and neck, moving down her body until he found her other breast. He closed his lips over her and tongued the fabric. It stuck to her nipple, and he suckled her through the linen. She clasped the back of his head as she moaned.

Desire pulsed between her thighs, and she lifted her hips, seeking more pressure. He ground down against her, answering her query. His length pressed against her sex, sending a rush of pleasure through her body.

"Please. Kit." She wasn't sure what she was asking

for, but she needed something.

He rolled to her side, and with the loss of his weight and pressure between her legs, she groaned with disappointment.

"Shh," he whispered against her breast. He pulled at the neckline of her night rail, dragging it down over her breast. It pulled taut against her neck, but it didn't hurt. Not that she would have noticed pain as soon as his mouth closed over her bare breast. His lips and tongue teased and tormented her all while his other hand moved up her leg, pushing her night rail to her waist.

Cool air rushed over her thighs, her sex. But then his hand was there, his fingers trailing through her curls. He traced around her opening, driving her mad with need.

"*Kit.*" Again, she wasn't sure what she wanted but knew it involved him touching her there.

Then he did.

Lightly at first, his fingertips tracing softly over the folds of her flesh. He stroked and pressed with his fingers, coaxing her desire to an even greater height. Then his thumb found that spot that had given her such pleasure when he'd settled between her legs, where his shaft had rested and moved, creating a friction she longed to feel again.

Just as she began to rotate her hips, seeking that abrasion of him against her, he slid his finger inside her sex. She cried out, surprised but also jubilant at the delicious sensation of him filling her.

This was nothing like she'd experienced before. This was expert, not clumsy, refined, not rough.

He sucked hard on her nipple, then grazed the flesh with his teeth. She couldn't be still. Her body writhed beneath his, her hands moving over him, urging him for more. She rose off the chaise, and her hips circled between the cushion and his touch. His hand worked faster, stroking her flesh, then filling her again. He pumped into her a few times, then withdrew and teased her from the outside, sending her spiraling into desperate desire.

When he entered her again, it was with two fingers—or so she thought. She began to lose herself. She just knew it was more—spectacularly more—and she rose up to meet his thrusts.

His mouth met hers in a deeply arousing kiss, wet and hot, and somehow mimicking what he was doing to her sex. He pulled back and whispered, "Come for me, Verity. Let go. Do you understand?"

She shook her head, her senses in a frenzy as her body tried to comprehend what he meant.

"You're going to fall apart—pleasure you never imagined. You're so close, I can feel it. Just give yourself over to me. Focus on me touching you here." He pressed that place at the top of her sex that felt so good. "And on my fingers inside you. I know you want to move more. Give yourself up to the movement. Rise up, take me deep inside you." His words enflamed her as he thrust into her, filling her. She began to understand. That thing rising inside her was reaching a peak. She could feel it too. She *was* close, whatever that meant.

And then she knew.

He squeezed her nipple as he thrust his fingers deep into her sex. Whatever was holding her together simply broke. She was no longer a whole person. She wasn't even sure she was still Verity. Nor did she want to be. She was a mess of sensation and pleasure, and there was nothing but ecstasy and joy.

It took long moments for her body to begin to quiet. She opened her eyes and stared up into his face, taut with his own unquenched desire. Rufus had always taken his pleasure, as evidenced by his shouts of satisfaction and the spilling of his seed.

"I should go," he said.

She caressed his face, gently running her thumb over his bruise. "Please don't. Come to my bed."

He inhaled sharply. "Verity, I don't wish to take advantage."

She narrowed her eyes at him. "I'm asking you to. Please. Take advantage."

His face cracked into a smile that made her heart flip over. She began to fully comprehend the love that her cousin Diana had for her husband. Not that she loved this man—not yet, anyway. But she was desperate to finish what they'd started, for so many reasons.

"You've done so much to erase a painful past, I suspect without even realizing it. Tonight you've given me a taste of what marriage could truly be, and I would ask you to complete the lesson."

"I know nothing of marriage."

"Then of sex. It seems you know plenty of that." She suffered a surprising flash of jealousy as she contemplated how that had come to pass.

He rolled from the chaise and stood. Disappointment curled in her gut. But only for a moment.

He offered her his hand. "My lady."

She gave him a half smile as well as her hand. "I'm a duchess. It's 'Your Grace.'"

He hauled her up and pulled her against his chest, his arm snaking around her waist. "I meant *my* lady. You're *mine*. Tonight." He kissed her, his hand twining in her braid and pulling her head back while he devoured her mouth.

She felt exposed and vulnerable and incredibly aroused. The satisfaction she'd felt moments ago faded behind a swell of desire so strong, her legs quivered.

He swept her into his arms and carried her into her chamber. Rather than deposit her on the bed, he set her down next to it and immediately pushed her dressing gown over her shoulders.

She shrugged out of the garment and let it pool to the floor. He made to remove her night rail, but she wanted him in the same state. She put her hands on his waistcoat and unbuttoned it with quick flicks of her fingers. He lifted her night rail to her hips, his hands grazing her bare flesh as she worked, waiting patiently for her to complete her task.

Struggling to ignore the sensations resulting from his touch, she focused on sliding the waistcoat over his shoulders. He had to let go of her gown to allow her to remove the garment. Instead of lifting her night rail once more, he tugged his shirt from his waistband and whisked it over his head, baring his chest.

He arched a sandy brow at her. "Is that better?"

"Much." She stared at his chest. He had far less hair than Rufus had, and it was lighter in color, just like the hair on his head. And she couldn't explain it away as being exposed to too much sunlight. Unless he walked around on the ship without a shirt... That image was incredibly enticing, however.

None of that mattered. She accepted this man wasn't Rufus. She was thrilled by that, in fact.

Then she noticed the scars.

One near the center of his chest—maybe two inches long. Another on his right shoulder, angrier looking, perhaps four inches. Small red spots at the top of his abdomen along his rib cage. A particularly long one, at least eight inches stretching from his left collarbone and disappearing into his armpit.

She traced that one with her fingertips. "What happened?"

"A battle during the war."

"You've seen many battles, I think."

"Yes."

She wanted to ask what had driven him to do such a thing, but perhaps he hadn't many choices available to him. As unyielding as her life had been, she'd had privilege. Clearly, he hadn't.

Yet, you would think he was born to this life. He carried himself as a duke ought, and he certainly knew how to talk. She'd pit his intelligence against Rufus's or any other nobleman she'd met. In fact, he'd held his own quite well with Simon.

"Have you looked your fill?" he asked.

She wasn't sure she ever could. He was a mass of muscle and sinew. She ran her hands over his flesh, wanting to memorize every plane, every dip, every scar. It was so easy to see him climbing the mast of a ship or fighting in battle.

He stared at her with keen lust blazing in his gaze. She shivered at the power of his desire and the strength of her own rising to meet his.

He kissed her again, his lips and tongue tasting hers. He was familiar now, which only made it that much sweeter. His hands came up and cupped her breasts, each massaging and squeezing, then lightly tugging on her nipples. Sensation shot straight to her sex.

She reached for his breeches, finding the buttons of his fall and working them loose as she'd done to his waistcoat, but with perhaps a bit more urgency. Her knuckles brushed his cock as she worked. When the fall came open, she reached inside his smallclothes and found his shaft. He moaned as he pitched forward into her hand.

Here was another way in which Kit was not her husband. She could tell he was…bigger. Longer, with more girth. She thought of how that would feel and decided she didn't want to think about it or compare him to what she'd known before. The whole point of tonight was to drive those memories away and replace them with something far better.

Wrapping her fingers around his shaft, she stroked him from base to tip, then back again. This much she knew how to do.

Kit lowered his head to her breast and held her flesh to his mouth as he licked and sucked. She squeezed him, perhaps a little too tightly since he gasped against her.

She loosened her grip. "Sorry."

"No, don't stop," he rasped.

He liked that, then. Emboldened, she gripped him firmly as she slid her hand along his flesh. He moved with her strokes, and she was reminded of the way his fingers had thrust into her. Soon, his cock would do the same, and she found she didn't want to wait any longer.

She edged backward and felt the mattress against her bare backside. "Kit," she urged, gently tugging his cock.

"Yes, my love?" His endearment made her shudder with need.

"I would like—" She cried out as he pinched her nipple, then sucked on it with great force. "I would like you inside me."

"I would like that too." He straightened, then divested himself of the rest of his clothing. As he peeled his breeches and smallclothes away, his shaft rose long and hard, his balls tight and round beneath. Yes, he was much larger than Rufus.

"You look very…big."

He stroked his hand between her legs. "And you are very wet. I don't think there will be a problem."

He spent a moment teasing her flesh, pressing his fingers to her opening and then driving inside. She clutched his shoulders as her legs threatened to give out. He seemed to understand, for he lifted her onto the bed, then climbed on beside her.

His hand returned to her sex as he leaned over and licked at her nipple. "Have you been kissed here before?" He slid his fingers over her folds. "I suspect not, but I don't want to assume."

"No. I never even thought of that." Which was perhaps silly since Rufus had required her to put her mouth on his sex—something she'd detested doing.

"Nor did your worthless husband, apparently. I, however, am not worthless, and when we are not in such a hurry to find our release, I will show you how pleasurable that can be."

The thought of his mouth and his tongue on her sex was simultaneously horrifying and arousing. And, shockingly, she thought she might like taking Kit's cock into her mouth.

He laughed softly against her breast as his fingers delved inside her. "I can see that idea excites you. You're even wetter now."

Kit rolled on top of her. "Part your legs."

She moved beneath him, doing as he commanded, and waited breathlessly for his invasion.

"Guide me, Verity," he said huskily. "Take my cock and put it inside you. Go as slow or as fast as you like."

His words aroused her even more, spinning her desire to an even greater height. She took his flesh in her hand and opened her thighs to receive him. His tip nudged her opening, and the start of ecstasy already flooded her body.

She pulled him farther, lifting off the bed to meet him. But it was still too slow. "I need you to—" She wasn't sure. "*Move.*"

"Like this?" He speared into her in one deft thrust, filling her so completely that she saw lights behind her eyelids after she squeezed them shut.

She clasped his backside, feeling the clench of his muscles and the velvet smoothness of his skin. "*Yes.* Don't stop. Please."

Bracing one hand near her head, he put the other on her hip, clutching her as he withdrew, then pushed forward again. "Lift your legs." He guided her to show her what he meant.

He slid even deeper, touching something deep inside that made her want to weep with the pleasure of it. She held him tight as he drove into her, hard and sure, over and over. Pressing her heels into his backside, she arched up to meet his thrusts, crying out as the friction sent her deeper and deeper into dark, passionate need.

His fingers dug into her, then he lifted his hand to smooth a curl back from her face just before his lips claimed hers. He swallowed her cries as their movements grew more frenzied. The pleasure that had built before in her study was nothing compared to this. She felt tossed atop a cresting wave, or at least imagined how that would feel.

His teeth snagged her lip as he broke the kiss. "Come

for me now, Verity. *Come.*"

She knew what that meant now and surrendered to the pleasure. Her muscles clenched around him, and he shouted as he thrust hard and deep. Wave after wave of ecstasy crashed over her. She was mindless with joy and never wanted it to end.

Gradually, he slowed, kissing her softly as her world came back into a dull focus. She caressed his back, her legs relaxing around him. After a few moments, he withdrew from her and moved to her side.

"Now, I should go," he murmured before dropping a kiss on her shoulder.

She turned her head to look at him. "I want you to stay."

He stared at her, their eyes communicating in ways their mouths perhaps could not. Not yet, anyway. His lips curved up into that heart-stopping smile she'd come to adore. "If you insist."

"I do." She pulled back the coverlet and slipped into the bed, holding the bedclothes open for him to join her.

He did, sliding his body next to hers and gathering her against him. He kissed her hairline, her temple, her brow. "Sleep, my love."

She did—and never more soundly.

Chapter Fourteen

❧❦❧

LIGHT WAS JUST creeping beneath the curtains on the windows as Kit awakened. It took him a moment to recall where he was—and why. He lay on his side with Verity nestled against him, her back pressed against his chest. She was warm and soft, and he smiled at the fortune he'd been dealt.

But it was so tenuous. His happiness faded a bit, which made him determined to hold on to what he'd found. Would she let him? It seemed they both wanted the same thing—to keep the family they'd become. And yet so many things stood in their way. They ought to go to London so that he could be officially declared the duke.

He tried to imagine what that would be like—balls and parties and clubs. Presumably, he was already a member. Hopefully, someone would know which one… He knew from the account books that Rufus hadn't kept a house in London, but then he'd been duke for only a short time before he'd disappeared. The prior duke—Kit's father—had leased one, according to the ledgers. That seemed an odd situation for a duke, but what did Kit know?

He inhaled the sweet violet fragrance of Verity's hair. The braid was still intact, but several locks had come loose. He longed to unravel the mane and run his fingers through the silken strands.

What was stopping him? She'd have to unbraid it when she awakened anyway. Or so he thought since he'd never seen her in a braid except when she was prepared for bed.

He untied the ribbon at the end and set it behind him. Then he carefully worked his fingers through the braid, unwinding the locks with care and relish. She stirred in his embrace, sighing softly as she pressed back against him.

The contact of her backside with his cock brought it fully erect. He finished unbraiding her hair and buried his face in the dark curls.

"What are you doing?" she asked, her voice low and heavy with sleep.

"Reveling in you." He found her neck and kissed her repeatedly, moving his lips along her flesh and feeling her shiver.

"That's a very flattering thing to say."

He moved his hand to her breast and cupped the warm globe before using his fingers and thumb to tease her nipple. "And what will my flattery earn me?"

She gasped softly as she wriggled her backside against him. "Nothing. I don't trade myself for pretty words. But since I know you're a man of more than just pretty words—" She broke off in another gasp as he trailed his hand down over her abdomen and stroked between the folds of her sex.

"Sometimes I prefer not to talk at all," he murmured against her neck before he suckled her flesh. He pressed his finger into her sheath and felt her contract around him. She was so very responsive—hot and wet and eager. He could just slide right into her. He moved his lips to her ear. "Is this all right?"

"No."

He stopped his hand and began to withdraw.

She turned in his arms. "Don't stop. It's more than

all right. But it's also not enough." She shook her head. "I'm terrible at this."

"Not true." He kissed her, smiling against her mouth. "You're wonderful at this."

She looked into his eyes, her irises dark. "I want to be. Show me." She rolled him to his back and moved onto his chest, splaying her hands over his nipples.

When she touched him, hell when she looked at him with that half-seductive, half-inquisitive stare, it was as if he were a young lad who'd never yet known a woman. As if he were a man who'd been too long without a woman, a sensation he was familiar with. But it was more than that. He'd been with many women who'd slaked the thirst of a long drought. Verity was wholly different.

She lifted her head to press her lips to his. "Can I be...on top of you like this?"

"You can be wherever you like." He kissed her back, snaring her lips and tongue in a blissful tangle. Putting his hands on her waist, he pulled his mouth from hers. "It's easiest if you sit up."

She rose from his chest and straddled his hips. "Like this?"

"Yes, just like that." He couldn't keep from staring at her breasts and the way they swayed as she moved. Round with pert, dark rose-brown nipples, they captivated him completely.

"Kit."

He heard the frown in her voice and jerked his gaze to her face. "Mmm?"

"Is it really easier for me to sit up, or do you just prefer this view?" She arched her brows at him as she took her hands and cupped the underside of her breasts.

Dear God, but the sight of her touching herself was almost his undoing. "It's, er, both." His voice sounded strained, as if he were holding on to the mast in the midst of a thunderous storm. "Could you, ah, keep doing that?"

"What?" She caressed her flesh, making her breasts move. "This?"

Blood rushed to his cock. "Yes. That. And maybe touch your nipples. If it's not too much trouble."

She blushed, hesitating before she pinched her thumb and forefinger together over each nub. "Like this?"

"God, yes. And pull them, just a bit."

She did, tugging her flesh and holding on.

He struggled to take a deep breath and simply couldn't. "Does that feel good?" He barely recognized the sound of his own tortured voice.

"Yes, but not as good as when you do it." Her tone had also lowered to a husky rasp. "But the way you're looking at me—"

He reached up and cupped her nape, dragging her down for an openmouthed, scorching kiss. He licked and sucked at her mouth, devouring her in an attempt to satiate his raging lust. She kissed him back with equal abandon and fervor until he feared he might burst.

He drew back with a sharp gasp. "Verity, I'm going to spill my seed if we don't commence."

"Show me," she repeated.

Putting his hands on her waist once more, he guided her back. "Raise yourself over my cock." When she did, he grasped the base of his shaft and pressed the tip to her wet sheath. "Now lower yourself."

She rested her hands on his chest, and he watched as she sank onto his flesh, impaling herself inch by delicious inch. Her channel tightened around him, encompassing him in dark, spectacular velvet. When she was flush against him, he groaned, putting his hand back on her waist.

Without direction, she began to move, up and down, going slowly at first. Her breasts taunted him, and he couldn't resist reaching for the globes. He massaged her, using his fingers to coax her nipples into stiff, tight peaks. Desperate to taste her, he moved one hand beneath her arm to her back and urged her forward.

She descended, changing the angle of their joining. As soon as she was close enough, he came up off the pillow and took her nipple into his mouth. He kissed and sucked her, and she began to move on him more quickly.

Cries of delight and anticipation flew from her mouth as he licked her. She pumped her body over his, taking him deep, then nearly relinquishing him from her flesh, then doing it all over again. Her speed increased as her muscles worked, and he sensed she was building to her release.

Then the world stopped for the briefest moment. She sat back slightly, pulling her breast from his mouth. Her hand cupped his balls, and he jerked with need. His climax had been building, but now it rushed over him. He gripped her hips and drove into her with mindless desire. She cried out, her moans filling the chamber as she met him thrust for thrust. She bore down around him, and he spent himself with a final cry of ecstasy.

She fell forward, collapsing onto his chest, her breathing fast and hard to match his own. He caressed her back and smoothed her hair as he fought his way back to full awareness.

After a few minutes, she slipped to his side and he clasped her tight against him. She rested her head on his shoulder, and Kit didn't think he'd ever felt more content. But he knew it couldn't last. Not until they surmounted the obstacles before them.

With regret, he pierced their veil of bliss. "I need to tell you about what I found at Cuddy's." He'd reviewed the ledger after she'd left him the other night.

She put her hand on his chest and lifted her head to look up at him. "What's that?"

"Cuddy kept a ledger detailing his embezzlement—receipts of what he stole and payments to multiple recipients."

Her eyes widened with alarm or interest or both. "To whom?"

"I don't know. There are amounts next to letters or numbers or, in one case, a symbol."

Her brow creased. "What sort of symbol?"

"A cross on its side."

"He couldn't have been giving money to a church." She scoffed, resting her head back on Kit's shoulder. "I'm not sure he ever went."

"I doubted that too, but what do I know of Cuddy? I wish I'd been able to get him to talk. I found one other thing—a letter from your father. In it, he said he would take care of matters regarding his dismissal and told Cuddy to remain in Blackburn."

Verity snorted, and Kit had to stifle a laugh at such an inelegant sound coming from her lips. "Of all the pompous things to say… But of course he would tell Cuddy he would handle it. I do believe he thinks Cuddy reported to him."

And because of that, Kit wondered if her father wasn't somehow involved in the embezzlement. That was another reason he wanted to go to London—to query her father. "Given your father's association and involvement with Cuddy, would it be a stretch to think he might know of the embezzlement?"

Verity stiffened, but only for a moment. "That would be…distressing. May I see the ledger and my father's letter?"

"Of course. I would appreciate your counsel." He kissed the top of her head and stroked her arm. He wasn't ready to leave their cocoon just yet. He was enjoying getting to know her without secrets and lies between them. "How did you come to marry Rufus?"

She took a breath and hesitated, but only for a moment. "We were invited to a house party here—I was just nineteen. My father was always soliciting invitations for us in the hope that I would catch the eye of an important nobleman."

"And you caught Rufus's eye." Kit had no trouble believing that. He would choose her from every other woman in the world.

She nodded. "Apparently. It was a terrible house party—that was when Augustus's son fell into the pond and drowned. Rufus tried to save him, but he was too late." She frowned momentarily, her expression turning pensive. "Actually, that's the only time I recall Rufus displaying any compassion or care. Augustus was devastated, and Rufus made a great effort to comfort him. I remember being impressed by that, and it's why I accepted his marriage proposal. He asked that we wait six months so they could observe a mourning period. I was, of course, more than happy—or at least relieved—to delay. I didn't even know him, but I looked forward to doing so based on what I'd seen. My father was overjoyed." She looked up at Kit. "It was such a coup—me marrying the heir to a dukedom. In hindsight, I wondered if my father employed some method of extortion to bring it about."

Her mention of the word extortion sent ice down Kit's spine. His suspicions regarding her father suddenly seemed more credible. "Why did you think that?"

"It was incredibly important to my father that I marry well. He craved a title so badly and did everything he could to make me attractive to suitors—tutors, deportment, dancing lessons. But I was still just the granddaughter of a baronet without particular wealth or influence. Without something beneficial to offer, how could he persuade the next in line to a dukedom to marry me?"

"Persuasion would not be necessary if I were the groom. One look at you, and I'd be lost. One day with you, and I'd be enslaved. One lifetime with you would not be enough." He felt her shiver.

She turned her head up to his, her eyes bright with desire. "*Kit.*"

In spite of their earlier activities, his cock hardened. "Isn't it possible Rufus saw you and was smitten?"

"It's possible, I suppose, and it's certainly what I believed at the time. He didn't reveal his true character until after we were wed. At the house party, he seemed a bit aloof, but that changed after Godwin died. We didn't remain long, but from what I could see, he was greatly affected."

"You said he was aloof—wasn't he courting you during the party?"

"Not particularly. We danced a couple of times, and I sat next to him at dinner one night. But he seemed to gravitate toward me after the tragedy occurred." She frowned. "I never realized that before."

"Perhaps he was looking for consolation and you were kind to him. At least that's how I imagine you were."

"You're sweet." She leaned up and kissed him. "I do remember my father encouraging me to comfort him."

Something about this felt off to Kit. "With Godwin's death, Rufus became the heir presumptive."

"Yes."

"And you say Godwin drowned. Did anyone witness it?"

Her forehead wrinkled as her features turned contemplative again. "No. The gentlemen had gone for a ride, and Rufus had stayed behind with him because he needed to take a break. He gave the boy some privacy, and when he didn't return, Rufus found that he'd fallen into the pond."

He recalled her anxiety the day they'd picnicked there. "You were thinking about that when we were at the pond with Beau."

"Yes, but I didn't want to say anything, not in front of Beau."

He could understand that. "So the only person who can definitely say what happened to Godwin was Rufus, who would directly benefit from the boy's death. How convenient."

Verity's eyes widened as she pushed up to a sitting position. "You think Rufus killed him?"

Kit lifted a shoulder. "I think it's impossible to know. Where was your father during all this? Was he on that ride?"

"He was, and now I recall that someone asked where he was because he'd been riding at the back—Augustus wanted to know if anyone had seen or heard anything.

My father said he hadn't." She blinked at him. "You don't think he was involved somehow?"

"I don't know what to think, but it all sounds very suspicious, as does Augustus's sudden decline before his death. He wrote a letter to my father before he died—the new vicar gave it to me along with some other items when I visited upon my return."

"That's nice that he saved some of your father's things."

Kit nodded, but his mind was on the letter. "He wrote about his sadness over losing his son and his regret over not doing more for me. He said he wasn't long for the world and that he wasn't ready to go, that he didn't like his heir and that he wished it were me instead."

Her gaze softened. "With an endorsement like that, it's no wonder you want to stay."

"It didn't sound like a letter written by a man dying of sadness—he wanted to live." Again, Kit wondered if something nefarious had occurred but doubted he'd ever know.

"Kit, I think we should go to London so that you can appear in the House of Lords and be recognized as the duke."

Kit sat up and tried to focus on her face instead of the curve of her breasts. "You do?"

"We must if we want to preserve our family."

His breath caught. "Do you want that?"

"More than anything." He reached for her, but she held him at bay, lifting her hand. "I don't want to lose you, and I'm in danger of that until you're declared the duke. Once you have the title, no one will be able to take it away."

"You're terribly confident." He wished he was.

Her gaze softened, but carried the courage he'd come to admire so much. "I have nothing else. I'm determined we will be a family."

Her bold declaration along with her fervor were the sweetest things he'd ever heard. "I love you." He clasped the back of her head and drew her forward for a deep, lingering kiss.

She jerked away, startling him. "What time is it?" She looked frantically toward a clock on the mantel. "I'm surprised Beau hasn't come in yet." She sprang from the bed. "You should clean up and put something on."

She briefly left the chamber then came back wearing a night rail just as he'd pulled his shirt over his head.

It was a near thing, for Beau came into the chamber just as Kit pulled his breeches on. Beau stared at him, blinking as if he'd just awakened—and Kit supposed he had—then he looked at Verity, who stood next to the bed appearing as guilty as Kit felt. Or maybe that was his imagination.

"Papa?" Beau turned his attention to him once more. "What are you doing here?" He took in Kit's attire. "Did you sleep here?"

Kit blinked, unsure of what to say. He looked toward Verity who cast a glance in his direction.

She saved him by answering. "Yes, Papa slept here."

Beau came toward him. "Were you scared, Papa? That happens to me sometimes."

"No. I was—" He wasn't entirely sure what to say, but in this case decided he didn't want to lie. Which was ironic since this was a situation in which it was likely more than acceptable to do so. "I wanted to kiss your mother."

Beau's look of utter disinterest nearly made Kit laugh. "Because you don't like to do it in front of people."

A chuckle escaped Kit's mouth. He couldn't help it. "Apparently." In truth, he'd kiss Verity wherever she'd give him leave.

"I'm hungry. Can we have breakfast now?" Beau asked.

"Yes," Verity said. "Let's get dressed." She looked at Kit, who gathered up the rest of his clothing. His shoes were near the bed, right next to Verity, in fact. He went to slide them onto his feet, and she turned toward him, her gaze locking with his. Her lips parted, and his body stirred once more.

Without thinking, he bent his head and kissed her. It was brief but enticing, a promise of what was to come.

Provided nothing went wrong before he became the duke.

◆Ɛ•3◆

AFTER SPENDING THE day preparing to leave for London, Verity said good night to Beau as Kit began to read to him. She watched them for a moment, her heart full, before turning to go to her chamber. It had taken a great deal of work, but they would leave in the morning in two carriages—the first carrying her, Beau, and Kit, and the second carrying Beau's tutor and her maid. She'd sent a letter to Simon and Diana informing them of their arrival. They'd be delighted to welcome them at their town house in Mayfair.

Due to the excessive activity of the day, she hadn't seen or talked with Kit since that morning. They had so much to discuss, to learn about each other. She was eager for their life together to truly begin. She was also apprehensive, particularly about Cuddy's death and whether Kit would be held responsible. Surely he wouldn't be, not when he was only defending himself. Perhaps they should visit the constable.

Yes, they *should*, but she was afraid to do so until he was declared the duke in the House of Lords.

She climbed into bed to wait for Kit. He hadn't moved into her chamber but they planned for him to do that when they returned. They had, however, planned for him to join her tonight. She didn't want to spend another night without him.

Apparently the day's work had been exhausting because she fell asleep and didn't awaken until the sun was peeking beneath the curtains. Blinking, she felt a warmth against her back and smiled. She rolled over to face Kit and was surprised to see his eyes were open, their dark pupils fixed on her.

"Good morning," he said softly, his deep voice sliding over her like warm bathwater.

She trailed her fingertips along the side of his face and along his jaw. "Why didn't you wake me last night?"

"You were very asleep and, frankly, too beautiful to disturb."

She caressed his shoulder. "I wish you had."

He reached for her beneath the covers, his hand stroking her hip. "I can disturb you now, if you like."

She lifted her lips in a seductive smile. "I like."

Keeping his gaze locked with hers, he guided her onto her back and came over her, his mouth taking hers in a soft but searing kiss. Leaving her breathless, he moved down her body as he pushed her night rail up. He disappeared beneath the covers and kissed her hip. She started with gasp, closing her eyes as she cast her head back on the pillow.

He trailed his lips over her flesh while he brought his hand to the curls between her legs. Instinctively, she opened her legs, knowing what he meant to do—he'd told her he wanted to.

His breath tickled her folds just before his fingertips stroked her there. She shuddered as desire quickened in her belly and settled low in her pelvis.

With a soft moan, she put her hand on his head to steady herself. Anticipation pulsed through her as sensation rioted within her body. Then he kissed her there, his lips teasing and gently sucking. Pleasure bloomed, and she shoved the covers away, baring his head between her thighs. She thrust her hands into his hair. His touch was light and caressing with his mouth and fingers teasing her flesh.

And then he stopped playing.

He gripped her hip and licked along her crease, and the addition of his tongue changed everything. What had been decadently wonderful was now darkly erotic, and the desire she felt became a deep and desperate lust for everything this man would give her.

She clutched at his head as he speared his tongue inside her. His thumb pressed and stroked her flesh while his fingertips dug deliciously into her backside.

Relentless in his pursuit of her pleasure, he replaced his tongue with his fingers, driving into her while he sucked on that nub at the top of her sex. She cried out as a wave of ecstasy slammed into her, but she wasn't ready for release. Not quite yet. Not when everything he was doing felt so good.

Alternating his mouth and fingers, he tormented her flesh, holding her hard and fast as her hips began to move. She felt utterly shameless, arching against his mouth and pleading for more.

He caressed her backside, urging her to move and working furiously to coax her release. Pleasure spiraled through her, moving up and pressing on her chest as her muscles began to contract. The control she barely held slipped and splintered, exploding in a torrent as she came around his fingers, his tongue bathing her heated flesh.

He rose and came over her. She slid her hands up around his neck, gliding her palms over his warm skin. He ducked his head down and kissed her, his mouth open and wet, his tongue seeking hers. She tasted herself and reveled in this new intimacy.

He pulled back, and she opened her eyes to find him staring down at her with that same intensity with which he'd looked up at her before. "You *are* my wife. In every way, Verity. I would fight for you at any cost."

The declaration stole her breath, and emotion clogged her throat. Swallowing, she caressed his nape and drew his head down to hers. "You don't have to fight—I'm yours."

Chapter Fifteen

※•3•※

KIT CLAIMED HER mouth once more, pouring his heart and his soul into their kiss. Now that there were no secrets between them, he felt freer than he had in ages. Maybe in his entire life.

Because love could do that, he realized. It could make you hurt and seethe one moment and fairly burst with joy the next. It was a tumult, and he wanted it every damn day of his life with her.

Her hand curled around his stiff cock, and he groaned into her mouth. His hips moved forward of their own accord, desperate to find her heat. She knew and guided him to her sheath. He slid inside, his shaft slickened by her wet channel.

He wanted to go slow, to savor their joining, but he couldn't. He was too overwhelmed with emotion and need. He cupped the underside of her jaw, his fingers tucking behind her ear as he drew his mouth from hers.

"I can't," he rasped. "Can't go slow."

Her eyes fluttered open, and he saw his own desire reflected in their earthy depths. "Don't."

He gripped her firmly but with great care as he drove into her. She wrapped her legs around him and raked her nails down his back, never breaking the lock of their eyes. Her lids slitted, but she watched him with her lips parted.

He couldn't look away. This moment between them was too powerful. "God, you feel so—" He couldn't come up with an accurate word to describe everything he was experiencing.

Her hands clasped his backside as she arched her hips and met his thrusts. "Harder. Please. Faster. It's just—" She interrupted herself with a low moan, and her eyelids fluttered.

Kit let himself go, slamming into her with strength and speed. Her muscles contracted around him, and he knew her orgasm was right there. He dragged his thumb over her lips and pushed it into her mouth, sliding the pad over her lower teeth.

She snagged his flesh then sucked on him as she bore down around his cock. She cried out, and he moved his hand back, cupping her nape as he came with astonishing force.

Kit pumped into her, and she rose up against him, their bodies moving in glorious concert as they crested the peak of pleasure together. He didn't remember a more satisfying—or humbling—moment in his entire life.

They eventually slowed and came to a stop, their breaths coming in loud gasps before settling to near normal. He collapsed on top of her, but when he made to slide to the side, she clutched him against her. "Don't move. Please."

He dragged his lips across her forehead. "Move. Don't move. You're a bit of an autocrat."

She gave him a saucy smile. "And don't you forget it."

He laughed against her temple. Her hair was loose, which she knew he loved. Had she left it that way on purpose? He hoped so.

Her fingertips traced circles on his lower back. "Now you can move. But not too far."

With a low chuckle, he slid to her side. Grabbing two

pillows, he stuffed them behind his head and scooted up to a partial sitting position. She nestled against his side and put her hand on his chest, again drawing circles over his flesh.

He brushed his lips across her forehead. "When did you know I wasn't Rufus?"

"Almost immediately, I think. I didn't know for *certain*, but you were just too different. He was…barbarous, and I suspect you don't have a cruel bone in your body."

He stiffened when she said barbarous. "How?" He realized she could interpret that question a number of ways, but she answered how he hoped she would—with what he *needed* to know.

"It started small—he would belittle me in act and deed. The physical intimidation started on our wedding night. He was a brute in the bedroom, but often drank himself to a degree of, er, nonperformance. Eventually, that became my fault too." Her hand pressed flat against his chest, and he could feel her pulse in her wrist. Steady and strong, as she'd had to be living with that monster.

"Did he hurt you?"

"Physically?" She nodded slightly. "Sometimes. But he preferred to torture me in other ways—making me stand in the corner all night and watch him sleep. I would ponder all the ways in which he might die." Her hand balled into a fist on his chest, and Kit covered it with his, squeezing her.

"He can't ever hurt you again."

She relaxed, her hand flattening once more against his chest. "Then he went to London, and shortly thereafter, I found I was expecting Beau. I was terrified for the child and thought of running away."

Kit's heart squeezed, and he longed to find Rufus Beaumont and kill him if he wasn't already dead. He hoped for the man's sake he was, because Kit would not make it quick or pleasant.

"But then he disappeared," she said, exhaling. "It was like a reprieve. For months, maybe even years, I was afraid he'd come back, but eventually we—Beau and I—settled into a comfortable routine."

She had to have been horrified when he'd arrived. "I'm so sorry for the anguish I caused you when I showed up," he said, stroking her back and shoulder. "If I'd known the truth, I wouldn't have tried to be him."

"Now you see why it was difficult to believe you were Rufus. You were so different in every way. Everyone noticed."

"Does anyone else at Beaumont Tower know— definitively, I mean?"

She looked up at him. "Not that I'm aware. I didn't tell anyone you're Kit. Did someone say something?"

"No, but I have to wonder who Cuddy was talking about when he said someone else knew my secret."

She pushed up to a full sitting position, her face creased with concern. "That's a problem. As is the constable. What are we going to tell him?"

Kit blew out a breath. He'd cocked that up for certain. "I should just have told the truth." Surely the constable would have believed a duke's account of what had happened. Kit needed to remember he *was* the duke and start bloody acting like it. "It was incredibly selfish."

She cupped his face, her touch gentle against him. "It's hard not to be selfish when we both just want to keep this happiness we've found." God, she understood. "I don't want to lose this either."

He turned his head and kissed her palm. "We won't. If the constable comes, I'll think of something." He didn't want her to worry about it.

She gave him a reassuring smile that didn't quite reach her eyes. "We'll be on our way to London in a couple of hours anyway. I doubt we'll have to speak with him."

She was, of course, wrong.

❖❖❖

DESPITE WORKING HARD on preparations the day before, it was past midmorning before the two coaches were ready to depart for London. Beau was beyond excited as they packed things into the coach for him to do along the way. Verity tried not to think about when he grew tired of the confines of the vehicle. Just as she helped him inside, her heart leapt into her throat as an unexpected visitor rode into the courtyard.

The constable.

He brought his horse to a stop near the coaches and dismounted. A groom rushed to take his reins, and the constable offered a nod.

Verity sidled closer to Kit, who stood beside her. "That's the constable. Mr. Jeffers."

Kit touched her arm. "Don't worry. And definitely don't let him see you worry. Do I know him?" He kept his voice barely above a whisper.

"Yes, but not well. Just act as if you do."

"Should I act...normal?" They'd discussed earlier whether he ought to behave differently in London. Though Rufus had visited for only a short time, he might have left an impression, given his general behavior of aloofness and scorn. They'd decided that he had to be who he was—which wasn't Rufus. To that end, he would likely find himself apologizing for quite some time.

"Act as you've been. Like we talked about earlier."

"Right." He took a deep breath and smiled as the constable approached. "Good morning, Mr. Jeffers. I would say I'm glad to see you, but I believe you're here because of a distressing matter."

Jeffers, a pock-faced man of at least fifty with a genial smile, bowed. "Good morning, Your Grace." He performed the same for Verity. "Your Grace."

"We were sorry to hear of Cuddy's death," Verity said.

"Yes, yes, such a shock for Blackburn," Jeffers said. "I know Mr. Strader was employed here until recently. Have you any idea as to who might have wanted to harm him?" He looked between Verity and Kit, but his gaze settled on Kit.

"None, I'm afraid, but then I've only been home a month or so."

"Rumor has it you were conscripted, but I can't see how that's possible." He chuckled, but there was a note of unease in the tone of it.

"In this case, the rumor is accurate," Kit said evenly. "I spent the last six and a half years at sea, and I'm glad to finally have my legs on land."

Verity knew that wasn't true. In fact, she suspected he missed his ship and sailing more than he realized. It wasn't being a captain—at least she didn't think that was it. She thought being duke and running an estate rather fulfilled his desire to lead. And he was so very good at it. Pride pushed at her chest as she slid a glance at him.

"I bet you are," Jeffers said. "And I'm sure everyone here is…glad to have you back." His slight hesitation before saying "glad" wasn't lost on Verity.

"Actually, we are more than glad," she said, tucking her arm through Kit's. "His Grace has returned quite changed."

Jeffers now looked mildly uncomfortable, but he summoned a smile just the same. "How splendid. Well, if you think of anything regarding Mr. Strader, I hope you'll let me know."

"Actually, I should tell you that we believe he was embezzling from the estate," Kit said, shocking Verity with his forthrightness. "That's why I dismissed him. A review of the accounts revealed discrepancies."

The constable's gray eyes narrowed, and his brow puckered. He nodded several times. "I see. I see. I must say I'm not entirely surprised to hear this. Mr. Strader's reputation in town was less than savory, particularly since he left your employ. I've learned he regularly met with a pair of miscreants at the Sheep's Head."

Kit leaned forward slightly with interest. "May I ask who? I should dearly like to recover at least a portion of the funds Cuddy stole. Perhaps these men could help."

"I doubt that—they seemed to be of a lower class. Or so Thompson—the barkeep at the Sheep's Head—said. He said they met Strader in the pub once a quarter or so. Oh, and they aren't from here, so good luck finding them."

"Did Thompson know where they were from?"

"He thinks London, based on their accents." Jeffers let out a soft chuckle. "Can't imagine you'd find them there, however."

Kit's answering smile was mild and brief. "No, I

can't imagine I would. Thank you for the information, just the same. Do you think it's possible these men had anything to do with Cuddy's death?"

Jeffers stroked his chin. "It's possible, I suppose, but Thompson said they were in town a week or so ago. He doubted they'd be back so soon—he was adamant they showed up once a quarter or thereabouts."

Beau stuck his head out the window of the coach. "Are we going or not?" He glanced toward the constable but didn't seem to care that they had a visitor.

Jeffers chuckled again. "Someone's ready to be on his way."

Verity narrowed her eyes toward Beau but then smiled. "Yes, we're going to London. He's never been."

Beau grinned. "I'm going to the museum and to have ices and to the Tower of London!"

The constable looked toward the coach. "Sounds like a wonderful trip. Have a grand time." He returned his attention to Verity and Kit. "I'll be on my way, then. Thank you for speaking with me. Safe travels to you."

"Thank you, Jeffers." Kit reached out and shook the man's hand, which elicited a flash of surprise in the constable's eyes.

Jeffers gripped his hand with a nod. "Thank you, Your Grace." He bowed to Verity once more before turning and going to his horse.

Verity waited until he was on his way through the gate before taking her arm from Kit's and turning to him. "Why did you tell him about the embezzlement?" she asked quietly.

"Because he could easily find out from Thomas." His gaze locked on hers. "I would have told him the truth

THE DUKE OF LIES

about killing Cuddy, but I know how badly you want to get to London."

She leaned into him. "So you will be the duke and our family will be safe."

He bent his head and kissed her.

"Now you kiss too *much*," Beau whined. "Can we *go*?"

Verity felt Kit smile against her mouth as laughter broke them apart. "Yes, we can go." She looked up at Kit with a surplus of emotion—some of which she wasn't sure she wanted to define, so she didn't. "To London, where everyone will welcome the returned Duke of Blackburn."

"To London," Kit agreed softly before helping her into the coach.

She could hardly wait to get there.

Chapter Sixteen

※·€·3·※

IT WAS A week that felt like a month, and Kit wasn't looking forward to the return—at least not right away. Traveling such a long distance with an energetic six-year-old boy had proven taxing, but also endearing. Every night, Beau curled up between Kit and Verity and fell immediately to sleep, and though Kit wasn't able to share any intimacy with his wife, he couldn't be annoyed by the lack of it when the resulting sense of family and connection were a different kind of intimacy that was both unexpected and incredibly satisfying.

And he supposed he couldn't say there hadn't been any intimacy of the sexual kind. They'd managed a rather brief coupling in a dark, shadowed corner of the stable while Beau had been inside the inn with his nurse. Kit smiled at the memory and looked very forward to having Verity alone that night. Hopefully, Beau wouldn't mind sleeping in his own chamber at Aunt Diana and Uncle Simon's.

It was just past noon on their eighth day of travel as the coach rolled to a halt on Upper Brook Street. Kit tried not to gape at the grand town houses lining the road. He knew Simon was particularly wealthy, but this was a level of elegance and prestige Kit had never seen.

Welcome to your world.

Beau tapped his foot impatiently as they waited for the groom to open the door. They'd long since abandoned trying to coax him to wait for his mother to depart first. On the contrary, they *wanted* him out of the coach as soon as possible.

He bounded forth the moment the steps were in place. Kit followed him and helped Verity descend. She looked at him with a heat that seemed to indicate her mind had maybe taken the same direction as his. He drew her hand close to his chest after she stepped down. "Soon," he murmured.

She grinned, then turned her head to the town house, where the door was already open and Simon and Diana were now stepping outside.

They exchanged hugs and greetings, and soon Beau was off with their butler, exploring the house. Randolph was a younger fellow and had explained he had four younger brothers and was up to the task of managing Lord Preston. He had, in fact, seemed eager for it.

Simon and Diana escorted Kit and Verity into the drawing room where the housekeeper delivered refreshments.

"Would you mind if we closed the door?" Verity asked.

Kit tensed. They'd discussed the need to have this conversation, but he was still nervous. Verity didn't want to lie to her cousin, her best friend, her confidant about who Kit really was. And Kit simply couldn't deny her a thing. He was, in a word, besotted.

"Not at all," Simon said, rising and closing the door. He retook his seat with a look of eager curiosity. "Though now my interest is quite piqued."

Verity sat beside her cousin on the settee while Kit and Simon faced them over a low table in a pair of chairs. She angled herself toward Diana. "We wanted to tell you something—something very important and very secret. We don't wish to put you in an awkward position, but this isn't something I could keep from you." She looked over to Simon. "And I know Diana would need to share it with you."

Simon exchanged a warm glance with his wife. "I would tell her she didn't have to, but that wouldn't make any difference."

This provoked Kit to laugh. He was new to this marriage business, but he already knew that trying to manage his wife would not turn out well.

"Which is why we're telling you both," Verity said. She took a deep breath and laid her palms flat atop her lap. She looked over at Kit, hesitating. "There's just no easy way to say this."

Kit glanced from Simon to Diana and back again. "I am not Rufus."

"Oh, thank God." Diana clapped her hand over her mouth and then laughed. And then it spread. First to Verity and then to Simon and finally to Kit, who really didn't know why it was amusing, but in that moment, he didn't think anything had been more humorous.

At last, their laughter began to die down, and Kit found his breath. He looked at Diana. "You're glad?"

"Oh yes. Rufus was awful. And you're not at all. It made no sense. And honestly, this is far more palatable."

"Who the devil are you, then?" Simon winced. "Er, sorry. I presume you mean to tell us. Or not," he added lamely.

"Of course we mean to tell you," Verity said. "Kit is Rufus's cousin—the illegitimate son of Augustus Beaumont. Kit is short for Christopher, which was one of Augustus's names."

"It's also one of Beau's," Diana noted. Her gaze fell on Kit and softened. "How lovely."

"Yes," Verity agreed. She'd brought the names up the first night of their journey after Beau had fallen asleep. She'd said she loved the fact that their son had his name—his real name. That she'd referred to Beau as *their* son had filled Kit with joy.

"That's why you look so much like him," Simon said. "You're rather closely related."

More closely than that, of course, but they'd decided not to disclose the part about him being Rufus's half brother. They didn't see the point in publicizing Kit's mother's adultery.

"That's where the similarity begins and ends," Verity said firmly. "Kit is nothing like Rufus."

"I should say not," Diana said.

"Well, I didn't know him, but I've heard some things, and let me tell you, they aren't good." Simon frowned. "Prepare yourself for any manner of reception now that you're here. Most are eager to see you and hear your tale of disappearing. I do hope you've cooked up something good."

"Something beyond conscription?" Kit asked. "That is the reason I've given, and the only one I think I can sell."

"From the time we spent together, it did seem as though you'd been on a ship," Simon said.

"Captain of a privateering vessel, actually," Verity said with a distinct tone of pride.

Simon turned sharply toward Kit. "The devil you say! I want to hear all about that."

Kit chuckled. "It's probably not as spectacular as it sounds." Oh, parts of it were—the sea, the command, the camaraderie aboard ship, the thrill of victory. Those were the parts he missed. The Thames wasn't far. He longed to go to the docks and at least look at the ships.

"I'm sure it's not as unspectacular as you would have me think." Simon cast a sly smile toward his wife. "But we'll discuss it later at the club."

Diana rolled her eyes. "While you do that, Verity can tell me all about why Kit pretended to be Rufus."

"It's not a secret—from you anyway," Kit said. "I needed a new ship after mine burned. I planned to ask my father—Augustus—for the funds. When I learned he was dead, I decided to just take what he'd once promised me."

"It's a rather long and involved story," Verity said.

Simon looked between Verity and Kit, his gaze uncertain. "Do you know what really happened to Rufus?"

Kit exchanged a glance with Verity before giving Simon a rather grim frown. "No, and I suspect we never will."

"I feel a bit awful for saying so, but I do hope he stays missing," Diana said with a slight shiver. "I don't wish him harm, but it would be better for everyone if he didn't return."

Kit suspected the man was dead, but didn't say so. He did find himself wondering about the particulars. Had he run into trouble on his way home from London? Had he suffered an accident? It wouldn't keep him up at night, but it would be nice to know, if only to resolve things for Verity and Beau.

Verity smiled brightly, and Kit wondered if it was entirely genuine. "Perhaps we should focus our energy right now on how to reintroduce Kit, er, Rufus, to Society."

Simon reached for a cake. "Most everyone I've spoken to is keen to recognize you in the House of Lords, but they want a chance to meet you. To that end, we must parade about as much as possible. I know you're tired, but since today was a shorter travel day, I wondered if you might be up for socializing this evening. We could start at a ball, and then I'll take you off to Brooks's."

"Am I a member there?" Kit asked.

"Yes." Simon frowned, then looked toward his wife. "I think Kit needs a speedy review of Debrett's."

Verity lifted her hand to her mouth as her eyes widened. "I should have thought to do that."

"It's quite all right," Diana said reassuringly. "We'll manage things."

Kit looked to Diana. "If you just give me the book, I'll read it."

"He's a fast reader," Verity explained. "He'll probably devour it in an hour. Or less."

"But will you remember it?" Simon asked.

Kit was never more glad for his particular skill with reading and memorization. "As if it were a picture in my mind."

Simon blew out a breath. "Bloody convenient."

Diana stood. "I'll get the book."

Verity joined her. "And I should go check on Beau."

Kit and Simon leapt to their feet as the women left arm in arm. Verity cast a smile over her shoulder at Kit. He was looking forward to finding her in their bedchamber later.

"It certainly looks as if marriage agrees with you," Simon said. "But then I'm a huge proponent of the estate myself."

"Verity far exceeds anything I imagined marriage to be. She and Beau mean everything." He looked Simon in the eye. "I'll do anything to protect them—and what we have."

"Your secret is safe here." Simon clasped his bicep in a firm, brief grip of friendship. "You're family now."

◆ξ•3◆

KIT IN CRISP black evening clothes was just about the most arousing thing Verity had ever seen. It seemed she wasn't alone in that estimation since nearly every woman in the ballroom kept sneaking glances in his direction. Only some weren't sneaking. They were blatantly staring and clearly discussing him with their companions.

When she and Kit had entered a short time ago, the room had fallen silent save the music playing in the opposite corner, but conversation had struck up almost immediately, and it was obvious they were the primary topic. Everyone was eager to see the long-lost Duke of Blackburn. She wasn't sure they even saw her at all.

They'd arrived with Simon and Diana, who were greeted with the occasional nod and smile. Moving to the side of the ballroom, Simon clapped Kit on the shoulder. "Welcome to London, where notoriety is the best currency. And right now, you're the richest man in the room. Can't say I'm sorry to pass on the honor."

Diana gave Verity an apologetic glance, but Verity shook her head. "I'm glad to divert attention from you."

"What am I missing?" Kit asked.

"I'm the Duke of Ruin, remember?" Simon said. "Furthermore, my lovely wife was previously engaged to my best friend. It was a bit of a scandal when they both married other people." His gaze focused across the ballroom. "Ah, here come Nick and Violet now."

Verity, her hand still tucked around Kit's arm, gave

him a squeeze. "You can see why Society has been focused on them."

"That and the antics surrounding that other fellow." Simon looked toward Diana. "The Duke of Seduction?"

Diana nodded. "It hasn't been a dull Season, to be sure."

Nick and Violet smiled in greeting as they approached, and Violet leaned over to kiss Diana's cheek.

"Allow me to present my dearest friend, the Duke of Kilve," Simon said. "Though I'll give you leave to call him Nick, whether he likes it or not. Nick, this is the Duke of Blackburn."

Kit offered his hand to Nick, and Verity finally let go of his arm. She should have done so already, but she found herself wanting to make sure everyone in the ballroom knew he belonged to *her*.

"Pleased to meet you," Kit said.

"This is my wife, Violet. If you're calling me Nick, you'd best be on the same familiar terms with her."

Violet took Verity's hand. "I've heard so much about you from Diana. I feel as if I already know you."

"She's told me of you too," Verity said. "I'm so glad she has such a good friend here in London."

"She has several," Violet said. "Not everyone here is shallow or unkind. And we'll be sure to point out to you which ones are." She gave Verity a conspiratorial wink.

Verity was pleased to have allies in such a foreign place. Over the next half hour or so, they met various people, and her head was soon swimming with names and faces she wasn't sure she could possibly remember.

Somehow, they'd split into two groups, with the

women together and the men together. The latest
arrival to their group was the charming Duchess of
Kendal. About ten years Verity's senior, she was
charming and kind and clearly well connected. "Now,
Duchess," she said to Verity, "you mustn't pay
attention to gossip and rumors. There are quite a few
circulating about you and Blackburn just now,
particularly about Blackburn."

Verity's brow puckered. "What are they saying? Not
because I care, but because it's better to be
forewarned."

"True," Diana agreed.

The Duchess of Kendal gave Verity a supportive
smile. "Remember, these are just rumors. Though
Blackburn's prior visit to London was brief, he
established quite a *reputation* for himself, apparently."

Verity could well imagine what that might be—
probably drink and perhaps gambling. Had he been
violent at all? "He was, ah, different before he
disappeared."

"Again, don't pay them too much mind, but when
you notice so many women staring at him, now you
know why."

Verity couldn't resist darting a glance toward him and
instantly felt a pull to move to his side. "Because he's
incredibly handsome?"

Diana exchanged a look with the Duchess of Kendal.
"I think Nora meant something specific by reputation.
I believe she means he carried on affairs."

"Affairs may be too formal a word," Nora said
gently. "He was known for rather loose behavior. I'd
stay clear of Mrs. Walthorpe if I were you."

So Rufus had been a rakehell along with all his other
sins. "Why?"

"She's telling anyone who cares to listen that she and the duke carried on a lurid affair before and that she looks forward to making his reacquaintance." Nora winced. "Sorry. As I said, better to be forewarned.

"I appreciate knowing, thank you. And Rufus will too."

"I do hope you'll call me Nora," she said with a smile. "Please let me know how I can help. I look forward to welcoming you into our set."

Diana lightly touched Verity's arm. "Simon became quite friendly with the duchess's brother-in-law, the Earl of Knighton, when we came to town. So naturally I became friends with the countess and then with her sister, Nora. As Violet said, there are plenty of lovely people."

"Indeed, and now I must be off," Nora said brightly. "I promised my sister I would meet her in the retiring room. I'll be sure to introduce you to Jo—you'll like her immensely." She departed with a friendly nod.

Diana leaned over and whispered, "Perhaps you and Kit should dance—to show everyone you're a happy couple. Sorry, *Rufus*."

Verity wasn't sure Kit could. She moved to close the gap between their groups and went to his side, indicating for him to lean down so she could speak close to his ear. "Diana suggested we dance. Do you know how?"

He winced. "No. You can teach me tomorrow. No dancing tonight."

She nodded, thinking she couldn't possibly teach him to master dancing in one day, but then Kit had proven himself adept at just about everything he tried, including practically memorizing Debrett's earlier. How else could a privateer pass himself off so convincingly as a duke?

"All right, but stay clear of someone named Mrs. Walthorpe."

He looked down at her with mild alarm. "Why?"

"Just trust me. I'll explain later." If Verity happened to encounter Mrs. Walthorpe, she might just give Society another interesting piece of gossip. She wasn't sure she'd be able to hold her tongue with regard to Mrs. Walthorpe's expectations with her husband—as in, they would never come to pass.

Verity's eye caught the next person heading in their direction and momentarily froze. She clutched at Kit's sleeve. "My father is coming. Be sure to act like an ass."

"I thought I was supposed to act like myself."

"Yes, that too, but you need to convince my father in a different way than you need to convince everyone else. With most people, merely acting ducal is enough to intimidate them into believing you're who you are—it worked with everyone at Beaumont Tower. But my father knew Rufus better than most. He'll be able to tell, just as I was." She tensed as he neared and quickly remembered to add, "Call him Horatio."

And then he was there, his long, narrow face pinching into a smile. "Good evening, daughter. I arrived a short while ago and heard you were here." He turned his focus to Kit. "And here is my son-in-law after so many years. I hope you'll forgive me for not coming to Beaumont Tower to welcome you home. It's such a long trip, and the Season is such a whirl." He laughed with a wave of his jeweled hand.

Kit offered a tepid smile. "Good evening, Horatio. How good of you to come over and welcome us."

"Even if you weren't family, I would have *had* to—you're the spectacle of the evening. And probably at least for the next week." He said this with a glee that made Verity grit her teeth.

"I'm sure it's quite gratifying for you to be at the center of gossip," she said rather too sweetly.

He narrowed his eyes slightly but didn't respond to her taunt. Instead, he turned his attention to Kit. "You look quite different, Rufus. Did you grow while you were away?"

"I worked hard aboard a ship. I'm bigger, yes." Kit kept his tone even and his eyes rather cold and expressionless. He'd definitely mastered ducal intimidation.

"A ship? So the rumors are true—you were conscripted?" Verity's father said this with considerable disbelief. "The nerve of someone kidnapping a duke. One wonders how they were able to do such a thing."

"You'd be surprised what criminals are capable of." Kit arched his brow. "Or perhaps not. You no doubt heard I dismissed Cuddy."

"You speak of criminals and then mention Cuddy—is this because he was murdered?" he blinked at Kit, but his gaze was hard, and Verity wondered if some sort of communication was happening between the two men. "Such a tragedy. I hope they catch whoever did it." He twitched his shoulders as he looked toward Verity. "What a macabre topic for such a fine evening. Forgive us, my dear. Come, Rufus, let us depart so we can speak without offending feminine sensibilities."

Anxiety spiraled in Verity's gut as Kit glanced over at her.

"Since it's our first night in London, I'm not sure I'd like to leave Verity's side."

Her father's gaze narrowed as he scrutinized Kit for a moment, then he nodded approvingly. "You've changed in more than just looks. There was once a time when you preferred to be anywhere but with my daughter. I'm glad to see your time away has shown you the error of your behavior."

Verity stared at her father, scarcely believing he was saying such things right in front of her. She couldn't keep her reaction buried. "*Father.*"

He gave her a brief, apologetic smile. "Oh, I'm sorry, dear. But I do care for you, and it's best for Rufus to know straightaway that I won't tolerate his nonsense."

Nonsense. Was that what her father thought of the way Rufus had treated Verity? Now she was shocked silent.

Her father blinked at Kit. "Ready, Rufus?"

Kit sent another glance toward her, and she nodded imperceptibly. He should go. To not go would only arouse her father's suspicions, and she feared they were already aroused.

"I'll be back soon," Kit said, leaning down to brush a kiss against her temple.

She watched them go and tried to curb a sense of foreboding.

✦⊱⋅⊰✦

EXPECTATION AND APPREHENSION curled through Kit as he followed Horatio from the ballroom. "Where are we going?"

Horatio looked over his shoulder with a pompous, tight-lipped smile. "To have a little talk—father to son."

"You aren't my father," Kit said. Regardless of what the man's relationship had been with Rufus, he would set new rules tonight. Starting with not upsetting

Verity.

"Close enough since yours died. And then you lost Augustus, who was a bit of a surrogate, wasn't he?" Horatio pushed open a door that led to a small sitting chamber. It was empty but moderately lit with a pair of wall sconces, a lantern, and a low fire in the grate. He held the door and gestured for Kit to precede him. "After you."

Kit looked at him warily as he passed and went into the room. The sound of the lock clicking into place made Kit turn. "You're locking the door?"

"I don't think we want to be interrupted. Or overheard. I'm afraid I must speak to you of a rather sensitive matter."

Kit's shoulders bunched with tension. There'd been an undercurrent to their conversation in the ballroom—Kit mentioning criminals and Cuddy, and Horatio responding with Cuddy's murder. Not death, but murder. Kit had already wondered about Horatio's involvement with Cuddy's embezzlement, and that grew into a full and weighty suspicion.

Horatio walked to the fireplace, where he seemed to study a figurine atop the mantelpiece. "First, let me say how pleased I am to see that you seem much changed with regard to my daughter. This is excellent, for I didn't want to have to remind you of the importance of not embarrassing her as you did last time you were here. I won't meddle in what you choose to do within your own home, but here in London you must behave appropriately. If you want to have affairs, be discreet. And for the love of God, don't drink and gamble excessively." He turned, and his nose wrinkled, as if he'd just stepped in horseshit. He looked like an arrogant prince with his embroidered coat, diamond stickpin nestled in the folds of his cravat, and the singular, but quite large, jewels he wore on each hand. How the hell did the second son of a baronet afford to dress like that?

Because he stole from a profitable estate.

"Second, and more importantly, now that you've returned, I'll need you to reinstate the stipend you agreed to give me when you wed my daughter."

Shit. What had Rufus agreed to? Had Horatio actually extorted him to marry Verity? It certainly sounded like it. Kit had to pretend he knew about it. "I'm not going to do that."

Horatio frowned. "We had an agreement. I know things. Things you wouldn't want made public."

And there it was. "I also know you and Cuddy embezzled thousands from Beaumont Tower over the past six and a half years. And I have proof."

The older man's eyes narrowed to dark, beady points. "That's unfortunate. I see we both have secrets we'd prefer to keep buried. I would argue, however, that yours are a bit more damning. You aren't the Duke of Blackburn, and I can prove that too."

Kit stalked toward him, stopping a few feet away when the man flinched. "How the hell can you do that? Unless *you* know where he is." Kit saw no point in trying to keep up the charade. They'd moved far past that. This man had other damaging information about Rufus that had nothing to do with Kit not being the duke. He could, it seemed, ensnare Kit as himself or as Rufus. Either way, he was damned.

"I don't, but Cuddy determined you weren't him, and, though our association has been brief, I concur. What I can't understand is how you fooled my daughter. I thought she was smarter than that, but perhaps she's just so relieved to have someone other than that blackguard, she doesn't care. Can't say I blame her."

His casual discussion of Verity's pain and suffering nearly drove Kit to hit him. "Whatever comes of this, you aren't to speak of her. She detests you, and I can easily see why."

Horatio drew back in offense, his lips parting. "She's my daughter. Of course I'll speak of her. But I'm glad you care enough to be protective." He cocked his head to the side. "In fact, I can see you care for her greatly. So agree to the arrangement—it works well for both of us. You have my daughter, and I continue to live in the manner in which I deserve."

"Deserve." Kit spat the word. "You deserve to be drawn and quartered for sacrificing your daughter to meet your own ends. Even now, you're willing to trade her to me—a stranger—for money. You don't know who I am or what I'm capable of."

"Murder, it seems," he said softly. "Yes, I'm convinced you killed Cuddy, especially since you knew of our scheme. And I know precisely who you are. You look far too like Augustus Beaumont, and I'm aware he had a bastard hovering about somewhere." He made Kit sound like an annoying insect. "Do you really want all of England to know Verity accepted the prior duke's bastard son into her bed as a replacement for her missing husband?"

Unable to contain himself a moment longer, Kit lunged forward and gripped Horatio by his lapels. His fingers crushed the expensive fabric as he drew the man inches from his face. "How can you claim Verity's happiness is important to you while threatening to ruin her life? You're despicable." Kit released him savagely, and Horatio stumbled backward until he smacked into the mantelpiece. If not for that protruding piece of wood, he might have fallen over the hearth and at least against the fire if not into it. Pity.

Horatio straightened, adjusting his clothing and smoothing his hands over his wrinkled coat. "Better behaved when it comes to my daughter, but also a brute, I see." He cleared his throat and calmly looked Kit in the eye, seemingly unaffected by Kit's barely leashed violence. "Your hands are tied here. Do you want to be the duke or not? Even without the prize of my daughter, you're gaining a powerful title and, as you said, a profitable estate. I daresay you'll barely miss the stipend you'll send me."

"Of course we'll fucking miss it. How do you think I discovered the embezzlement? And rather quickly, I might add. There are many improvements that have been ignored and tenants who need assistance. But you don't comprehend any of that because it doesn't affect you. And stop calling her your daughter. She's nothing to you." How Kit longed to wipe the arrogance from the man's gaze.

"She is, however, everything to you. What is it going to be?"

Fury raged through Kit. "I will not be extorted.

"Don't think of it like that. It's a mutually beneficial arrangement."

Kit couldn't help prodding for definitive confirmation for his many suspicions. "Like the one you made with Rufus when he wed Verity? What did you have on him? Did he kill my half brother Godwin?"

Horatio wrinkled his nose as if he were smelling vinaigrette. "Let us not revisit ancient history. None of that matters. You aren't Rufus. But you *can* be. Take the deal I'm offering. The alternative would crush Verity and likely see you in jail for fraud, if not something worse."

The walls seemed to close in around Kit. "Verity will never agree to give you funds from her estate."

"So don't tell her. I'm quite confident in your ability to deceive. With the exception of me and Cuddy, you seem to have done rather well with your masquerade. All you need do is sign the contract I'll send over in the morning, shake the Lord Chancellor's hand, and take your seat in the Lords. Then you'll be the Duke of Blackburn forevermore."

"Until you decide to change the terms," Kit spat.

"Not at all, which is why there will be a contract. I will testify from now until my death that you are the right and honorable Duke of Blackburn."

Of course he wanted to put it in writing, lest Kit renege as soon as he took his seat. Without the contract, it would be the word of a duke against the word of this social-climbing sycophant. Kit realized they were alike—both wanting to be something they weren't. Horatio wanted to be wealthy and important while Kit wanted the dukedom and everything that came with it, especially Verity. Who also—desperately—wanted him to be the duke. He suddenly hated himself.

Because he was going to take the fucking deal.

"You're a self-serving prick, Horatio. But for Verity, I will accept your terms. Send the contract and be sure it includes the following: you are not to visit Beaumont Tower or otherwise contact her or me unless I give you leave. Do you understand?"

Horatio pouted, and Kit longed to wipe that pathetic

look from the man's face permanently.

He exhaled dejectedly. "I suppose if I must."

Kit turned and quit the room before he gave in to the violence rioting through him. As he approached the ballroom, he nearly collided with Simon.

"Oh, there you are," Simon said. "I was just coming to rescue you from Verity's father." He looked past Kit. "Where were you?"

Kit ignored the question. "I've had enough for one evening."

"Yes, I find balls tedious. Let's go to the club."

"No. Not tonight. I'm tired from traveling." He wasn't tired at all. In fact, he would have gladly sailed out to sea right that very minute.

"Of course. I understand. Come, let's fetch the wives." He turned and they went into the ballroom, where Kit put on his best performance to date—that of a man who wasn't about to commit to a lifetime of lying to the person he loved most in the world.

Chapter Seventeen

AFTER CHECKING ON Beau, who was asleep in the chamber next to hers and Kit's, Verity opened the door to see Kit staring into the fire. His face was blank, but his frame was tense—his shoulders high and the muscles of his neck tight.

He'd been quiet since leaving the ball, and when she'd questioned him upon arriving back at the town house, he'd blamed it on fatigue. Since she was rather exhausted herself, she hadn't questioned it. Now, however, she wondered if his time with her father had affected his mood. She wouldn't blame him if it had.

He turned his head as she closed the door with a soft click. He wore a silk banyan, which he'd donned while she'd gone to check on Beau. "How is he?"

"Sleeping quite soundly," she said, tightening the tie that held her dressing gown closed.

"Good. We should probably do the same." He turned toward the bed, and she knew something was bothering him. All day, they'd exchanged glances and touches that seemed to promise of reclaiming their intimacy now that Beau wasn't sharing their bed.

She was more convinced than ever that her father was to blame. "What happened with my father?"

"He's an ass." The vehemence of his answer startled her, but she wasn't surprised by his summation.

"Yes. What did he say?"

"He thanked me for being different, for being a better husband—he said he cares greatly for you.

That's horseshit, however." He winced. "Sorry. He *should* care for you."

She walked around the bed and went to stand in front of him, placing her hand on his chest, which was bare in the V of the opening of the banyan. "He should, but he doesn't. I have no illusions about that. I'm sorry you had to spend time alone with him."

"It's all right. God willing, I won't have to ever again."

"That would be lovely," she said, smiling softly. "He believed you were Rufus, then?"

"He seemed to. We shall have to be on our guard." He looked down at her, his eyes narrowing slightly. "You were going to tell me about Mrs. Walthorpe."

Verity made an inelegant sound and briefly closed her eyes. "Apparently, Rufus carried on an affair with her when he came to London, and she hopes to rekindle the association. So be on your guard."

He put his arms around her waist and drew her close. "It's becoming evident that I shall have to proclaim my love and adoration for you from the rooftop of every building in Mayfair. Or perhaps I should just make love to you in plain view of everyone so they can be assured my heart—and my body—belong to you and you alone."

"*Kit.*" The vision of him shouting on high and then taking her into his arms in front of the entire ton was both terrifying and arousing. "You can't do either."

"No? Then what can I do to prove to everyone that I am yours?"

"I don't care if everyone knows." That wasn't entirely true—she wanted the Mrs. Walthorpes of the ton to know definitively. "All that matters is that *I* know."

"And do you?"

She narrowed her eyes at him and pushed the banyan from his shoulders. She sucked in a breath as she realized he was completely nude beneath. "What I know is that as stunning as you look in your evening wear, you look even better just like this." She flattened her palm against his chest and slowly walked around to his back. She skimmed her hand over his shoulder and then down the blade until her fingers caressed his lower back. She dipped her hand lower, cupping his smooth backside, a body part she'd never imagined to be attractive but couldn't seem to stop looking at or touching when she had the chance, like now.

She dragged her hand over his hip as she circled back to his front. She kept her hand low, bringing it to the sac between his legs, where she fondled him.

"Verity." His voice was low and dark, almost a growl.

"I know you make me happier than I've ever been and that I'm so proud to be your duchess. You've returned honor and integrity to the title and to Beaumont Tower. Augustus would be proud too."

He cupped her face and kissed her, his lips and tongue claiming hers with a ferocity that scorched her soul. It was a very long moment before he came up for air. "I love you."

"I love you too." It was the first time she'd said it out loud, though she'd felt it for him for so long. Fear—of losing this dream—had kept her silent, but she wasn't afraid anymore.

He looked into her eyes, his fingers stroking her face. "God, I don't know what I ever did to deserve you. I'm not entirely sure I do."

She clutched his neck, bringing him down to kiss her again. "We deserve each other."

His fingers dug into her hips, pulling her pelvis flush against his as their mouths met and joined. She ground against him, seeking the feel of his cock against her sex.

He tore her dressing gown open and pushed the fabric from her shoulders. She'd forsaken a night rail, anticipating that wearing one would only be a hindrance.

His hands came up and cupped her bare breasts, his thumbs dragging over her tightening nipples as desire spiraled to her core. She tingled everywhere—from her mouth where his tongue danced with hers, to her breasts where he teased her flesh, to her core where she desperately wanted him to touch.

Perhaps sensing her need, he trailed one hand down to the apex between her thighs and stroked along her heated flesh, provoking a moan low in her throat. He pushed a finger into her and she gripped him harder as she spread her legs. Tearing his mouth from hers, he swept her onto the bed. He followed, his mouth clamping hard on her breast as he slipped his fingers into her. She moaned, closing her eyes as she reached for and found his cock. He was hot and hard and so deliciously smooth. She pulled him forward, more than ready for him to drive into her.

He didn't hesitate, his cock finding her sheath with fast and eager abandon. He speared into her, filling her completely. She wrapped her legs around him as pleasure rushed over her, pushing her toward release.

She grasped his backside, squeezing his flesh as he thrust deep into her body. Crying out, she urged him harder and faster just before he claimed her lips once more. They fought to kiss and breathe and drive the other to the edge and beyond.

For Verity, it came quickly, ecstasy slamming into her

in waves. She moved with him, never wanting the sensation to end. As it began to ebb, she was tossed again into the darkness of passion, ascending to the peak of pleasure alongside him.

Stroke after stroke, he filled her with rapture and love. When she came again, she cried out his name over and over as nearly unbearable sensation swept her away.

He pumped into her one last time and shouted before collapsing over her. She held him close, kissing his cheek, his temple, his lips.

He rolled to his side and carried her with him, keeping her tight against his chest as he stroked his hand along her back. "I swear to you, I will spend my life making you and Beau happy. Nothing else matters to me."

She listened to the strong beat of his heart, slowing into a steady, reassuring rhythm. As she drifted to sleep, she didn't think she'd ever felt more secure, more protected, more loved.

⚜

KIT JOLTED AWAKE with a start. His skin was flushed, his heart pounding. After staring at the canopy most of the night, he must have finally fallen asleep. For a time, anyway—long enough to dream.

No, to have a nightmare.

In it, he became the Duke of Lies, a man who kept things from his beloved wife. A man Kit couldn't bring himself to be. He'd embarked upon this miraculous journey under the shadow of deception, but he'd pledged to be honest with Verity, and by damn, he would do that.

He waited until his pulse slowed and his body calmed. When he was able to draw a deep breath, he crept from the bed and found his banyan. Drawing it around his body, he turned back to the bed where Verity slept.

Rather, where she had been sleeping. She sat up and brushed her hair from her face, blinking at him. "You're awake rather early," she said in a sleep-roughened voice.

He'd realized many things in the night: He loved Verity and Beau; he'd do anything to protect them; he wanted her father to burst into flames. And he couldn't sign the contract and lie to her again.

Moving to the bed, he perched on the edge near the end, angling his body toward her. "I didn't tell you everything about my meeting with your father last night."

"But you'll tell me now." There was a hint of question in her suddenly alert eyes.

"Yes. I promised you I would be honest, and I'm sorry I wasn't last night. I'd thought to try to protect you from your father's machinations, but you're strong enough to know—and you should know. You've every right."

She paled slightly. "You're worrying me."

How Kit hated her anguish—damn her father. And damn him for complicating her life. "He's the other person who knows I'm not Rufus."

"How?"

"He says Cuddy told him, so I must assume he realized my deception. However, the night I went to see Cuddy, he gave me the impression someone had told him. I have to suspect your father somehow knew without even meeting me. How is that possible?" Kit had an idea, particularly since Horatio said he could *prove* Kit wasn't the Duke of Blackburn.

"It isn't possible." Her eyes widened. "Unless he knows what happened to Rufus." Her jaw dropped for a moment. "How can that be?"

Kit shook his head, his mind swimming. "I don't know, but I mean to find out."

They were both quiet a moment. At last she broke the silence. "What does my father plan to do?"

"He wants me to continue the stipend Rufus agreed to when you wed."

Her eyes widened. "Rufus gave him a stipend?"

"Apparently. Now I'm to sign a contract giving him a lifetime allowance. In exchange, he'll testify that I am the Duke of Blackburn."

Her eyes filled with disgust. "And if you don't?"

"He'll tell everyone who I really am—Augustus's bastard—and that you were all too eager to welcome me as your husband's replacement. He's absolutely despicable." Kit didn't bother disguising the vitriol he felt.

"Truly," she agreed darkly, her gaze casting about the room before settling on him once more. "I'm sorry, but I refuse to give him money."

"Good."

She blinked in surprise. "What about the dukedom? It should be yours. I want it to be yours."

He shook his head sadly. "But it isn't. And if I take it, I'll be the Duke of Lies. I can't do that to you or to Beau. We must tell him the truth, and I can't ask him to hide it. Besides, the title is his. Once Rufus is officially declared dead, Beau will be—and should be—the Duke of Blackburn."

Lines creased her face as defeat filled her eyes, and

he knew she agreed. "What do you want to do?"

"Aside from declaring the truth that I'm Captain Christopher Powell, I'm not sure. It depends on what your father will do when we tell him we won't consent to his extortion. He's used to getting his way, I think." While Kit didn't have definitive proof of his embezzlement, he was certain of it. And now there was the matter of Rufus's disappearance and whether Horatio had played a part.

"Can't we just threaten to have him arrested for embezzlement?"

"Would you want to do that to your own father?"

Her eyes darkened. "He's guilty of the crime—of stealing from me. He may also be guilty of worse," she said softly. "What if he had something to do with Rufus's disappearance?"

Kit moved forward and took her hand, hating the anguish in her gaze. "I'm so sorry about all this."

"I don't like my father very much—or at all really. But I never imagined he'd be guilty of actual crimes. And for what? So he can have an extravagant life and buy his way into Society. Wealth and position have always been his passion."

If he didn't practically despise the man, Kit would have pitied him. "We can't prove any of this right now."

Lifting her chin, she stared at him with hardened eyes. "We must. I won't allow him to interfere in my life any longer, Kit."

God, he loved her so much. "You're beautiful when you're enraged."

She cocked her head to the side and flattened her lips, causing him to chuckle softly. "Sorry," he murmured. "I'll talk with Simon about how to proceed.

We may not have the evidence we need yet, but perhaps Simon can help decipher the codes in Cuddy's ledger." The sideways cross, the number twenty-two, and the letter G.

She nodded with enthusiasm. "That's an excellent idea. There must be a way to tie my father to the embezzlement. Should we go in person to tell him we won't be extorted?" She pressed her lips together. "On second thought, I don't want to see him. Did you say he's sending you a contract?" At his nod, she continued. "Let's return it with a note telling him we won't give him a farthing."

He inclined his head. "I bow to your discretion." His tone was light but now, he looked at her with gravity. "Verity, I want you to make the decisions about this. You've had far too much stolen from you—by your father, by Rufus, by me."

She pulled on his hand, and he inched closer to her on the bed. "You haven't taken a thing—you've given me, and Beau, so much."

"I want to give you both the world. If you'll let me."

She smiled softly. "I just want you." She launched herself forward and as he caught her, he held her close, looking down into her face.

"There is one other thing. I expect to be accused of fraud—for impersonating a duke. Your father will surely lead that charge."

She didn't even take a breath before saying, "I will say you did so to protect me and Beau and Beaumont Tower from my father's crimes. If not for you, we wouldn't have discovered the embezzlement."

"We have to prove it first."

"We will," she said firmly. "You must work on your optimism."

He laughed, drawing her close. "How you still have a wealth of it is beyond me."

She curled her arms around his neck and pressed against his chest. "I credit you. You came from nowhere and gave me and Beau something we never had—love and family."

He felt precisely the same. "No, you gave it to me."

She laughed softly. "We gave it to each other." She kissed him then, her lips molding to his and easing the anxiety rioting through him. Pulling him, she fell back onto the mattress and brought him with her. Her eyes were dark with love and desire. "This will all come out right. You'll see."

He wanted to, but right now, he saw charges of fraud and a potential prison cell. "We have to find proof of your father's crimes."

She gazed up at him reassuringly. "We will. He's guilty, and the truth will win out."

Kit wanted to believe her, but with that came the dread that he was guilty too.

❧❦❧

THE CONTRACT ARRIVED the following day while Kit and Verity were at the park with Beau. As soon as they arrived back at Simon and Diana's town house, Randolph handed him an envelope, and he and Verity exchanged a knowing glance. They went upstairs to their sitting room and promptly wrote a note telling Horatio they'd burned the contract.

Then they burned the contract.

That afternoon when Simon arrived home, Kit asked if they could speak in his office. After grabbing the ledger from upstairs, Kit informed Simon of all that had transpired.

Simon now sat behind his desk, his eyes wide with disgust. "Her father's a right son of a bitch. But I shouldn't be surprised. Diana's father is equally so, and they *are* brothers." He let out a rather virulent curse. "It's amazing to me how two such abominable men fathered such wonderful women."

"Now you see why I'd like you to help me find evidence that will keep him out of our lives for good."

"I can see that, all right. I only wish I could do the same for Diana's father. Not that he's tried to communicate with us since I tossed him from Lyndhurst back in January."

Kit opened the ledger and set it down in front of Simon. "Do you see him here in London at all?"

"No, but I imagine he tries to stay clear of me. He would if he's smart, and honestly, I don't know if he's that smart. He may just be lucky." Simon brought the ledger closer. "Let's see how we may prove *this* Kingman is a scoundrel of the criminal order." He studied it for a moment, slowly turning a few pages, his brow furrowed. "The CS is your steward?"

"Cuthbert Strader, yes. That leaves twenty-two G and the odd sideways cross."

"I don't suppose he was giving money to the church?" Simon asked wryly.

"We discarded that idea," Kit said with a half smile.

"Brilliant." Simon returned his gaze to the ledger, frowning. "The amounts to twenty-two G are higher overall, and they vary. Whereas the payments to the steward and this cross symbol never seem to change."

"Yes, and the cross payments don't start until several months after Cuddy was hired."

"That should tell us something," Simon said, looking

up once more. "What does it tell us?"

"If it's extortion, it started sometime after Rufus disappeared. I wonder if the two are somehow related."

Simon sat back in his chair. "How do we investigate that?"

Kit exhaled. "*That* is what I'm trying to determine."

A commotion in the entry hall drew Simon's focus toward the door. "Wonder what that's about?"

The door opened without a knock, and Simon's young butler, his face pale, stepped inside. "I'm sorry to disturb you, Your Grace, but I'm afraid there are Bow Street Runners in the hall."

Simon stood. "Runners? What the devil for?"

Kit's stomach sank even as he rose from the chair. "I'll wager they're here for me."

The butler turned his wide-eyed expression to Kit. "You're correct, Your Grace. I did tell them you were busy."

Kit managed to laugh. "I imagine they didn't much care."

Randolph shook his head. "No, sir."

"Come along, then," Kit said with resignation.

Simon moved quickly around the desk and grabbed Kit's arm as he walked toward the door. "You can't mean to go with them?"

"What else can I do? I'm not going to make a scene and have Beau witness anything. Let me go with them quietly. Talk to Verity and puzzle out that damned ledger. I'm confident Horatio is behind this. It's more crucial than ever that we reveal his crimes." Kit hadn't even had a chance to tell him about Horatio's potential involvement in Rufus's disappearance. "Ask Verity about the possible connection between her father and Rufus going missing."

Simon's eyes widened. "This is a bloody novel." He frowned. "I don't like you going."

"Nor do I. Rally the troops and work quickly, please." Kit stepped into the entry hall and greeted the Runners warmly. One was a tall, beefy fellow with a ruddy complexion, while the other was leaner with a long nose and a foreboding stare. "Good morning. I understand you're here for me."

The leaner fellow glowered at him. "You're being charged with fraud—impersonating a duke—and murder."

Kit had expected the former but not the latter. "Whose?" he asked, surprised at how calm his voice sounded.

"Cuthbert Strader and His Grace, the Duke of Blackburn."

Holy hell. Horatio was going for the jugular, then. And Kit was suddenly dead certain he'd had something to do with Rufus's disappearance.

Kit turned to Simon. "He wants money—he'll try to get it from Verity. Use that to flush him out."

Simon nodded vigorously.

"You coming peaceably?" the beefy Runner asked.

Kit accepted his hat and gloves from Randolph as if this were just another excursion instead of transportation to Bow Street. "Yes. Let's go." He set his hat on his head and pulled his gloves on with a final look at Simon. "Tell her not to worry."

Simon shook his head. "She will."

"I know." And with that, Kit marched out as if he were walking the plank.

Chapter Eighteen

VERITY COULDN'T MANAGE to stop shaking as she sat with Diana in the drawing room as Simon welcomed four guests—Nick, Bran Crowther, Earl of Knighton, Titus St. John, Duke of Kendal, and Daniel Carlyle, Viscount Carlyle. Simon introduced the latter three ending with Lord Carlyle, a rather tall gentleman with steely, blue-gray eyes and thick, dark hair. "We're lucky Bran has become friendly with Carlyle who was, until recently inheriting his title, a constable."

"How fortuitous," Diana said brightly, giving Verity's hand a squeeze.

"I've told them all what's happened," Simon said, clutching Cuddy's ledger in his hand. He looked pointedly at Verity. "All of it, including Kit's true identity."

They'd agreed that was necessary. There was no reason to keep it secret, not when Kit had been prepared to announce it. She and Kit still hadn't determined how things would play out—there hadn't been time. But she'd meant what she told him: she just wanted him.

Verity looked at Lord Carlyle, who sat in a chair near the settee. "You know all the charges against him?"

"Yes. The murder accusations are, of course, the most concerning. However, am I correct in understanding that he did commit fraud?"

Verity shook her head. "Not precisely. He pretended to be my husband so we could uncover my father's crimes." It was her turn to lie, and she would do so willingly to keep her family together and safe.

"So he never intended to claim the dukedom?" Carlyle asked, glancing toward Simon.

"No." The lie scalded her tongue, but she didn't care.

"He did not," Simon echoed. Before he'd gone to solicit help from these men, she'd talked with him and Diana, and Simon had pledged to do whatever necessary to keep Kit from jail—or worse. They were, he'd said, family.

Carlyle nodded. "Then that shouldn't be a problem either. Do you know if Mr. Kingman has proof that Mr. Powell killed either of these men?"

"Captain Powell," Verity corrected softly. "He captained his own ship. No, I can't believe he does." But since Kit *had* killed Cuddy, she feared it was possible. Oh, why hadn't he gone directly to the constable? She knew why, and she told herself to stop fretting about things they couldn't change. "If we can prove he was embezzling from my estate, he may drop the charges."

Lord Carlyle's eyebrows rose. "You plan to extort him? I can't be a party to that."

"Of course not," she said. "But if I can prove my father's criminal activities, we may be able to show that he was trying to cover them by falsely accusing Kit. There's something else." She took a deep breath. "We suspect my father may have had something to do with my husband's disappearance nearly seven years ago."

"I see." Lord Carlyle tapped a finger against his chin. "Your father is accusing Captain Powell of killing the Duke of Blackburn. It's not uncommon for a man to accuse another of that of which he is guilty. I've seen it many times."

Diana let out a soft gasp, and Verity clasped her hand.

"Let us try to find the evidence we need, then," Lord Carlyle said. "May I see this ledger?"

Simon opened the book and handed it to him. "We know who the CS is."

The former constable studied the ledger. "The sideways cross is likely the Blades, a group of criminals that does favors for middle- and upper-class folks—for a price." He flipped through a few pages. "These are quarterly payments to them in the same amount. Looks like extortion to me." He glanced up at Simon. "Is that correct?"

"That's what we suspect. But we didn't know what the cross represented."

"My apologies," Lord Carlyle said with a faint smile. "I shouldn't have called it a cross as you did. It's a sword. If it were a cross, it would be vertical. And the longer line has a bit more length than your typical cross."

Verity now wondered why they'd ever thought it was a cross to begin with. Had they missed something obvious with the twenty-two G? She thought hard and, as realization hit her, brought her hand to her forehead. "The final code is my father's address. Twenty-two Grafton Street. You've made me think of something else." On the journey from Beaumont Tower, she and Kit had discussed the pair of men from London who had visited Cuddy on a regular basis. He suspected they'd come to collect the money that was catalogued in the ledger. She rose from the settee as excited energy pulsed through her. "Every quarter, two men came to Blackburn from London to see Cuddy. Kit thought they might be collecting payments. Perhaps they're from this Blades group."

"It's possible," Lord Carlyle said. "That would be a strong connection to make. However, it would be even better if we could discover what these payments to the Blades and to Cuddy were for. They're static." He gave her a pointed look. "Quarterly, in fact, which seems to indicate an extortion schedule. Do you know the basis for the extortion?"

She shook her head. "I'm not sure Cuddy was extorting anyone. I think that was simply his fee, but I doubt we'll ever know since he's dead." She inwardly winced. Kit was accused of his death, and of that, he was guilty, even though it was in self-defense. What were they going to do about that? She worked to ignore a fresh stab of fear. "I don't know about the Blades. Other than they may have come to Blackburn each quarter."

"I think I know," Simon said. "The payments to the Blades started after the duke disappeared. Kit thinks it may have something to do with that. And if your father was also receiving money and was somehow involved with Rufus's disappearance, it's all just a bit too coincidental now, isn't it?"

Verity felt as if the floor was evaporating beneath her. Diana had stood with her and now, sensing Verity's distress, put her arm around Verity's waist.

"What must we do to free Kit?" Verity asked as the fear curdled in her gut.

"We need to discover what your father was paying to hide—if indeed that's what he was doing."

Verity was certain of it. And she was becoming more and more certain it had something to do with Rufus. "I know it is. How would my father even know to hire such people?"

"It's often done through retainers," Lord Carlyle explained. "They may have a connection to the criminal classes. To expedite matters, it would be best for us to interrogate your father's staff."

"Do you have time to help with that? Please, I'm quite desperate." Verity hated to beg, but she'd do whatever it took.

Lord Carlyle smiled. "Of course. We'll need to occupy your father, however."

Verity narrowed her eyes. "I'll dispatch a note to him immediately and ask him to come here."

"You're a smart woman, Your Grace," Lord Carlyle said. "Make him think he's won. Perhaps you'll even get him to admit his crimes."

Verity doubted that, but oh, she would try. "Please just save Kit. Beau and I need him back."

❧❦❧

WHILE DIANA PROMISED to keep Beau occupied upstairs, Verity waited impatiently for her father to arrive. After what seemed a lifetime, Randolph showed him into the drawing room. He looked as smug and irritating as ever. No, he looked more so. And then he frowned, pitching his entire expression downward as if he meant to push his features from his face. She might have laughed at his exaggeration if she wasn't so distraught.

"Good afternoon, Father. Thank you for coming. Shall we sit?" She was still shaking, though not as much as before. They had a plan, and, God willing, it would be executed flawlessly. She just had to do her part.

"How magnanimous of you, my dear," he said cautiously, eyeing her with skepticism. He sat in a brocade chair as Verity perched on the settee. "I expected you to rail at me."

She clasped her hands together and hoped he couldn't see her mild tremors. "I wanted to, but I find I'm feeling differently about Kit now. I see he was using me, and that I subjected Beau to his machinations." These lies came easily as she worked to ensnare her father.

"That's right. I'm so sorry." Except nothing about his supercilious demeanor supported that sentiment.

"Still, I don't want him to hang. I don't think he killed Rufus—why would he wait six and a half years to return and claim the title?"

Her father seemed to contemplate that for a moment. "I've wondered that too, but I doubt we'll ever know why. He won't ever tell the truth anyway. I'm so glad you've come to your senses. Now that we've put that horrid matter behind us, let us speak of the future."

She couldn't pretend she didn't know about his request for funds—not after the response Kit had sent to him yesterday. "You want to know if I'll provide you with an allowance from the estate."

"It's only fair, my dear. How am I supposed to live?"

Within your means would be a good start. She forced a smile so brittle, she felt her face might break. "Yes, well, I do think you could perhaps curb your expenditures somewhat. The money you siphoned from the estate was greatly missed, and many things were ignored over the past seven years since you talked Rufus into hiring Cuddy."

His eyes narrowed, and Verity knew she was treading close to the edge. "Rufus was more than happy to take my counsel. And allot me funds. *He* gave me an allowance."

"Did he? Unfortunately, I was not aware of his arrangements."

He sniffed. "I suppose I could take a bit less than I do now."

"I'm not sure what you mean by a bit, but I'll pay you the amount in Cuddy's ledger that was entered beside the sideways cross."

He coughed and shook his head. "No, no, that's not nearly enough. That will barely satisfy my…creditors."

She tipped her head to the side and plunged ahead with audacity. "I did wonder what those amounts were for. The CS was for Cuddy, obviously, but I'm confounded as to the other two. Presumably one of them was what he paid to you?"

He smiled broadly and waved his hand. "Never mind that now. It doesn't matter. If you'll just pay me twice the amount as the sideways cross, that will be fine."

She frowned. "That may be a strain. I'll need to speak with Thomas."

Her father leaned forward, his lip curling. "I require that amount, Verity. If you want me to try to keep the imposter from hanging, you'll need to agree to that."

She blinked at him, adopting an air of naïvete. "Could you do that? Then I suppose I must agree to your terms. Thank you, Father."

She glanced at the clock, thinking they hadn't had nearly enough time. How could she keep him occupied? Standing abruptly, she gave him a bland smile that hopefully disguised her hatred. "I think I require some cheer to improve my mood. I know how much you like to shop. Shall we go to Bond Street?"

He stared at her. "You wish to shop. With me."

"Unless you'd rather not. I'd like to find something

special to surprise Beau. I'd invite him to come with us, but he is with his tutor. I hope you don't mind that I didn't interrupt him to come down to see you." She didn't think her father would care one way or the other, and she didn't want Beau in his presence ever again.

"I'm just surprised." He rose from the chair and smoothed his coat. "We can take my chaise."

She bit her tongue before she could ask what else Beaumont Tower had purchased for him. "Splendid. I'll just fetch my hat and gloves and meet you in the entry hall." She swept from the drawing room and hurried upstairs, where she found Diana and quickly told her what had transpired.

"I'll have them find you on Bond Street when they've finished," Diana said. "Don't worry about Beau," she said softly, casting her gaze at where he sat drawing a picture. "I'll take good care of him."

Verity touched her hand. "I know you will."

"Who would have thought that between our fathers, yours would be the one to commit a crime?" Diana shook her head in disbelief. "My money would always have been on mine."

Verity kissed Beau good-bye and dashed back downstairs, where she met her father with a false smile and a belly full of anxiety.

⚜

THE BURLIER OF the two Bow Street Runners opened the door of the coach. "Come on out."

Kit blinked into the bright sunlight as he stepped onto the street. "Where are we?"

"The residence of Mr. Horatio Kingman."

Kit pivoted and took in the charming façade of the

town house. The number twenty-two stared boldly at him from the brick, and the code in the ledger was suddenly clear. He had to assume that Verity, his brilliant love, had puzzled it out.

"Why did you bring me here?" When they'd loaded him into the wagon, they'd only said his presence was required somewhere.

"Your day is about to improve," the bulkier of the two Runners said enigmatically, leading Kit to the front door, where it was quickly opened by a butler who admitted them inside.

"Follow me," the butler said nervously as he guided them through the small house to the rear, where a door opened out onto a stone patio. Beyond was a square patch of garden, which was currently in a state of disorder as no fewer than four noblemen dug in the dirt.

Simon looked up from where he wielded his shovel and grinned. "The conquering hero returns."

"I'm no hero." Kit looked at his escorts in question, still confused as to what was going on. "Why am I here?"

"We'll let Lord Carlyle explain." The leaner Runner pointed to a rather tall fellow standing off to the side of the garden.

Kit edged toward Simon. "What are you doing in Horatio's garden?"

"Digging for treasure," Simon said. "Allow me to present Lord Carlyle, a former constable who has graciously provided his assistance today. You will owe him a great deal."

Kit pivoted toward the side of the garden where Carlyle stood with another man. Judging from his garb, he looked to be a groom. He also looked to be rather defeated given the downward cast of his eyes and the slump of his shoulders.

"We aren't digging for treasure, of course," Carlyle said evenly. "We're exhuming the body of Rufus Beaumont."

Kit sucked in a breath and turned his head toward the…grave. "How do you know he's there?"

Carlyle indicated the man beside him. "This is Luton, Mr. Kingman's head groom. Six and a half years ago, he arranged for a criminal organization known as the Blades—whose symbol we found in your former steward's ledger—to intimidate the Duke of Blackburn. It seems Mr. Kingman didn't like the man's rakehell behavior and sought to ensure he changed his ways."

Kit could understand Horatio's motivation but wanted to clarify the man's intent. "Intimidate him or kill him?"

"Apparently the objective was to intimidate, but according to Luton, the Blades claim he changed his mind and asked for them to kill him. They've been extorting money from Mr. Kingman ever since."

"Why would they bury him here?" Kit suspected he knew the answer, but wanted the full story from Carlyle.

"To ensure Mr. Kingman's compliance. If he failed to meet their demands, they needed only to point the authorities to the garden for proof of the man's crime. And as I've explained, he had motive."

"I had motive too." Kit gestured toward the groom. "Will this man's story be enough?"

"I believe so. Which is why I asked the Runners to bring you here. You can't very well have murdered the duke. You've never even been to London, have you?"

Kit shook his head. "I have not."

The groom lifted his head, his eyes full of tears. "I'll do whatever is necessary. I never meant for anyone to get hurt. I was only following Mr. Kingman's orders." He turned toward Carlyle. "I'm a dead man for sure when my cousin finds out."

"His cousin is one of the Blades," Carlyle explained. He pressed his lips together and regarded the groom. "You've done your part for them. Explain that Kingman was arrested—for I expect he will be when he arrives—and that the money has stopped. That is not your fault, and that will be the end of it. And then don't contact them again. I might even suggest looking for employment outside London."

"Yes, my lord," the groom said, nodding enthusiastically.

Kit looked to Carlyle. "When Kingman arrives... Where is he?"

"On Bond Street with his daughter. We sent one of his footmen to fetch them here."

Fear gripped Kit's gut. While Kingman hadn't perpetrated any violence himself, the man was apparently capable of heinous crimes, and Kit hated thinking of Verity in his company.

Carlyle seemed to read his concern, for he smiled encouragingly. "I believe Her Grace is fine. She was quite prepared to lead her father on a merry chase to keep you safe."

Kit's heart swelled even as apprehension maintained its hold. "What of the other charges against me?"

"I understand there was no fraud, that you never intended to claim the dukedom. You were simply protecting Her Grace and the estate."

"Yes." Kit could scarcely believed Verity's plan had worked, but then she was exceptionally clever.

Carlyle cocked his head to the side. "As for the other murder, did you do it?"

Kit wanted to lie—hell, he needed to lie. But the words wouldn't form. Just as he couldn't get the truth to form after he'd accidentally killed the man. "I didn't murder him. We fought."

"I see."

"I went to see him and found evidence of his crimes. He attacked me, and I defended myself." Kit winced. "I regret what happened, but it was Cuddy who was intent on murder. I also regret not informing the constable at the time."

"We'll sort that out," Lord Carlyle said. "The way this all seems to be falling into place, I doubt you will be seen to have any culpability."

"Found something."

Kit turned at the call from one of the men. It was the Duke of Kendal who'd spoken. He bent and picked something up from the dirt. Kit rushed to his side.

"Looks like a signet ring," the duke said. "Recognize it?" He dropped the piece of jewelry onto Kit's palm.

The bright afternoon sunlight glinted off the gold. Kit held it up and instantly knew what it was. "This was my father's ring. The ducal signet."

"I've found bone," Nick said grimly.

"What is the meaning of this!" The sound of Horatio Kingman's voice drew everyone to turn toward the door to the house. As they did so, the man's face lost all semblance of color. He clutched the doorframe as Verity rushed past him.

She ran directly into Kit's arms, and he gathered her close, kissing her forehead, so glad to have her safe and whole in his arms. She touched his face and looked up into his eyes. "Are you all right?"

He curled his hand into a fist around his father's ring. "Never better."

She arched a dark brow at him. "Never?"

A smile dashed across his lips. "Maybe not never, but this is a fairly good moment."

Lord Carlyle turned toward Horatio, his hands clasped behind his back, and announced in an authoritative tone, "Mr. Kingman, you are accused of killing Rufus Beaumont, Duke of Blackburn."

"I didn't! It was him!" He pointed wildly at Kit. "He wanted to claim his father's title! He's a bastard! He has the motive!"

Kit took a few steps toward him, and Verity stayed close to his side, her arm wrapped around his waist. "As do you, Horatio. While your intent may have been well placed, you chose to do business with the wrong people. And you threatened the wrong people too."

"What was his motive?" Verity asked.

Kit looked down at her. "He wanted Rufus to behave in a more ducal manner, and when he refused, Horatio hired brigands to frighten him into behaving. There is some dispute as to whether he wanted them to kill Rufus or merely intimidate him."

Horatio's eyes were huge in his pale face. "I didn't mean for him to die. But you should be glad he did— Rufus was a murderer. He watched Godwin drown so he could inherit the title, and I'm confident he poisoned the duke, starting at that house party."

Verity gasped. "And yet you did nothing. You may not have killed anyone directly, but you are guilty of terrible things."

Carlyle cleared his throat. "Regardless of what happened, the discovery of the duke's body in Kingman's garden will reflect poorly on him." He looked toward Kit. "And you can prove he embezzled—that alone would cause him to hang."

"No!" Horatio cried. He brought his hands up and covered his face, tipping his head down as sobs racked his body.

Verity's forehead creased, and she shook her head. "I don't want him to hang."

Carlyle's gaze was tinged with sympathy. "We can ask for mercy and seek transportation instead, but it will be up to the judge. Take him to Bow Street, lads."

The Runners, who'd been loitering near the house after escorting Kit to the garden, took a still-sobbing Horatio by his arms and dragged him back through the house.

"What of the Blades?" Kit asked, feeling Verity stiffen as she slowly turned back toward the garden.

"We're always trying to catch them for one crime or another," Carlyle said. "Rather, *they* are. That's not my job any longer." He nodded toward Verity. "I'm sorry for the way this turned out."

Verity pressed closer to Kit and shuddered. "I don't know what to say."

Kit held her tight against him. "You don't need to say anything. This is a great deal to comprehend. I'm not sure I do fully yet."

"What are they digging up?" she asked. "Is it…him?"

Kit pulled back to open his hand and showed her the ring. "Titus found this. It was my father's."

"I recognize that. Rufus wore it after Augustus died." She looked toward the garden. "So he really is there?"

"Yes." He didn't offer any condolences because he didn't think she'd want them. "Are you sad?"

"No. I'm relieved to know, and I hope he's at peace. We should take him back to Beaumont Tower and bury him properly there. For Beau."

Oh God, Beau. What were they going to tell him?

"I agree. I... I don't know what to say to him."

She turned in his arms and looked up at him. "About his father?"

"About him, about me, about any of it."

"We won't tell him everything at once." Her forehead creased. "I think I'd like to take him home as soon as possible."

"Not until we take him to the museum and Gunter's and the Tower. He'll be devastated if we don't."

"I'll be devastated too," she said. "I was so looking forward to doing all that. As a family."

Despite the events of the day, hope and peace made Kit smile. "And I so wanted to take you to a play."

She smiled back. "You will. Someday."

Simon came to the edge of the garden and leaned on his shovel. "This is going to be an even bigger scandal now. Nick, I do believe the focus may finally be off us permanently." He winced and ducked his head. "Sorry, perhaps that was too soon."

Verity surprised Kit by laughing. "No, and you're right. We'll need to complete our sightseeing and be on our way as soon as possible."

"We could cause an even bigger scandal and get married," Kit said softly.

She looked up at him, her eyes glowing. "Yes, please. The sooner the better."

"As soon as we get home," Kit vowed.

"Home. I like the sound of that." Her brow creased slightly. "And you're fine with it being on land?"

"Home is with you and Beau, wherever that is. You have my whole heart and my entire soul, and I don't ever want them back."

She leaned up and put her lips on his. "Good, because you can't have them."

Epilogue

THE WARM SUN roused Verity from her nap atop the blanket. She blinked as she rose from the pillow Kit had thoughtfully brought along and looked out to the pond, where Beau was rowing the boat. Even from this distance, she could see how hard he was working to get them back to the dock.

It was a blissful sight—her son and her husband together in a happy activity. Kit had spent the summer building the dock and teaching Beau to swim. He'd also taught Verity, but she didn't like to put her head under like Beau did. He was, she decided, part fish.

And now, with her belly swelling with Kit's child, she much preferred to nap. It had been like this with Beau too, but the persistent need to sleep had lessened at some point, and she anticipated it was happening now as she hadn't felt the need to nap in a few days. Today, however, with the sun and the birds and the overall sense of contentment, she'd easily drifted off.

The boat hit the dock, and Beau jumped out to lash it to the side as Kit had taught him. He'd learned so many things from his father over the past few months.

And yes, Kit was his father in every sense of the word.

Telling Beau had gone well. He'd been sad to hear that his real father was dead, but glad that they were bringing him home. They'd decided not to tell him of his grandfather's involvement. He'd learn of it some day, but not yet. And he'd never see him again, for Horatio was already on his way to Australia on a convict ship after Verity had pleaded—via letter—for that sentence instead of hanging.

Simon had been right—the ensuing scandal had been massive. Everyone was talking about the shocking discovery of the Duke of Blackburn's body in his father-in-law's garden. People clamored to catch sight of the widowed duchess and the man who'd pretended to be the duke. That he'd done so to flush out her father's crimes was a particularly scrumptious bit of the gossip, of which there was plenty to devour.

After cramming their sightseeing into a day and a half, Verity and Kit had swept Beau, who was now the Duke of Blackburn, out of London. He wouldn't take his seat in the Lords for many years, and so there was no need for them to return to London any time soon.

The scandal in Blackburn was far less, though they did attract attention wherever they went. The staff at Beaumont Tower and the retainers didn't particularly mind that Kit was Captain Powell and not His Grace. In fact, a few had even said they were glad to know he *wasn't* the duke. They were, to a person, including Thomas, delighted for Verity and for their obvious happiness.

So it was that they'd settled into an idyllic peace in which their family would gain a new member come early spring. In the meantime, they were to journey to Lyndhurst in a few days so that Verity could attend Diana's birth. Nick and Violet would be there too, and Violet was also expecting a child around the new year.

Beau bounded along the dock and ran to the blanket. "Did you watch, or were you sleeping the whole time?"

"Not the whole time. I saw you row to the dock quite expertly and then tie up the boat. You've become quite accomplished."

His little chest puffed up, and he glanced at Kit as he walked up behind him. "Thank you. Papa says so too."

"You're a natural sailor," Kit said, clasping Beau's shoulder briefly before depositing himself on the blanket next to Verity.

"I can't wait to take a boat on the ocean when we visit Aunt Diana and Uncle Simon!"

They'd planned a side trip to Southampton, where they would take a boat to the Isle of Wight for a couple of days. Kit was ridiculously giddy about it and Verity terribly excited to see him in his element.

Kit turned his head to Beau with a grin. "Maybe we'll convince your mother that we need a ship." He tossed a wink toward Verity.

"Papa, we are far too busy here at Beaumont Tower for that." Beau sounded as if he were thirty-six instead of six, causing both Verity and Kit to burst into laughter. Beau looked between them. "What's so funny?"

Verity managed to draw a breath. "Nothing, dear. You are just incredibly wonderful. Do you want a cake? There are still some in the hamper." She inclined her head toward the picnic basket on the edge of the blanket.

"Yes, please. I'm just going to go check on the bird nest over there. I suspect they'll be flying south soon." He went to the basket, found two cakes, and began munching as he walked a short ways from the blanket to survey his avian friends.

"We're going to have a bird in the house some day," Kit said. "Mark my words."

Verity sighed as she lay back on her pillow and looked up at the clouds floating across the pristine blue sky. "Probably."

A shadow fell as Kit came over her and dropped a kiss on her lips. "Are you feeling all right?"

Mornings could be a challenge, but by afternoon, she was usually just fine. "Yes, thank you."

"And did you really watch Beau, or were you asleep?"

She laughed softly and swatted his arm. "I've never lied to you—not like you lied to me."

"Ouch." He fell to his back beside her. "A direct hit."

She rolled to his side, pushing herself flush against him and placing her hand on his chest. "I was teasing."

He smiled up at her, his green eyes brilliant in the sun. "I know."

"I love you."

"I know that too." He curved his hand around her nape and drew her down for a short but penetrating kiss that made her toes curl.

When she drew back, she was a bit breathless. "We should stop before Beau makes fun of us."

"Probably, but you're irresistible." He kissed her again, their lips lingering until they heard Beau cough.

Verity sat up and looked over at her son as he ambled toward the blanket. "Ready to go back to the house? It's almost time for your afternoon lessons with Mr. Deacon."

Beau exhaled with regret. "Yes, if we must."

Kit helped Verity to stand, then folded the blanket. He'd adopted a bad habit of refusing to let her carry anything but their child so he toted that, the pillow, and the basket while they each took Beau's hands. It was how they always walked around the estate together.

"Where will my baby brother go when we walk?" Beau asked.

"Your baby sister will walk wherever she likes, and we'll let her," Kit said, convinced, like Simon, that he was going to have a daughter.

Verity didn't care what it was. She was just thrilled to have another child and this time with the man she loved. "Your baby sister or brother can decide. But for a while, I'll carry her or him. Or perhaps she or he will ride on Papa's shoulders."

"Like I do sometimes?"

Kit nodded. "Yes, but you're growing too tall and heavy."

When they reached the house, Beau went reluctantly upstairs while Kit returned the basket to the kitchen and the blanket to the laundry. He met Verity upstairs in her study, where she was about to read a letter from Diana.

"Oh, you're busy," he said, turning to go.

"Never for you." She rose from the chair and glided across the room. "I've waited my entire life to share my days with someone like you, and I am grateful for every moment."

"Not as grateful as I am. And lest you decide to argue, I am prepared to prove it. Right now." He gave her a seductive, suggestive smile that stoked her desire.

She slid her hands up his coat and curled them around his neck. "Then do."

THE END

Thank You!

❧

Thank you so much for reading *The Duke of Lies*. I hope you enjoyed it!

Would you like to know when my next book is available? You can sign up for my newsletter, follow me on Twitter at @darcyburke, or like my Facebook page at http://facebook.com/DarcyBurkeFans. I also have a reader group on Facebook called Darcy's Duchesses, which is a great place to hang out with other readers and chat with me. Find us at http://facebook.com/groups/DarcysDuchesses.

The Duke of Lies is the ninth book in The Untouchables series. The next book in the series is *The Duke of Seduction*. Watch for more information! In the meantime, catch up with my other historical series: Secrets and Scandals and Legendary Rogues. If you like contemporary romance, I hope you'll check out my Ribbon Ridge series available from Avon Impulse and my latest series, which continues the lives and loves of Ribbon Ridge's denizens – So Hot.

I appreciate my readers so much. Thank you, thank you, *thank you*.

Author's Note

❦

  This was a complicated and challenging story to write, in no small part due to the issues surrounding what happens when a duke disappears. I did a lot of research to try to determine what would happen as far as someone claiming the title after a disappearance and someone else inheriting the title (it all became much easier once Rufus was found dead!). There's a great deal of gray area, and I incorporated what I learned to the best of my ability. Any mistakes are my own.

  Beaumont Tower is based on Hoghton Tower located near the actual town of Blackburn in Lancashire, England. The floor plan is almost identical, though I did wall in some bedrooms for privacy and I changed the name of the King's Room to the Knight's Room so as not to confuse it with the King's Hall. It was great fun to be able to visualize Beaumont Tower so completely!

Books by Darcy Burke

❧❦❧

Historical Romance

The Untouchables

The Forbidden Duke
The Duke of Daring
The Duke of Deception
The Duke of Desire
The Duke of Defiance
The Duke of Danger
The Duke of Ice
The Duke of Ruin
The Duke of Lies
The Duke of Seduction
The Duke of Wishes
The Duke of Mischief

Secrets and Scandals

Her Wicked Ways
His Wicked Heart
To Seduce a Scoundrel
To Love a Thief (a novella)
Never Love a Scoundrel
Scoundrel Ever After

Legendary Rogues

Lady of Desire
Romancing the Earl
Lord of Fortune
Captivating the Scoundrel

Contemporary Romance

Ribbon Ridge

Where the Heart Is (a prequel novella)
Only in My Dreams
Yours to Hold
When Love Happens
The Idea of You
When We Kiss
You're Still the One

Ribbon Ridge: So Hot

So Good
So Right
So Wrong

Praise for Darcy Burke's
Secrets & Scandals Series

HER WICKED WAYS

"A bad girl heroine steals both the show and a highwayman's heart in Darcy Burke's deliciously wicked debut."
                    –Courtney Milan, *NYT* Bestselling Author

"...fast paced, very sexy, with engaging characters."
                    –Smexybooks

HIS WICKED HEART

"Intense and intriguing. Cinderella meets *Fight Club* in a historical romance packed with passion, action and secrets."
                    –Anna Campbell, *Seven Nights in a Rogue's Bed*

"A romance...to make you smile and sigh...a wonderful read!"
                    –Rogues Under the Covers

TO SEDUCE A SCOUNDREL

"Darcy Burke pulls no punches with this sexy, romantic page-turner. Sevrin and Philippa's story grabs you from the first scene and doesn't let go. To Seduce a Scoundrel is simply delicious!"

                    –Tessa Dare, *NYT* Bestselling Author

"I was captivated on the first page and didn't let go until this glorious book was finished!"
                    –Romancing the Book

TO LOVE A THIEF

"With refreshing circumstances surrounding both the hero and the heroine, a nice little mystery, and a touch of heat, this novella was a perfect way to pass the day."

–The Romanceaholic

"A refreshing read with a dash of danger and a little heat. For fans of honorable heroes and fun heroines who know what they want and take it."

-The Luv NV

NEVER LOVE A SCOUNDREL

"I loved the story of these two misfits thumbing their noses at society and finding love." Five stars.

–A Lust for Reading

"A nice mix of intrigue and passion...wonderfully complex characters, with flaws and quirks that will draw you in and steal your heart."

–BookTrib

SCOUNDREL EVER AFTER

"There is something so delicious about a bad boy, no matter what era he is from, and Ethan was definitely delicious."

-A Lust for Reading

"I loved the chemistry between the two main characters...Jagger/Ethan is not what he seems at all and neither is sweet society Miss Audrey. They are believably compatible."

-Confessions of a College Angel

Legendary Rogues Series
LADY of DESIRE

"A fast-paced mixture of adventure and romance, very much in the mould of *Romancing the Stone* or *Indiana Jones*."

-All About Romance

"...gave me such a book hangover! ...addictive...one of the most entertaining stories I've read this year!"

-Adria's Romance Reviews

ROMANCING the EARL

"Once again Darcy Burke takes an interesting story and...turns it into magic. An exceptionally well-written book."

-Bodice Rippers, Femme Fatale, and Fantasy

"...A fast paced story that was exciting and interesting. This is a definite must add to your book lists!"

-Kilts and Swords

LORD of FORTUNE

"I don't think I know enough superlatives to describe this book! It is wonderfully, magically delicious. It sucked me in from the very first sentence and didn't turn me loose—not even at the end ..."

-Flippin Pages

"If you love a deep, passionate romance with a bit of mystery, then this is the book for you!"

-Teatime and Books

The Untouchables Series
THE FORBIDDEN DUKE

"I LOVED this story!!" 5 Stars

-Historical Romance Lover

"This is a wonderful read and I can't wait to see what comes next in this amazing series..." 5 Stars

-Teatime and Books

THE DUKE of DARING

"You will not be able to put it down once you start. Such a good read."

-Books Need TLC

"An unconventional beauty set on life as a spinster meets the one man who might change her mind, only to find his painful past makes it impossible to love. A wonderfully emotional journey from attraction, to friendship, to a love that conquers all."

-Bronwen Evans, USA Today Bestselling Author

THE DUKE of DECEPTION

"...an enjoyable, well-paced story ... Ned and Aquilla are an engaging, well-matched couple – strong, caring and compassionate; and ...it's easy to believe that they will continue to be happy together long after the book is ended."

-All About Romance

"This is my favorite so far in the series! They had chemistry from the moment they met...their passion leaps off the pages."

-Sassy Book Lover

THE DUKE of DESIRE

"Masterfully written with great characterization...with a flourish toward characters, secrets, and romance... Must read addition to "The Untouchables" series!"

-My Book Addiction and More

"If you are looking for a truly endearing story about two people who take the path least travelled to find the other, with a side of 'YAH THAT'S HOT!' then this book is absolutely for you!"

-The Reading Cafe

THE DUKE of DEFIANCE

"This story was so beautifully written, and it hooked me from page one. I couldn't put the book down and just had to read it in one sitting even though it meant reading into the wee hours of the morning."

-Buried Under Romance

"I loved the Duke of Defiance! This is the kind of book you hate when it is over and I had to make myself stop reading just so I wouldn't have to leave the fun of Knighton's (aka Bran) and Joanna's story!"

-Behind Closed Doors Book Review

THE DUKE of DANGER

"The sparks fly between them right from the start... the HEA is certainly very hard-won, and well-deserved."

-All About Romance

"Another book hangover by Darcy! Every time I pick a favorite in this series, she tops it. The ending was perfect and made me want more."

-Sassy Book Lover

THE DUKE of ICE

"Each book gets better and better, and this novel was no exception. I think this one may be my fave yet! 5 out 5 for this reader!"

-Front Porch Romance

"An incredibly emotional story...I dare anyone to stop reading once the second half gets under way because this is intense!"

-Buried Under Romance

THE DUKE of RUIN

"This is a fast paced novel that held me until the last page."
-Guilty Pleasures Book Reviews

" ...everything I could ask for in a historical romance... impossible to stop reading."

-The Bookish Sisters

Ribbon Ridge Series

A contemporary family saga featuring the Archer family of sextuplets who return to their small Oregon wine country town to confront tragedy and find love...

The "multilayered plot keeps readers invested in the story line, and the explicit sensuality adds to the excitement that will have readers craving the next Ribbon Ridge offering."
    -Library Journal Starred Review on YOURS TO HOLD

"Darcy Burke writes a uniquely touching and heart-warming series about the love, pain, and joys of family as well as the love that feeds your soul when you meet "the one."
                        -The Many Faces of Romance

I can't tell you how much I love this series. Each book gets better and better.
                        -Romancing the Readers

"Darcy Burke's Ribbon Ridge series is one of my all-time favorites. Fall in love with the Archer family, I know I did."
                        -Forever Book Lover

Ribbon Ridge: So Hot
SO GOOD

" ...worth the read with its well-written words, beautiful descriptions, and likeable characters...they are flirty, sexy and a match made in wine heaven."
                        -Harlequin Junkie Top Pick

"I absolutely love the characters in this book and the families. I honestly could not put it down and finished it in a day."
                        -Chin Up Mom

SO RIGHT

"This is another great story by Darcy Burke. Painting pictures with her words that make you want to sit and stare at them for hours. I love the banter between the characters and the general sense of fun and friendliness."

-The Ardent Reader

" ...the romance is emotional; the characters are spirited and passionate... "

-The Reading Café

SO WRONG

"As usual, Ms. Burke brings you fun characters and witty banter in this sweet hometown series. I loved the dance between Crystal and Jamie as they fought their attraction."

-The Many Faces of Romance

"I really love both this series and the Ribbon Ridge series from Darcy Burke. She has this way of taking your heart and ripping it right out of your chest one second and then the next you are laughing at something the characters are doing."

-Romancing the Readers

About the Author

❦

Darcy Burke is the USA Today Bestselling Author of hot, action-packed historical and sexy, emotional contemporary romance. Darcy wrote her first book at age 11, a happily ever after about a swan addicted to magic and the female swan who loved him, with exceedingly poor illustrations.

A native Oregonian, Darcy lives on the edge of wine country with her guitar-strumming husband, their two hilarious kids who seem to have inherited the writing gene, two Bengal cats and a third cat named after a fruit. In her "spare" time Darcy is a serial volunteer enrolled in a 12-step program where one learns to say "no," but she keeps having to start over. Her happy places are Disneyland and Labor Day weekend at the Gorge. Visit Darcy online at http://www.darcyburke.com and sign up for her newsletter, follow her on Twitter at http://twitter.com/darcyburke, or like her Facebook page, http://www.facebook.com/darcyburkefans.

Made in the USA
Middletown, DE
07 September 2018